TEACHER'S PET

WENDY SMITH

Edited by LAUREN CLARKE

Cover Design by MOSS DESIGNS

Photography by GOLDEN CZERMAK / FURIOUSFOTOG

Cover Model ANTHONY MAINELLA

This is a work of fiction. Names, characters, businesses, places, events, and incidents are either the products of the author's imagination or used in a fictitious manner. Any resemblance to actual persons, living or dead, or actual events is purely coincidental. Wendy Smith is in no way affiliated with any brands, songs, musicians or artists mentioned in this book.

This book is written in New Zealand English.

ISBN-13: 978-1-991303-07-3

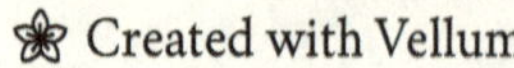 Created with Vellum

GLOSSARY

This book has been written in New Zealand English, so some phrases or words may be unfamiliar. If you find anything else, please ask. :D

Bonnet - Hood of the car

Pepi-pod - A small, portable sleep space that allows parents to co-sleep safely with their baby

Torch - Flashlight

Hair of the dog - Having an alcoholic drink in the morning to help get over the hangover from the night before.

Nappy - diaper

Box of fluffies - good, feeling great.

Gear stick - Shifter

1

JAMES

Students sometimes have a reputation for partying.

Not me.

It's rare for me to come out, but somehow tonight a few of my classmates talked me into it.

I already regret it.

The bar's packed with uni students, and a headache's started creeping across my forehead from all the noise.

It makes me miss home.

I'd always looked forward to moving to the big city for uni, but there are times when it's too big and noisy. Especially compared to the peace of Copper Creek. A quiet drink at the pub with my brothers is a far cry from the chaos here.

"Want another beer?" Cody asks.

I shake my head. "Nah. I'm going home."

"It's still early."

"Yeah, but if I drink any more I can't drive home, and I'm not leaving my car parked where it is."

He laughs. "You could always catch the bus and leave the car at home."

"I like driving." *I also like using it as an excuse not to be out all night.* "I'm just going to finish my food and get out of here."

"It's not anything to do with *her*, is it?"

I don't need to ask who he's talking about. While I haven't seen Ashley tonight, there's only one person Cody talks about like that. He knows how heartbroken I was when she left me, and while it was months ago, it hurt for a very long time.

"She's not here. Is she?"

He nods to the right, and my gaze sweeps past the others at our table, over the room until I see her. She's sitting at a table on a barstool, and the guy sitting right next to her is practically groping her in public. His hand is on her breast, and she's resting her head on his shoulder, a look of complete and utter contentment on her face.

I'm not going to pretend seeing that doesn't hurt.

But it hurts a lot less than it used to.

I'm still not sure what happened to us. She was the reason I came to Auckland Uni in the first place. But she chose to break it off with me for someone else. We've barely spoken since.

Her gaze flickers up and meets mine. I've known her since we were kids, but she's like a stranger now.

She smiles at me. *Does she think we're friends now?*

Then she drops her gaze and turns back to the man who's got his arm around her.

I don't want her back. Not when she hurt me so much. I'd hoped one day we could still be friends.

I'm not sure, despite her smile, that's ever going to be a possibility.

I push my plate away and stand.

"Do you want that?" Cody asks. There's still half a plate of nachos, but I've lost my appetite. I'm not still hung up on Ashley, but a lifetime of friendship reduced to nothing hurts.

"You're welcome to them." I turn to the others at the table. "See you later, guys."

"Are you leaving?" Sara asks.

"Yep."

She screws up her face. "Do you have to?"

I know she likes me, and she's cute. Really cute. But I'm just not feeling it, and I don't want to lead her on. "I'm gonna go home and crash."

She reaches across Cody and puts her hand on my arm. We've been down this track before when she wanted me to take her home. "Stay for another drink."

"I'm driving. Don't let Cody eat all the nachos. See you next week." Pulling away, I turn and walk to the door of the bar. I don't look back.

My thoughts turn to my car. If I'm lucky, I haven't been towed.

There are few places to park around the university, but I found a quiet little side street with a two hour parking limit. Hopefully no one's noticed my car there.

There's traffic on the street, but the car park is dark and quiet. A sob stands out above the background noise.

As my eyes adjust to the low light, I spot the shape of a woman on a bench. The lighting's so bad around here, and my stomach lurches. *What if something happened to her?*

"Excuse me. Are you okay?"

She raises her head.

When I draw closer, I recognise her.

Doctor Mia Scott.

I'm not in her class, though there's a good chance I'll be in it next year when I study for my master's. She's the queen when it comes to biotechnology, and one of the youngest lecturers at the university. Not to mention the fact that she's fucking gorgeous. I've been looking forward to being around and learning from her.

But right now, she looks distressed. "Doctor Scott?"

She sniffs. "I'm sorry."

I take a seat on the bench beside her. "For what? Are you okay?"

"My car's not starting." She lets out a sob, and I get the feeling this is about more than her car breaking down.

"Want me to take a look?"

"Do you know anything about cars?"

I smile. "My brother's a mechanic, and he's taught me a few things. I can't promise I can get it going, but it won't hurt to try."

"You'd do that?"

"Sure. I'm James Campbell, by the way."

She nods. "I know who you are."

"You do?"

"You've got a very promising career ahead of you. I didn't think it would be in mechanics, though." The smile she gives me is small, but it's better than seeing her sad.

"Where's your car? Let me take a look."

She stands, and I follow her to a nearby late model Subaru. After opening the driver's door, she pops the bonnet.

"There's not a lot of light around here," she says.

"No, but we'll work that out. Can you get in and try starting the car?"

Mia walks back to the driver's side and gets in the car.

When she turns the key, I hear the click of the starter motor. And that's it. It doesn't turn over.

I fish my phone out of my pocket, and flick on the torch function.

"Try again?"

The result's the same.

She gets out of the car.

"I think you need a new starter motor. I could replace it, but of course I don't have the part."

Mia nods. "I can get a garage to look at it. Get it towed tomorrow."

"Want a lift home?"

Her eyes widen. "Oh, I can get a taxi."

"I'm happy to give you a ride. My car's parked in the side street."

Uncertainty crosses her face. "Are you sure?"

"I was just on my way to my place. I'm happy to take a detour."

She smiles. "I'd appreciate that. Thanks."

"Where do you live?"

"Sandringham."

I nod. "That's not too far. Come on."

She grabs her bag and locks up the car. I lead her through the remainder of the car park and out into the street.

Thankfully, my car's still there.

"Isn't it a bit risky parking here?" she asks.

I shrug. "Probably, but there aren't a lot of places to leave a car around here. I should take public transport, but I can't be bothered."

She laughs. "As long as you know there's a risk."

"Live dangerously, that's me." I press my key fob and unlock the car. Opening the passenger door, I smile as she climbs in before closing it and rounding the car.

"Thanks, James. I can't tell you how much I appreciate this. I've had some pretty useless moments in my life, but melting down in public is taking the cake right now."

I start the car. "I wouldn't class this as useless. It's not like I can fix it right now. Maybe you don't know much about cars, but you're a freaking genius in a lot of other ways."

She laughs. "I'm not sure about that."

"Are you kidding? You're one of the reasons I came to this university. I want to syphon that knowledge from your brain." I grin.

"That doesn't sound creepy at all."

I glance at her as I pull out into the quiet street. After her tears, it's nice to see a smile on her face. "I'm not a creepy guy. I don't think so, anyway. I've been called a lot of things in the past, but creepy's never been one of them." As we pull up to the traffic light at the end of the street, I take a longer look at her. She's wearing a suit, but the jacket doesn't look very thick. "Are you warm enough?"

"It's a little chilly out there. But I'm fine now."

"I'll turn on the heater. It'll warm us up pretty quickly."

Turning onto Symonds Street, I pull up at the next set of lights. "Where am I going?"

"Aroha Ave. It's off Sandringham Road. Behind St Luke's shopping mall."

I nod. "Okay. I'll get us to Sandringham Road, and you can point me in the right direction."

She smiles, and my heart pounds much harder than it should.

Why did it have to be her? Why couldn't it have been Professor Strawbridge, who is perfectly nice, but about sixty and doesn't look like sex on a stick?

I swallow a laugh.

"James? Are you okay?" Her hand touches my arm, and I swear to god the skin goes numb. I guess I didn't keep that laugh as quiet as I thought.

"I'm fine. I'm just glad to be heading home."

"And now I've derailed those plans."

Shit. "No, that's not what I meant. It's Friday. That's all." I shoot a smile at her. "I'd much rather get you home safe than leave you there waiting for a taxi."

"I don't usually have crying meltdowns in the car park." She lets out a nervous laugh.

"I've never seen you have one before, so I'm sure you don't. I'm glad I could help out."

"Better you than Garrett finding me."

"Garrett?"

She nods. "My ex-husband. Or rather ex-husband to be. I'd never have heard the end of it."

"Does he hang around the university after hours often?" I expect a laugh, but instead there's silence. Following the end of Symonds Street, I turn into New North Road.

"He starts work at the university on Monday." She sighs.

I lick my lips. "I'm sorry. I gather that's not good."

"Well, I don't think he took the job because he had a sudden interest in education."

"I'm sorry to hear that. I hope he's not giving you a hard time."

She shrugs. "It's okay. Just something I have to deal with. So he tells me that, then I come out, find my car not starting, and end up a big, snotty mess."

I laugh. "That's the last thing you are."

"It's what I feel like."

"Trust me. That's not what it looks like from here."

The drive is silent for the next ten minutes until we draw close to her street.

"It's right here."

I flick on the indicator, and pull into the right-turning lane. It's Friday night, but there's not a huge amount of traffic around, and it doesn't take long for me to be able to turn.

"My place is just down here on the left."

I slow.

"See that rubbish bin there? That's my place if you want to pull up outside."

I nod, coming to a stop right by the bin. "Is that yours? Do you need me to take it in?"

She smiles. "I can. Thank you for everything."

She turns her head. I've never been so close to her before. She smells sweet, and my stomach flips at her being near.

"You're welcome. Do you want some help with the car tomorrow? I can take you to the garage. I'm not doing anything."

Her lips curl into a smile. "I couldn't ask you to do that."

"It's no bother."

She swallows hard as her eyes search mine. What's she looking for? "You really mean that, don't you?"

My eyebrows knit. "Why wouldn't I?"

She shrugs. "I'm not used to men saying what they mean." Dropping her gaze, she takes a breath. "I'd appreciate your help. I know nothing about cars. My ex used to take care of anything to do with the damned thing."

"I can come with you and make sure the garage isn't ripping you off."

"You would do that for me?"

I smile. "Sure. I was just going to study otherwise."

Mia grins. "I shouldn't really distract you."

"It's way too late for that." I'm nervous, and maybe it's showing. I don't want to cross a line with her, but I also don't want to find out the car's failed and she's been stranded or worse.

She licks her lips. "Want to come in for a coffee?"

"I'd love to. I'll even grab your bin on the way." This is wrong. So very wrong. But why does it feel so right?

I'm not sure what to make of her.

She shouldn't be asking me in, and I shouldn't be going inside, but I throw all that out of my head as I get out of the car and grab the handle of the wheelie bin. "Where do I put this?"

Mia climbs out of the car, and smiles as she closes the door. "You're keen."

"Just trying to be helpful."

Before she does anything else, she seems to scan the street. What's she looking for?

"Okay, Doctor Scott. Tell me where you want your bin."

"It's Mia. Bring it this way."

After leading me down the driveway and toward the

house, she indicates a spot next to the side step. I roll it against the wall while she unlocks the door.

"Take a seat in the living room, and I'll put the jug on. How do you take your coffee?"

"Milk, one sugar, thanks."

I slip my shoes off on the doorstep and step into the kitchen. There's a large archway leading into the living room, and I walk through and sit on the couch.

It's an old villa, like a lot of the houses around here, but the inside is modern and fresh. It's not overly decorated, but at a guess, the lounge suite wasn't cheap. It's large and leather, and so comfortable I could probably fall asleep.

"Won't be a minute," Mia calls.

"Take your time. I'm not in any hurry."

I lean back on the couch. This isn't where I saw my night going. I thought I'd be at home by now, a ball of resentment because of the way Ashley treated me. That smile was the first recognition I've had from her in months.

"James. Here you go." Mia breaks me out of my thoughts by handing me a mug. She sits beside me on the couch. "I'm so glad to be home. I would have pulled myself together and got a taxi eventually, but it all got a little too much."

I nod. "I understand. From the sounds of it, today was a little overwhelming."

"You could say that." Her expression falls. I'd love to know what she's thinking, but there's a fine line I have to walk here. Mia Scott's a beautiful woman. She's dressed in a pantsuit, like she always wears to uni. Her long, dark hair hangs straight, and when she flicks it back, I suck in a breath.

I have a crush.

She runs her fingers around the rim of her coffee cup. "So, you're planning on doing your master's next year?"

I nod.

"Good. Like I said, I've heard great things about you. I think you'll do well."

I shrug. "I do okay."

"Your work is good, James. Don't underestimate yourself."

"That means a lot, coming from you."

Her cheeks flush. "I'm glad. And it's true. You've got a big future ahead of you if you want it."

"I'm not sure if I do."

She frowns. "What do you mean?"

"I'm not sure what I want to do with my life. I mean, I thought I had some ideas, and I wanted to study, but I still don't know what my end goal is."

Her lips twitch. "I didn't know either for the longest time."

"And you decided to teach?"

She nods. "It was something I kind of fell into. I'd been a student for so long, it just seemed like a natural progression."

"Do you ever think you'll do anything else?"

Mia shrugs. "I've got a publishing company interested in me writing a text book. I have this image in my head of finding some remote retreat and immersing myself in the process."

"Sounds great."

She looks back up, penetrating me with her blue-eyed gaze. "What were you up to before I derailed your trip home?"

"I was out tonight, and planned on leaving early anyway,

but my ex turned out to be in the bar. That helped give me a push out the door."

Mia grimaces. "That must have been uncomfortable."

I shrug. "We broke up months ago, and I'm not still hung up on her, but seeing her out with someone else sucked. I've been friends with her since we were kids, and now we don't even talk."

Mia's eyes are full of sympathy. "I'm so sorry."

"It is what it is. I moved on from being miserable, but there are still those moments when it hits me in the face that I lost her friendship."

She studies me for a moment. "It's funny, I've never felt that way once about Garrett. I used to think we were friends, but there was a shift in our relationship a long time ago." Looking down at her coffee cup, she sighs. "I'm not sure why I'm talking to you like this. Lord knows it's not appropriate."

"It's probably because I'm not a creepy guy."

Mia laughs. "Probably. I really do appreciate your help tonight. Sorry I was such a mess."

"You're allowed to be. I'm happy I could help." I smile.

"I'm glad you did."

"I'll give you my number, and you can text me when you want help tomorrow if you like."

She licks her lips. "Are you sure it's okay?"

"Seriously, I'd much rather know that you're not going to get stuck in a dark car park than anything else."

"You're a good man, James."

"I like to think so." I sigh. "I should probably get going. Before I make a James-shaped indent on your couch."

She grins. "I think you're a long way from that. But thank you again."

"You're welcome. Give me your number, and I'll text you mine."

For a moment she hesitates, but I tap her phone number into my phone when she gives it to me, and her bag buzzes nearby.

"See you tomorrow," I say.

When she walks me to the door, she looks outside. Is it her ex she's worried about? Despite our conversation inside, I'm not sure I want to pry.

"Good night, Mia. Make sure you lock the door." I'm sure she's well aware of her personal safety, but I feel responsible now I've been here.

"I will. Good night."

For a moment, I take in the sight of her. She's obviously older than me from what I know of her qualifications and experience. It's difficult to tell from just looking at her. Her smile lines are beautifully pronounced, and if I had to guess, I'd think she was maybe early thirties. She seems quite delicate, and I don't know if it's her manner or whatever she's been through that makes her so.

Whatever it is, I like it. It makes me feel protective.

But I shouldn't be feeling this way.

Not about her.

2

JAMES

It's close to midday when my phone buzzes. I've not moved from the couch since I woke up, knowing this was coming. Is it wrong to look forward to this moment? To want to spend more time with Mia?

Mia: *The car's at the garage.*

Me: *Want me to come and get you?*

Mia: *I'd appreciate it.*

I throw a clean shirt on, and pick up my keys from the coffee table. My heart beats faster at the thought of seeing her again. It shouldn't, but I can't help it.

It doesn't take me long to get over to her place. Before I can get out of the car, Mia comes running from the house. She opens the passenger door and sits, shooting me a dazzling smile that takes my breath away. She's in tight, dark blue jeans and a crisply ironed white shirt. It's like her clothes are moulded to her body. It's distracting.

"Let's get going."

I nod. "Sure thing. Just tell me where."

She gives me an address in Mount Roskill, and I programme it into the GPS of my phone. It's in a side street of an industrial area, and I'm not familiar with it, but it's not too far from her home.

"Did they have any issues picking up the car?" I ask.

"Not that I know of. I phoned them and told them where it was. They stopped in and got the keys, and then called me to let me know they had it back at the garage." She pauses. "How was the rest of your night?"

I shoot a glance at her. "Quiet. I just went home after your place and watched some TV."

"That's what I did too. It's also my plan for tonight."

I laugh. "Really? Me too."

She grins. "I want to say thank you for helping me. Want to find a movie to watch tonight? It's pretty lonely watching by myself, and I'll supply the popcorn."

"Are you asking me out, Doctor Scott?"

We pull up to a red light. Her expression's turned serious.

"I'm kidding, Mia. I'd be happy to watch a movie with you. I'll only be at home doing the same thing."

She nods, her lips curling into a smile. "I warn you. I don't like emotional movies. I'd much rather watch an action film or a comedy."

"Me too. Sounds like plan. I'll pay for the pizza."

She smiles again, and my stomach flips. So much for keeping my cool. "I think that's fair."

It is fair. And I'm not going to let myself feel bad about hanging out with her, even when she makes my heart beat faster.

The light goes green, and we go forward. And despite my

reassurance that it's not a date, I like the idea of spending time with her.

Anyone would be a fool not to.

THE GARAGE IS GROSS. It's tucked in behind a bunch of other commercial buildings. It's so grungy and awful compared to Adam's place. He'd have a fit if his guys let his workshop look this bad.

"Mrs Scott." An older man in overalls walks toward her. He gives her a kind smile.

Mia's not having any of it. "Doctor Scott."

He nods. "I think it's going to be a costly repair, love."

Her face falls.

"Why?" I ask.

The mechanic shifts his gaze to me. "There's a lot of work that needs to be done. I can itemise it."

I take a look at his name sewn onto his overalls. "Well, Joe, to me, it looked like just the starter motor. How about replacing that and then we'll take it from there?"

The older man looks like he's been slapped. "Know a bit about cars, do you?"

"My brother's a mechanic. I've worked with him."

He nods, looking me over. "Okay. We'll get right on that."

Mia stares at me as the mechanic walks away. "What was that about?"

I smirk. "If they've been the ones working on your car, I suspect that you've been paying a lot more for work than you needed to."

Her mouth falls open. "Really?"

"We'll see, but if they put in a new starter motor, and it fixes the issue, then I'll help you find a new mechanic."

A smile spreads across her face. "Maybe I can ask your brother to look after my car."

"He's in Copper Creek. It'd be a bit of a commute."

Her eyebrows dip. "Where's Copper Creek?"

I dig out my phone and pull up Google Maps. Her eyes widen as I trace from Hamilton to the east coast of the island, and scroll across the screen to what must look like the middle of nowhere. I guess it is.

"Well, that's out of the question." She laughs. "Does he make house calls?"

I laugh. "Not this far."

"Want us to bill this to the account, Mrs Scott?" the mechanic calls.

Mia straightens up. "Doctor Scott, and no, I'll be paying for it."

"You have an account here?" I ask. These guys could have been playing her for years.

She shakes her head. "Garrett does. My ex."

"Oh, so he's the one who's probably been overpaying for services."

Her cheeks pinken, and she seems to bite down a laugh. "Probably. He took care of it all, but he wouldn't know a spark plug from a starter motor."

I grin. "I can teach you that."

She laughs. "And he said I'd never cope on my own. All I needed was to bump into you."

"Why would you not cope on your own?"

Her face drops, and she looks away. "It doesn't matter."

"Yeah, it does. You're amazing."

She looks back at me, her eyes wide.

"I mean, that paper of yours on fermentation changed my life."

Her eyebrows creep up. "Is this a joke about brewing alcohol and student life?"

"No. I'm serious. I'm interested in agricultural biotechnology, and using fermentation, among other methods, for increased food growth."

She bites her bottom lip. "Uh-huh."

"Maybe it's from growing up in a rural area. Copper Creek is surrounded by farming property with all kinds of different crops."

"Sounds to me like you could have done well doing botany too."

I nod. "I thought about going to Otago for that. But I followed a girl …"

She laughs. "I understand."

We stand in comfortable silence. I like being with her. She's so easy to talk to. I can't imagine having conversations like this with any of my lecturers.

"We've got the part. Want me to give you a call when it's done?" Joe calls out.

"That'd be great." Mia says. She walks over to him, and when she's done she walks back toward me with a smile.

"I'll take you home, and bring you back later if you need me to."

She shakes her head. "I don't want to put you out."

"I'm not doing anything else. I've got some books in the car so I can do some study."

For a moment, she looks unsure.

"Doctor Scott, I'm happy to do it."

"Mia," she says. "I thought we'd worked that out last night."

"I'm not sure if I can call you that."

She laughs. "That's my name. I don't know if I can deal with you calling me Doctor Scott if you're acting as my taxi service."

"So, you're accepting my offer to drive you."

Mia nods. "I'd like that very much."

I grin. "Let's get you home, then."

"I'm starving. If you want to stop somewhere, I'll grab us some lunch."

———

WHEN WE GET BACK to her place, she retrieves the garage remote from her bag and presses it. The door swings open.

"Drive in and park here."

I shoot her the side-eye. "In your garage?"

She licks her lips. "If my ex goes past, it's better that he doesn't see a strange car parked in the driveway."

Confused, I drive forward. Coming to a stop, I turn off the car and pull the keys from the ignition. "Let's go and eat. I'm starving."

She grabs the large bag of food that she grabbed from the bakery we stopped at along the way.

"Does your ex drive past here often?" I pick up my books from the back seat.

Mia sighs as we walk the short distance from the garage to the house, flicking a glance toward the road. "He has a habit of turning up whenever he feels like it."

"I parked on the road last night." I gape at her. "That's why you were looking around."

"To see if I could see his car. His visits are usually during the day, but Garrett can be unpredictable."

After unlocking the door, she walks into the kitchen and dumps the food bags on the kitchen bench.

"Take a seat in the living room, James, and I'll plate this and bring it in."

"Do you need a hand with anything?"

She turns, her eyes widening, and I realise I've invaded her personal space. I'm too close. I take a step back.

"No, I'm fine. Unless you want to grab the drinks out of that bag and take them to the living room." She points at the bag that contains the two bottles of Coke she picked up.

I nod. "I can do that."

Mia smiles, before looking down. "You have books with you?"

"I thought I could get some studying done while we wait. If that's okay."

"I don't mind. I hope the conversation's not that boring."

Laughing, I shake my head. "No, I just need to get some reading in. I work the night shift at a petrol station four days a week, so those nights are out for studying."

As if it's hinting, my stomach grumbles, and Mia laughs. "Go sit on the couch and I'll bring you some food. I'm sure it'll be easier to read with a full stomach."

"Yes, boss."

Her smile lights up the room. "That's better. Get to work."

I laugh as I carry the bottles into the living room in one hand, my books under my other arm.

"I've got some marking to do anyway, so I'll go and get that. How long do you think they'll take to fix this car?"

"Not too long. At least, they shouldn't. Though, I wouldn't put it past them to try and drag out the labour charge."

She smiles. "At least it's not as bad as it would have been if I hadn't had you with me."

"I can't believe people are so dishonest. I mean, I know it happens, but …"

Mia walks into the room, a plate in each hand. One plate has sausage rolls on it; the other has doughnuts.

"Wasn't sure if you wanted savoury or sweet."

"I'm starving. I'll eat anything."

She laughs. "Are you still growing at your age?"

"I'm not a teenager anymore." I roll my eyes, and she just laughs harder.

"I'm going to go and grab my papers. Back in a minute." She drops the plates on the coffee table and turns. I can't help watching her leave the room.

Her jeans fit snugly around that beautifully shaped arse. I let out a long, silent breath at the sight of her.

I pick up a sausage roll from the plate and take a bite. My stomach grumbles.

Mia reappears, a pile of papers in hand, which she places on the coffee table. Opening a drawer in the table, she pulls out a glasses case and takes from it a pair of reading glasses. She sits in a nearby chair, kicks off her shoes, and curls up with her feet under her. Plucking a sheaf of paper from the pile, she starts reading.

I can't take my eyes off her.

Academic Mia is even hotter than she was five minutes ago when she was enjoying-a-quiet-lunch-with-me Mia.

When she reaches the end of the page, she licks her finger. It's the most erotic thing I think I've ever seen. And she has no idea.

She flicks it, never taking her eyes from the paper. There's the odd nod, or a murmur of agreement, but other than that she's engrossed in whoever's report that is. It stirs something inside me.

It's not just lust. Although, that's a big part of it.

I have so much respect for her. Her reputation precedes her. It was a coup for Auckland University to get her as a lecturer. Rumour had it that there was a lot of competition. But part of me wonders how much of that was a sacrifice by her for her marriage.

I'm not sure if her ex realised just how precious she is.

Not just because she's beautiful, sweet and kind. But because she's down to earth, humble, and she's made me feel like more of a man just by being in her presence.

She reaches for a doughnut and takes a big bite, her gaze meeting mine.

There's a layer of icing sugar around her mouth, and I'm taken by the urge to lick it off.

This isn't good.

I'm not sure how I'm going to get through this afternoon.

SHE DOESN'T GET a call for around three hours.

I've distracted myself with my reading, and she's marked

about half the papers she took out. It's easier if I don't look at her. Because all I want to do is kiss her.

I carry my books back out to my car and dump them in the back before we drive to the garage.

Joe the mechanic has done the work, and he grimaces as I look over the invoice. But it doesn't seem that bad.

I get in Mia's car and start it for her, smiling as it purrs like a kitten. "Sounds good."

She pays, and I drive back to her place, following her in her car. I pull into the garage beside her.

Her expression is pensive when she gets out of her car. "You saved me a lot of money. Thank you."

"You're welcome. If you have any more issues, you have my number now too, so call me."

Her lips curl into a wide smile. "I will. Let's get inside. Your shout for pizza for dinner, right?"

I laugh. "That's right."

"Do you need to go home for anything first? You've been here all day."

Shaking my head, I smile. "No. I'm good."

"Then let's work out what we're getting and find a movie."

I follow her inside and into the kitchen.

"I've got Netflix. We can pick something on there if you want."

"Sounds good."

She licks her lips. The simple action sends all the blood from my brain and straight to my cock. She's such a distraction. "I can't thank you enough for helping me today."

"It's really no problem."

"I think there are a couple of beers in the fridge. Want one?"

I nod. "I can grab it."

Mia places one hand on my chest. The contact makes me suck in a breath, and I hope she doesn't notice. "Go and take a seat. I'll get it. It's the least I can do."

I grin. "Yes, ma'am."

"You can stop with that too. It makes me feel old."

Laughing, I turn into the living room. "Sorry, Mia. I've got the Dominos app on my phone. Sound good?"

"Anything that doesn't involve me cooking sounds good. With the car and everything else going on, I don't really feel like it."

"I'm not surprised." I take a seat on the couch. "What kind of pizza do you want?"

"Not too fussed."

I scan the app for deals. There's one with a couple of pizzas and sides delivered. I choose a supreme and a barbeque chicken pizza, showing her the phone screen as she walks into the room with the beer.

"Looks good to me."

"Comes with garlic bread and fries."

She places the beers onto the coffee table and nods. "That sounds really good."

"I'll order it for six?"

She nods.

With a few taps of the buttons, I put my phone on the table and pick up the beer. "It'll be here then."

Mia sits beside me on the couch. "I guess we have some time to kill."

I lean forward a little. Being this close to her is nice. "We do." I lick my lips. This feels like a date, even though I know it's not. "So, tell me more about you."

She blushes. "There's not a lot to tell."

"I bet there is. You're a leader in your field. There has to be a story behind that."

She's so humble, she just shrugs. "I enjoy what I do. I always loved learning."

"Me too. I think with the possible exception of my brother, Drew, my other brothers preferred getting their hands on things. Drew became a doctor. He's an obstetrician."

She smiles. "How many brothers do you have?"

"Four."

Her eyes widen.

"Corey's the oldest. He's a real mountain man. He does pest control, like possums and ferrets. Adam's the mechanic. Drew's a doctor, and Owen's the Copper Creek town baker."

"I don't have any siblings. My childhood would have been very different to yours."

"I spent a lot of time alone when I was a kid. My brothers are all a lot older than me. I think Owen was ten when I was born?"

She nods. "I bet they dote on their baby brother."

Laughing, I shake my head. "They were pretty resentful when I was younger. I think I was more of a nuisance than anything else. But I get on well with all of them these days. They're pretty protective of me."

"I always wished I had that." She looks down at her drink. "Or someone to protect. I wasn't planned for. My parents had decided not to have kids."

"And they told you that?"

She lets out a long breath. "My mother made sure I knew it. I guess that's what made it so easy for them to basically disown me."

"That's awful."

Mia shrugs. "I wish things had been different. I'm not sure if my life would have gone the way it did if they'd been supportive."

"You married young."

She nods. "Young enough. Garrett was studying at the same time I was, but for a career in finance. By the time I moved onto my master's and then my doctorate, we were married and still in the honeymoon stage of our relationship."

"And at some point things went bad."

Mia looks up, meeting my gaze. The blue of her eyes hits me, and I'm sucked into her emotions. "I'm not sure if things were really ever good. Maybe I had rose-coloured glasses. But having a higher-qualified wife suddenly seemed to become a problem. Like he was angry that I'd completed my studies when he never seemed to care about me being a student."

"He sounds like a complete moron to me."

She laughs. "I'm not sure if I should be offended by that."

"I mean, clearly the smartest thing he did was marry you. He should have cherished you, not been bothered by your career."

With a sigh, she nods. "I know you're right."

I bite down on the inside of my cheek. "Is he a threat to you?"

She turns. There's panic in her eyes. Her ex must be a real

douche to put it there. "Garrett wouldn't understand me spending any time with another man."

"What? That I drove you to get your car fixed?"

She licks her lips. It looks like a nervous gesture more than anything else. I'm probably not the most appropriate person for her to be discussing this with.

"While we're waiting for the divorce, I'm trying not to get on his bad side." She seems to choose her words carefully.

"Did he hit you?"

Her eyes widen. "No, nothing like that." She swallows. "He just likes to be in charge."

My blood boils. He's clearly still got her shaken even though they're apart.

I lean forward. This is none of my business, but I have this overwhelming urge to protect her. "Was he abusive?"

She blinks rapidly. "I just know I couldn't live like that anymore."

Maybe he didn't hit her, but she's been wounded. I can see it in her eyes. Heat runs from the top of my head to the soles of my feet, anger at whatever she's gone through.

"Let's turn on the television. There must be something on," she says.

We sit in silence but for the television for more than an hour. It's not uncomfortable, but something weird hangs over us. Maybe it's the fact that I want to smack the living daylights out of the douchebag she was married to.

"I'm sorry for all the questions," I say. "The thought of you being hurt just makes me angry."

She places her hand on my arm. "Because you're a good man."

"My mother would have castrated me if I'd treated a woman badly." I laugh "She liked being mean herself."

Mia's mouth falls open. "Really?"

"No one's ever been good enough for her boys. I think she's trying to be protective, but it comes out all wrong."

"It sounds like she cares a lot."

"She does." I frown. Mum's illness is always in the back of my mind. We were so close when I was little, and I was the one at home with her and Dad when she was diagnosed. The thought of losing her stabs me in the heart.

"What's wrong?"

"Mum has cancer. I'm not sure how much longer she'll be around for."

Sadness fills her expression. "Oh, James. I'm so sorry."

"She's tough. This is the second time she's been ill, but I think this is it."

A knock on the door interrupts us, and I'm glad for the disruption. Mum is in my thoughts a lot, but while I'm studying I can't get home that often.

"I'll get it. That'll be the pizza," I say.

She shakes her head. "Garrett doesn't usually turn up in the evenings, nor does he knock, but I'll get it just in case. I'll bring it in here."

I watch as she goes to the door and take a deep breath.

I'm in over my head with her, but I'm going nowhere. This should be all kinds of awkward with her being who she is, but it's not. I feel more comfortable with her than I have with anyone else for a long time.

"Here we go." She carries in the pizza boxes with garlic bread and chips on the top, and sits them on the coffee table.

I separate the boxes and open them while Mia opens the bread and chips and places them just inside the boxes.

"I haven't had pizza in forever." She smiles as she picks up a slice of the chicken pizza.

"I don't have it often. I usually cook for myself. Nothing too fancy, but I can't afford to eat out all the time." I say it before I think. All that does is highlight the differences between us. It's hardly an impressive thing to admit.

She touches my arm. "I'll pay you back for this."

I shake my head, then take a bite. "No, you won't. I'm just glad I have someone to share it with."

"You usually eat alone?"

I nod. "I broke up with my girlfriend a few months back. It's been just me for a while."

"I'm so sorry."

"She was one of the reasons I came to Auckland, so it's not all bad."

She laughs. "Thank heavens for small mercies. Or something like that."

"I'm glad I'm here."

Her lips twitch. "I'm glad too." She takes a bite of the pizza and moans in such a way it makes my toes curl. "This is so good."

I don't want to eat anymore. I just want to watch her. She takes such pleasure out of something so simple.

After another bite, she gives me the side-eye. "You're not eating."

I laugh. "You're enjoying it enough for both of us."

She shakes her head. "I usually cook. Even if it's something simple. But this is divine."

"Maybe next time it's your turn to choose what we eat."

Her lips twitch. "Next time?"

Shrugging, I take another bite to avoid answering. I'm overthinking this. I know I am. But she doesn't seem to be put off by my attempts at flirting, and even seems to be flirting back a little.

She smiles, placing her hand on my arm. The spark for me is undeniable. Does she feel it too? "Thanks for dinner."

"You're welcome."

"There's some juice in the fridge. Want some?"

"Sounds great."

I wolf down another piece of pizza while she's gone. It doesn't help the nerves in my stomach. When I first saw her yesterday in the car park, she was Doctor Scott. Today, she's Mia.

She returns to the couch with a glass of juice in each hand, and passes one to me. I take a drink while she sits and place the glass on a coaster on the coffee table.

Mia smiles as I study her again. How on earth was I lucky enough to end up here with her?

I already worship her work. God, how I want to worship this woman.

I know I shouldn't.

I can't do this.

This isn't me.

But I do it anyway.

This is what I need.

I lean in and kiss her. It starts soft and lingering, but she opens her mouth and lets me in. My tongue meets hers. Our kiss is slow, sensuous. It's so much more than just a kiss—there's meaning behind it. Or is just that way for me?

When we break apart, she stares at me, but doesn't pull

away. I take her drink from her hands and place it on the coffee table beside mine. "Mia."

"James," she whispers. "We shouldn't."

"I know."

I take her in my arms and kiss her again. Her lips are so soft and welcoming. She stiffens, but doesn't stop me. I deepen the kiss, and she relaxes.

"I … thank you for helping me with my car," she says softly, and I know that's as far as this is going to go.

"I'm not sorry for kissing you."

Her lips spread into a smile. "I'm not really sorry you did. But you can't."

I nod. "I'm sorry I overstepped. I'll get going."

As I turn, she grabs hold of my arm. "Thank you for everything."

"You're welcome. You've got my number if you have any more car trouble. Use it if you need it or for anything else."

Mia nods.

I walk out to the garage, and the door opens as I approach. As if on autopilot, I start the car and back out of the driveway.

Leaving Mia makes me feel empty.

I'm such an idiot.

3

———

MIA

I SPEND half of Sunday pondering the night before.

I'm not sure what to do.

Ever since I finally got the courage to walk away from my marriage, I've been finding my feet in so many ways. Garrett took care of everything, which left me woefully inadequate at dealing with any stressful situation.

Sometimes, I feel like a child.

I spent years being controlled, manipulated, being made to feel like I was the weak link in our relationship. And then it took years to gain the courage to get out.

Even now, I'm trapped.

Garrett agreed I could live in the house until the divorce was final, but it takes two years to get to that point. There's no way to speed it up. At the end of it, we'll sell the place and split the proceeds, and then I'll be able to leave and live the life I want.

But Garrett won't let go.

On Monday, I not only have to continue to deal with waiting for our divorce, he'll also be working at the same place as me. I'm not stupid. This is his way of trying to control me still.

And now there's the added complication of what happened last night.

James Campbell has thrown me for a spin.

I didn't expect anyone to come to my rescue with my car. When I'd finished my breakdown on the bench, I would have gotten in a taxi, gone home, and probably called the garage to take care of it. I would have returned to the mechanic who has probably been ripping us off for years.

But there's so much more to James than I expected.

James genuinely cares.

He's sweet and caring. I haven't dated since leaving Garrett six months ago. The last thing I need is my control freak of an ex making my life difficult before I can completely sever ties. And he would.

Besides, James is a student.

That doesn't stop me being attracted to him.

He's the stereotypical tall, dark, and handsome guy. Solidly built, he has mischief in his eyes that are a soul-melting brown. It'd be so easy to drown in those eyes, and it doesn't help when his emotions are reflected in them.

My stomach's still flipping over the kiss.

I'd thought that reading the opposite sex would be hard when it came to starting again. It's not like I've had that much experience with romance, but James likes me as much as I like him. I knew that before he kissed me.

And that kiss.

He was gentle, but it was intense. It was no quick peck. Instead, it was filled with longing. *With lust.*

My entire lower body clenches at that thought.

I can't act on it, but I can't stop thinking about it.

My phone rings loudly, and I jump in surprise. When I pick it up, I smile when I see who it is—*Kelly Swanson.* We became friends a few years ago through Garrett. Kelly's husband met Garrett through work, and he was as big a douchebag as my own husband. When she left him, I looked closer at my own life and realised I didn't like what I saw at all.

"Hey," I say.

"I thought I'd catch up with you before another crazy week started. Want to get dinner somewhere?"

"Tonight?"

"Yeah. Nothing too flashy. Maybe we can go to that steak-house we went to last time? I could do with a big piece of meat."

I roll my eyes and laugh. "Trust you. That sounds amazing."

"I'll give them a call and make a booking for six if that works. Do it early so we can both get a good night's sleep before work tomorrow."

"That suits me."

AT FIVE-THIRTY, the taxi I ordered shows up outside.

I usually take one to meet Kelly when we go out. Inevitably, we drink a little too much, and I've already had enough hassle with my car without having to leave it in town for the night. There's not usually much parking around the restaurant anyway.

She's waiting by the door when I arrive, and beams as I walk up. After throwing her arms around me, she gives me a squeeze before letting go. "Look at you. Is that the happy glow of single life you have going on?"

I laugh. "Something like that. I'm so glad you called."

"It's been forever. Let's get inside." Once we're seated at the table, she reaches across and squeezes my hand. "You look amazing."

The waiter places a bottle of water on the table, and I pour myself a glass.

"Can we order a bottle of the house sav?" Kelly asks. She looks at me. "You still drink, right?"

"That sounds great to me. I could do with one or four."

She laughs. When the waiter's gone, she turns back to me again. "So, how is it all going?"

"Good. I'm biding my time until the divorce and keeping my head down. For the most part."

She grins. "So, you've met someone?"

I shrug. "Kind of. But it's complicated."

"It'll always be complicated when you still have that dick-head in your life."

I nod, and I'm not about to argue. She's right.

"After twenty years, I can't wait to get him out of my life. There's still a year and half to go until that happens. I'm so looking forward to it."

Kelly smiles. "I bet. I have some news of my own. I'm going overseas for a bit. Got a job offer in the UK, and my visa sorted out. So, I was thinking we could do tonight, and then catch up next week before I go."

"That soon?"

Her smile grows. "It was just one of those things that popped up. I'm grabbing the opportunities when they come. I think I've missed out on so much life."

I nod. "I understand. I'll miss you."

"I'll be back before you know it."

We've been out twice since my marriage breakup. When I was with Garrett, it was rare for me to have a night out without him. And when I did get one, I'd spend the evening being bombarded by texts asking when I was coming home.

I'm not sure now why I put up with it for so long. I guess I thought that was love.

I bet James wouldn't do that. He'd leave me to have my freedom, and then I'd come home to … *shit.*

What am I doing?

"Mia? Are you okay?"

I blink a couple of times, just staring at Kelly. My hand's gone to my lip without me even meaning to. *That kiss.* That's what I want. More of that.

But I shouldn't want more with James Campbell.

"Uhh, I'm fine. Just busy right now and a bit tired." I let out a long breath. "Garrett starts work at the university tomorrow."

Her eyes widen. "What?"

I nod. "Yep. All of Auckland, and by some miracle, the job he finds is at the place I work."

"It must be so tiring, dealing with his mental gymnastics. Why on earth does he think that it's appropriate?"

Shrugging, I take another sip of my drink. "It's not like I can do anything about it."

"Maybe now you can take up one of those overseas offers you got. I bet anything they're still keen."

I lick my lips. As much as that appeals, I like living in New Zealand. Maybe in a few years' time I'll consider a move, but right now I'm not giving up ground because of my ex.

"I'm here for what's left of this year and next year to sort out all the legal stuff with Garrett at least. I like my job. I'll see what happens when the dust settles."

She nods. "I can understand that. If you ever need an ear, day or night, I'm here. You know that, right?"

I smile. "Of course I do. And I appreciate it so much. I'm not sure what I would do without having you to talk to."

The wine appears, and we take a look at the menus.

"Eye fillet, medium rare." I smile at the waiter.

He nods.

"Same." Kelly laughs. She shifts her gaze to me.

We spend the rest of the night talking and catching up, but the whole time I'm keenly aware of this buzzing in my body.

Anticipation.

Excitement.

Excitement caused by James.

It's not late when I get home, but it feels like it. I head straight to the bedroom.

I pull off my clothes and put on my pyjamas. It's a cute little shorts-and-tank-top set I treated myself to a while ago. I always wore silky nighties before, even though I hated them. It's sad how much of yourself you can put aside when you love someone.

Returning to the living room, I fall onto the couch. I shouldn't have done this on a Sunday night. I have an early lecture tomorrow morning, and while I'm not drunk, I'm quite tipsy.

Reaching for the remote, I turn on the television. I'm not sure what the movie is, but it's got Tom Cruise in it, and he's running. So much running.

My mind wanders to the night before and James's kiss. Kelly would have wanted to go out and celebrate if she knew. James Campbell is so hot.

So fucking hot.

I've never been attracted to a student, and he should be no different.

But.

What's wrong with a little fantasy? Besides, he's not in my class. *Yet.*

I close my eyes. Memories rush forward from the night before. His soft lips, the way they tasted, the feel of his tongue against mine.

Holding my breath, I slide my hand down the front of my shorts and into my panties. I'm wet—surprisingly so. I never took the time to get to know my own body. Maybe it's time to change that.

I let out the breath, stroking my clit with my fingers.

My eyes are still closed, and I'm picturing James. It's not fair. I've been in a cocoon for nearly twenty years, never giving myself a chance to learn about my own sexuality—to grow into it.

I wish I was fifteen years younger.

When I first left Garrett, I'd never even thought about there being another man in my life. It was an act of self-preservation.

James's dark eyes burned a hole in my soul. They pierced through the facade that I've had in place for so many years. Maybe this is a chance to unlock the real Mia, the Mia who should have always been. Maybe this is a part of learning about that Mia.

I slip my other hand up under my shirt. Cupping my breast, I squeeze my nipple between my thumb and index finger. Involuntarily, my thighs squeeze together, trapping my hand.

I dip a finger into my pussy. It's for James. It's all for James. In this moment, I no longer care about right or wrong. I don't care that he's a student and I'm a teacher. I don't care about the age difference.

I want him.

He's woken something in me.

And I want to grab hold and enjoy it.

He's parting my legs, lowering his head and licking me. He can't get enough, and neither can I. This is what I've always needed —to feel wanted and appreciated.

I curve my fingers back over my clit and rub. Rolling to my side my gaze falls to the movie I was watching. The actors move and talk on the screen, but all I can think about is finding my own pleasure.

With James's help, of course.

I suck in my bottom lip, trapping it with my teeth. My breath quickens, and I fight the urge to close my eyes again.

My stomach clenches as the waves roll over me. I buck, letting out a moan. I close my mouth, my eyes widening as I look around. Of course no one can hear me. *What if Garrett walked in right now?*

I let out a long breath. My face is blazing. I don't need to touch it to know my cheeks are pink. From exertion or embarrassment, I don't know.

I just masturbated on my couch thinking about a student.

There's no way I can ever tell anyone about this.

4

———

JAMES

I CAN'T STOP THINKING about Mia. It's Friday, and nearly a week since I kissed her.

Maybe if she'd been angry, I wouldn't be thinking about her so much.

Instead, all I think about is the way she felt in my arms, how soft and warm her lips were, and the way she opened her mouth as if inviting me in for more.

It's confusing.

We used to pass each other in the corridor and not meet each other's gaze. Now, I can't help but look.

Twice, we cross paths, our hands brushing against each other. There's a spark, an electricity between us, and I know I'm not the only one feeling it. I just hope no one else has noticed her blushing.

I came to Auckland following my heart, only to have it broken. The feelings I now have for Mia bring me hope. I'm not sure if that's a good thing or not, considering who she is.

Irrational thoughts fill my mind. I don't care about my master's. If I have to, I'll finish up this year and pursue her. I am consumed by Mia Scott.

This is either the most stupid thing I've ever done, or it'll be the best.

Her office door is open, and for a moment, I take in the sight of her.

She's dressed professionally, like she always is. Some lecturers dress down in jeans and a shirt, but not Mia. It's so fucking hot. I don't think she has a clue.

I tap on the door. "Have you got a minute?"

She looks up. Her red-painted lips part when her gaze hits mine. "I …"

"I really need to talk to you."

She swallows hard and licks her lips. It's not helping.

When she nods, I step into the room and close the door behind me. "I can't stop thinking about you." I need to tell her and end the torment I'm feeling either way. There's no point in holding back. I need to say it, and hope for the best.

She drops her gaze and nods. "I'm the same."

"What do we do about it?"

She fidgets, her fingers intertwining. She's struggling. "I don't know."

"If I have to give up my studies, I will."

Mia stares at me. "James, that's crazy."

"I know, but I feel this really strong connection with you. It's not like anything I've ever had before."

"Me too," she says, "but I'm so confused. I'm not sure if it's because of something between us, or because I've just spent nearly twenty years in a shitty marriage with someone who didn't want me the way you seem to."

I sit on the chair opposite her desk, maintaining my distance. I can't push her. "If you tell me that it's that, and I'm imagining things, I'll go home and we can forget what happened."

"I'm not sure I can forget." She picks at her fingernails. "It wasn't just a kiss."

"No, it wasn't."

Her jaw ticks for a moment. "What if we spend some time together and see what happens?" she asks.

I nod. "I'd like that."

"Maybe we'll find it was just a case of you coming to my rescue and feeling chivalrous."

I laugh. "Well, while I would have helped anyone, it meant more to do it for you."

"And not just because of who I am?"

Shaking my head, I lean closer. "I didn't know you. I mean, I'm an admirer of your work, but I saw the real Mia Scott."

"I'm not sure if the real me is worth—"

"Don't you dare say that. That's not you talking—it's your piece-of-shit ex."

Her cheeks flush.

"You are worth so much more than he ever gave you credit for, Mia. And I'm not talking about your research. *You* are worth everything."

"James, you don't know me."

"I know enough. And I know I want more."

She smiles. "Are you always this forward?"

"Honestly? No. But I've also never had such a reaction to another human being as I have to you."

She shoots a glance at the door, but it's still firmly closed.

"Me either. I find you really easy to talk to, which is weird. I'm not that good at making friends that I can just chat with. And then you appear out of nowhere."

I laugh. "I find it really easy to talk to you too. There's a small group I hang out with from time to time, but I've not made that many friends since I moved to Auckland."

She nods. "I know what you mean. Garrett managed to isolate me from all of mine. Then he always twisted things to make it seem like I was at fault." She sighs. "If nothing comes of this, at least I think I've made a friend."

I smile. "So, let's explore this. It's not against the university rules."

Mia pales. "I know, but …." She sighs. "This has to be well under the radar. It took everything to leave Garrett. And if he finds out I'm dating anyone, he'll do his best to make my life hell."

"He got a job here to follow you. He needs to sort out his own issues."

She nods. "I know that. He's been told that. But until the divorce is over and the house is sold, we're tied together. I think he thinks if he's close to me, I'll change my mind."

Irritation builds in me. If it was that bad, he has no right to be anywhere near her. "Wow."

"But I can't live that life anymore, James. I can't spend my whole time being run down and made to feel inferior." She sighs. "Even our marriage counsellor thought he was a narcissist."

"Shit. That just makes you even more amazing."

Her smile is small, but it's there. "How?"

"Look at you and all you've achieved over those years.

While dealing with his shit. No one should ever make you feel small."

Tears well in her eyes. God, how I want to kiss her and feel her body pressed against mine again.

"What are you doing for dinner tonight?" I ask.

She shrugs. "Probably fish and chips in front of the television."

"I'll come over to your place if you want. It's probably safer than you being in my building where I'm surrounded by other students."

She still looks unsure.

"I'd like that," she says. "I'll leave the garage door open."

Standing, I grin. "I'll bring the fish and chips. Anything you want in particular?"

She shakes her head. "Just a piece of fish and some chips."

"I'll be there about six." Leaning forward, I peck her on the cheek. She freezes, and I realise what a dumb arse I am. We're on university property.

"I'm terrified, James. I hope you know that." She seems to force a smile.

"I'm not. This feels right."

She nods, and I leave her office feeling happier than I have in months.

It's a little after six when I pull into Mia's place. The garage door's open, and I drive straight in. It closes behind me.

Grinning, I step out of the car and grab the parcel of fish and chips. She knows I'm here.

She's waiting at the door with a big smile on her face. "You're here."

I walk past her into the kitchen, dropping the package on the bench. "Did you think I was going to stand you up?"

"Is this a date?" She sucks in her bottom lip.

"I'd like to think so." I take a step forward as she walks toward me. When we meet in the middle of the kitchen, I lean and plant a kiss on her cheek. "I hope so, anyway."

She's so cute when she blushes.

"What did you get?" She nods toward the bench.

"Four fish, two scoops of chips."

"That's a lot." She laughs.

"I'm starving. I didn't have lunch."

She shakes her head. "You have to take care of yourself."

"I was pretty excited about tonight."

Mia grins. "Me too."

I take one of her hands in mine. "I'm glad I came to see you. It was driving me crazy."

She lets out a long breath. "I was the same. I'll grab some plates."

I unwrap the food while she pulls out two dinner plates.

Mia shakes her head as she watches me grab two pieces of fish and pile my plate up with chips.

"What? I'm a growing boy." I laugh. I bite down on my lip. Highlighting our age gap wasn't what I wanted to do. But Mia seems to take it in her stride.

She rolls her eyes, making a grab for my stomach. I twist away, laughing louder.

"Where does it all go?" she asks. "My mother used to say I had hollow legs."

"Mine did too. Nothing hollow about mine."

Her palm rests flat against my abs. "I don't think there's anything hollow about any of you."

Placing the plate on the bench, I grasp her arms. "Are you coming onto me, Doctor Scott?"

"Don't call me that."

"Sorry, Doctor Scott."

Her mouth falls open, and she pinches my waist.

"Ouch." I laugh. "Sorry, Mia."

Her cheeks dimple as she smiles at me. With each passing minute, I like her more.

"I'm not even sure why I'm acting like this." Her smile grows bigger.

"Because you're so hot for me. Duh."

She laughs. "Stop it." Her cheeks go pink, and her eyes are so full of life.

"I like it when you're playful." I grin, picking up my plate. "Don't let the food go cold."

It only takes a few minutes for her to join me on the couch, and she's carrying a large bottle of tomato sauce.

"That's what I forgot. You distracted me by feeling me up."

"I did not." She gapes as she sits and hands me the bottle. "Stop casting aspersions on my character."

I chuckle. "You're allowed to feel me up. Just not in public."

Mia smiles. "This sneaking around thing is not going to do anything good for my blood pressure."

"I wish we didn't have to."

"Me too, but … it's what I have to do for my own sanity, as screwed up as that might sound. At least for a while. It's some time before the divorce is final."

"How long is that?"

She sucks in her bottom lip.

"Mia?"

"We have to be separated for two years. Which means we still have eighteen months to go."

"Shit."

She nods. "Want to change your mind?"

I shake my head. "Hell, no."

A smile spreads across her face. "I'm glad to hear it."

"As if I could walk away from you." I hold my hands up. "I didn't mean that to sound so stalkerish."

Mia laughs. "I know. I took it in the way I'm sure it was meant." Her eyes are so full of life, and it's a far cry from the way she was when I found her in the car park. She looks relaxed and happy.

I like her. Really like her.

THE MOVIE'S PLAYING, but I'm not paying attention.

Mia sits next to me. Not too close, but close enough that I can smell her. She's wearing fragrance of some sort. It's light, and I'm not sure what the scent is, but it suits her. I like her being this close.

Licking my lips, I slide my arm onto the back of the couch and around her. I don't try the sneaky yawn when I do it—that's way too corny, and I don't want her to think I'm playing with her.

She smiles and snuggles closer.

"Are you okay?" I ask.

"Very okay. I like this."

"Are you watching the movie? I have no idea what's going on."

She laughs. "Not really."

"Me either. Is this weird?" I ask.

"A little. But it's a good weird." She cups my cheek. "I like having you here."

"I like you being in my arms." I lick my lips. "I really want to kiss you."

Mia smiles. "What's stopping you? You didn't hesitate last time."

I laugh. "Can I kiss you, Mia?"

"I thought you'd never ask."

There's no more hesitation as I cover the small distance between us and press my lips to hers. She opens up, and I slip my tongue into her mouth, probing hers with gentle touches. She tastes like the sweet wine she's been drinking, and it spurs me on. I want this woman more than anything.

Mia sighs when I end the kiss.

"Still okay?" I ask.

"Even more so than before." Her eyes radiate happiness. "The way you kiss me. It's like … well, I don't know how to describe it. You're so gentle, and caring."

"It's the least you deserve."

"I want more."

"So do I." I run my finger down her throat. She closes her eyes, and I take a moment to look at her. She's so delicate she looks like she might just break if I'm too rough, but I know she's tough. Mia's had to be to do what she did. Walking away from a marriage after all that time must have been hard.

She opens her eyes. "What?" Her smile is intimate. We're

already sharing so much, but it doesn't freak me out. It feels natural.

"Just taking in how gorgeous you are."

Blush rises in her cheeks. I love making her blush.

Claiming her mouth, I push her gently back onto the couch. I'm so fucking hard just by being near her. I want Mia Scott more than I've ever wanted anyone or anything in my life.

My tongue tangles with hers, but I take the lead. Pulling off her mouth, I drop my head to her neck, kissing and sucking my way down.

"James." Her hands are on my chest, but pulling me closer. She wants me too.

I kiss all the way to the top of her breasts before I sit back up. Her eyes are wide, and her chest heaves as if she's run a marathon.

"You don't have to stop," she whispers.

"I think I do."

Her lower lip wobbles. Not much, but enough for me to see.

"I should go."

She licks her lips. "You don't have to."

"Are you asking me to stay?"

Mia swallows hard. "Yes," she whispers.

"I really want to, but I think we should take things slowly."

She smiles. "Has anyone ever told you how sweet you are?"

"I don't want you having any regrets."

Mia nods. "I understand."

I grasp her chin, pulling her gaze to mine. "This isn't a

rejection, Mia. You know that, right? I could stay here and kiss you all night. Or I could indulge in every single fantasy I've had this past week. But I don't want you waking up in the morning and freaking out about it."

"I don't think I would." She sucks in her bottom lip. "Fantasy?"

"Oh, I'm not ready to talk about that yet." I laugh. "But I want you to know that spending this evening with you hasn't dampened whatever this is for me."

"Me either."

"It's made it stronger."

God, how I love it when I make her smile. Her whole face lights up. *How often did she do that in the past if her ex was that bad?*

I want to be the opposite to whatever he was.

I want to make her smile like that all the time.

"We need to do this again, and soon," she says.

"Yes. Next weekend? Monday to Thursday night is out because of work. But Friday or Saturday."

She nods. "It feels like so far away."

"Well, we could do something tomorrow night if you want to as well. If it's not too much."

She nods again before letting out an exasperated sigh. "I've got plans with a friend tomorrow night."

My right eyebrow won't stay down.

"A girlfriend. We made plans last week. So, Friday next week, then?"

I grin. "Sounds good. Enjoy your night tomorrow."

Lingering on her lips, I reluctantly let her go. "Good night, Mia."

"Good night, James."

For a moment, we just look at each other. It's all I need. To know she's feeling the same way as I am. It's written all over her face.

In a lot of ways, it would have been better for both of us if this night hadn't worked out. Then she could have gone back to her life and me to mine, and next year and her ex wouldn't be issues.

Instead, I only want her more.

And I know she's feeling the same way.

5

———————

MIA

I'M DISTRACTED while at dinner with Kelly the following night.

I barely notice when the food arrives at the table, and she's half finished her steak before she looks up, her eyebrows raised. "Earth to Mia."

I shake my head. "Sorry, what?"

"Are you going to eat that?"

I nod, picking up my knife and fork.

"I like doing this with you, and it's the last time for a while with me going away, but it's not much fun when you're not here in spirit."

"Sorry. I've just got a lot on my mind."

"Is this to do with the 'it's complicated' guy?"

I look up and meet her gaze. Giving her a short nod, I cut a slice of my steak and pop it into my mouth. It's cooled, but still just as nice.

"I'm not going to ask you anymore because I don't think

you want to tell me, but I want you to know you deserve to be happy."

I put down my cutlery and take a sip of wine. "That's the thing. I think I really could be. It's just not the greatest of circumstances."

"Is he good to you?"

I nod at the thought of how sweet and gentle James is. What scares me is that things with Garrett started the same way, and look where that got me.

"He's perfect. Kind and caring, and he wants me. God knows why because I'm old enough to be his mother."

Kelly's mouth falls open. "He's a student?"

I look around, but either no one's heard her or they don't care.

"Yes. He's twenty-two."

"Well, you're only just old enough to be his mother. Legally. I'm so jealous."

I laugh. I know Kelly's had a lot of sex since she's been single. But she's got no hang-ups about sex with no commitment, whereas I do. Although, after my fantasy the other night, I'd take James any way he wanted me to.

"I asked him to stay last night, and he went home instead."

She cocks her head. "I'm so sorry."

"He was right. It's too early." I take another sip of wine. "Might have to wait until next week."

She laughs, reaching across the table to place her hand on mine. "As long as you're happy and not getting into another Garrett situation. One of those arseholes is enough for one lifetime."

I join in the laughter, but I still worry in the back of my head. Is James who I need and not just who I want?

THERE'S a single pink rose on my desk when I get in on Monday morning.

I smile. It can't be James. Can it?

I pull out my phone.

Me: *Did you leave something on my desk?*

The reply comes straight back.

James: *Guilty as charged. I had to "drop a book back that I'd borrowed".*

I grin. This isn't helping me fight this, even though I know deep down that I should. James is a guilty pleasure for me, and he makes me feel desirable and wanted. It's been a long time since I felt that.

What I need to work out is if he's good for my ego or if it's something more.

Me: Thank you. It's beautiful.

James: So are you.

My body tingles with anticipation for Friday. I want more kisses. I want more caresses. Even the simple act of him holding me brings me joy.

It's becoming clearer with every passing moment just how much I've missed out on for years.

Me: You're good for my ego. Talk to you later xx

I pick up the rose, breathing in its scent. This is the best ever start to the day.

But I have work to do, and I tuck the rose into a desk drawer and lock it away.

I have two lectures for the day, and once they're done, I head back to my office to get some marking done before I go home.

Garrett's sitting in my office. I managed to avoid him the first week he was here, but now he's seeking me out. I'm sure he has the admin staff falling all over him. He has all that charm for people who don't know the real him. He's a dark-haired, blue-eyed snake.

"I guess I forgot to lock the door." I place my bag on my desk and muster the dirtiest look I can.

"Thought I'd pop in and say hi. Wanna go for a drink?"

"No."

He smiles. "Come on."

"I'm not interested, Garrett. I didn't want you to come here, so why would I celebrate with you?"

He leans forward. "Do you miss me?"

"Are you even listening?"

He lets out a sigh. "I thought maybe if I was close to you, you'd see what a mistake you've made. I've got plenty of others interested."

"Then go fuck one of them. They can have you."

This isn't me. It was never me. But Garrett brings it out. I realised a long time ago that I had to be blunt with him. But this, like every other conversation we have, will fall on deaf ears.

"There's something wrong with you, Mia. This isn't like you. Have you seen someone about it?"

"Get the hell out of my office."

He stands, straightening his tie, and I'm really glad that the rose James left me is locked in my desk drawer. The last thing I need is Garrett sniffing around my love life.

"Garrett. Now."

He gives me a steely glare, the one that used to end all our arguments. The one that used to reduce me to an apologetic groveller. Usually for something I had nothing to apologise for.

Not this time.

I drive home, the rose on the passenger seat of my car. My constant reminder that there's something better out there for me. Unless James turns out to be just like him. I glance at the rose again out of the corner of my eyes. I'll just need to protect my heart until I know I can trust James.

I hate that Garrett leaves me feeling so raw and vulnerable.

But I also can't shut myself off.

AFTER A QUICK STIR-FRY DINNER, I sit down with a glass of wine.

Work is going to be tough from here on in. I'll have to remember to lock my office whenever I leave it just to keep Garrett out. Which sucks. Usually I lock it at night, and the cleaners unlock in the morning, but I don't lock it between lectures in case any of the other staff need to drop anything off.

My life is about to change again.

But it's not all bad. When I close my eyes, I feel James against me, his lips on mine, his tongue seeking entrance and telling me that he wants more. He wants *me*.

I jump when my phone rings, and smile when I see who it is. "James."

"I just got home, and I wanted to hear your voice."

I grin. I can't help it. "It's good to hear from you."

"How was your day?"

Taking a small sip of my wine, I give a little contented sigh. "Made better by you. By the way, my office will be locked during the day if I'm not in there from now on. Garrett paid me a visit."

"Shit." His tone grows serious. "Are you okay?"

"I'm fine. I'd tucked the rose away to avoid any questions anyway, but I have to be more careful. On the way out, I asked if the cleaners could make sure the door was locked when they were finished in the morning. I don't want him in there."

"Understandable. What did he want?"

I sigh. "Just to tell me what a mistake I'm making, and I guess to reiterate that he's working there now."

There's silence for a moment. I'd love to see his face.

"But you're okay? Did he upset you?"

"A little, but I'm home and I just ate. Right now I have a glass of wine, so all is right with the world." I lick my lips. "I'm just missing you."

I swear he growls, but it's hard to tell over the phone. "I'm looking forward to Friday."

"Me too. I went to Cody's this afternoon to study, but I thought a lot about you."

My heart thuds, but not because he's thinking about me. "You didn't tell him about us, did you?"

"No. Of course not. I'm not going to risk your career or my education. We're in this together, Mia."

I suck on my bottom lip. "I told a friend about you. Well, not about you per se, but she knows I'm seeing a student. But she's supportive and she's not looking for your identity. She just likes seeing me happy."

He chuckles. "I hope this makes you happy. But I don't think we should tell anyone else. Not yet anyway."

"I don't think we should either. My friend Kelly hates Garrett, if that helps."

He laughs louder. "I'm glad you have her, then." He pauses. "I should get going. I have to get ready for work. Working nights really screws me up."

"What hours do you work?"

"Eight until four in the morning."

I grimace. "Ouch."

"Won't hurt as much this week because I have Friday to look forward to."

"I'm going to finish this glass of wine and get to bed."

He lets out a loud breath. "There's an image. Don't get into any trouble. Have a good night, Mia."

I laugh. "The only time I think I'll get into trouble is when you're around."

"I like the way you think. Save it for Friday. Good night, Mia."

"Good night."

6

JAMES

MY STOMACH IS in knots by the time Friday comes.

Fridays are usually pretty good. My only lecture is in the afternoon, so after my Thursday-night shift I get a decent sleep. It still leaves me tired.

But today is different.

Tonight is date night with Mia.

I'm not sure how things are going to go, but I can imagine there'll be more kissing. How far will that take us?

We've talked on the phone every night this week, and the anticipation has built between us to the point where she's all I can think about.

And I know she's feeling the same way.

I pull into her garage, and there's a few moments before the door closes behind me.

She's waiting in the kitchen, and I don't hold back. I take her in my arms and kiss her, the tiredness disappearing when I'm holding her. Her body's tight against mine, and that's just the way I like it.

"James." She gasps when I let her up for air.

"How did you think I was going to greet you after a whole week?" I press my forehead to hers.

"I'm not complaining." She pecks me on the lips. "I made dinner."

I grin. "You didn't have to."

"I know, but I've been fidgeting since I got home, so I needed to do something." She laughs. "I hope you like the meal."

"I'm sure I'll love it."

Her eyes are so full of life, and her dimples are on full display. I love seeing her like this—so vibrant and full of excitement. "But before that, do you want a beer?"

"That would be great. It's been such a long week."

Mia squeezes my hand. "For me too."

She lets go of me and crosses the kitchen to open the fridge. My heart feels as if it's about to burst, but I'm not nervous. It's weird for me. I remember how awkward I was when Ashley and I first got together, but with Mia, it's so easy.

Maybe it's because I feel so protective of her, and that's overriding everything.

"Here you go. Dinner won't be long."

"Thanks." I take the beer she offers and with my free hand, pull her toward me again. Kissing her feels natural, and I intend to do it a lot more. She relaxes against me, and it's the best feeling in the world.

"Take a seat at the table. I just have to mash the potatoes and we'll eat."

"Good, because I want to get on with the rest of our night."

Her grin lights up the room. "So do I."

MIA'S A GREAT COOK. It's a simple meal—crumbed lamb chops with mashed potato and fresh vegetables, but it's perfect and tasty.

Afterward, I help her put the dishes in the dishwasher, and I wipe down the bench while she wraps her arms around me from behind. Her palms are flat on my stomach, and I sigh at the contact.

"I like having you around," she says.

I turn. "I like being around. Let's go to the living room and see what's on TV."

She nods. "Or we could talk."

"Or that. I'm not sure we'd see much of anything."

Mia laughs, taking me by the hand and leading me into the living room. "I've missed you all week." She pulls me down onto the couch beside her.

"I'm not sure I can go another week without seeing you." I reach up and palm her cheek.

After licking her lips, she purses them with a look in her eyes that tells me she has something big to say.

"Are you okay, Mia?"

"I need to know that you're doing this because you like me. Not because I'll be one of your lecturers next year and you're trying to get brownie points."

She needs to know I want her for her, but how do I

convince her of that? "I'll drop out next year if that's what it takes to prove it to you. I like you. I *really* like you."

She lays her hand on my arm. "You don't have to drop out next year. We'll work this out."

"So, that's a yes?"

Her lips curl into a smile. "A yes to what?"

"Wherever this night takes us. Slowly, but surely."

Mia laughs. "I like that idea."

I claim her mouth again. The kisses in the kitchen were tame compared to this. I need to show her how much I care for her.

My hand rests on her shoulder, and I run it down her arm. When she leans into me, I brave cupping her breast. She breaks the kiss with a gasp.

I look into her eyes.

She nods.

I run my thumb over her breast, grazing her nipple.

"Is this what you want too?" I ask. "I don't want to rush things, but this feels so right."

"For me too."

"All I want to do is touch you."

"I'll let you." She gives me a bashful smile, and I feel it in my groin.

"We'll go slow."

She nods, and I kiss her, fondling her breast through her clothing. When I pinch her nipple, she gasps again, and I swallow it in my kiss.

I slip my hand up under her shirt, pushing aside her bra. As I stroke her bare skin, she melts under me.

"James." She breaks away, and I push up her shirt. Her

breast is full with a light pink nipple that's pebbled under my fingers.

"Too much?" I ask.

She shakes her head. "I'm fine. I just want …"

I bend my head, tonguing her nipple before sucking it into my mouth. Mia strokes my back as I graze my teeth over it.

"I want you," I say, raising my head.

Her eyes search mine. "I want you too. How do we do this, James?"

I smile. "It's simple."

I drop to her other breast, repeating my actions. She lets out a contented sigh, her fingernails raking my back. I want to be inside her while she does that to my bare skin. I want to give her every little bit of pleasure that I can.

Taking a deep breath, I run my hand up her thigh and under her skirt. She sucks in a breath, and I meet her gaze, maintaining eye contact as I slip my hand into her panties, seeking her clit with my fingers.

There are no words.

There's no need for them.

Her expression softens as her eyelashes flutter. I stroke her clit with my index finger as we gaze at one another. I'm so fucking hard and can't wait to taste her, to be inside her.

She slides down the couch, giving me better access. When I slide my middle finger into her pussy, she gasps.

"You like?" I ask.

"Very much."

I chuckle, slipping my index finger into her and using my thumb to rub her clit. "We should go to bed."

Her eyes widen. "I guess the way the night's progressing, we're not taking things slowly."

"I was all for that, but right now I have two fingers in your pussy, and I'm not sure that's going slow."

She laughs, and I wince as her pussy tightens around my fingers.

"Are you okay?"

"Apart from having this desperate need to be inside you?"

Mia palms my cheek. "It's mutual. Believe me. I'm just a little scared."

"Of what?"

"This. Us. I never planned on having sex with a student."

I pull my fingers out of her. "I thought it was more than that."

"We still barely know each other, James. Are you worth being reckless and irresponsible for?"

My lips twitch. "You tell me." I slide my fingers back into her and pump them slowly, my thumb grazing her clit.

"Oh, you're playing dirty."

"I don't think I've ever wanted anyone so much." I lean over and nuzzle her neck. She squirms underneath me.

"I'm going to … ohhhh." Her body jolts as she comes. My fingers are soaked and all I can smell is her. That scent is my favourite aphrodisiac.

She pants. "Okay, that was …"

I grin. "Are you going to finish any of your sentences?"

Her chest rises and falls rapidly. "I'm beginning to realise I've lived a really sheltered life."

"You've come before, right?"

"Not like that." Her cheeks are flushed, and her hair is

mussed. If anyone showed up right now, they'd know what we'd been up to. "Not so … consuming."

"Consuming?"

She laughs. "I'm not sure how to describe it. Less functional and more emotional."

"I'm not sure if I can handle sex with you if you're going to be all scientific about it."

"James?"

I smile. "Yes?"

"Let's go to bed."

I pull my fingers out of her, and smile as she straightens her skirt when she stands.

"I'm not sure why you're doing that. It's just going to come off in a few minutes."

Her cheeks flush and she laughs. "I'm not sure either."

Taking my hand in hers, she leads me up the hallway and into the large master bedroom.

"The bed is new, in case you're wondering," she says.

"My brain's not working too well right now, so I wasn't."

Laughing, she turns to face me. I reach for the hem of her shirt, pulling it over her head. Her bra's sitting awkwardly above her breasts and as she reaches for the clip, I take in the sight of her.

When she realises, she crosses her arms over her breasts.

"What's wrong?"

"Maybe this was a mistake."

I frown, grasping her arms and pulling her toward me. "Why?"

"I'm thirty-nine years' old, James. I'm no spring chicken. My body's not what it used to be."

"It looks amazing to me."

Her worried expression softens. "I think we both know you don't mean that."

"But I do. You're beautiful, Mia. I want to make you feel that."

She sucks in her bottom lip. It drives me crazy how she's so confident one minute and withdraws the next, but I know it's her past that causes her to doubt herself.

Doubt is one thing she never needs to do with me.

I let her arms go and she uncrosses them. Her breasts are perfect. As perfect as they were a few minutes ago when I tasted them. "Let me see the rest of you."

She shakes her head. "Not yet. You're still wearing all your clothes."

I grin as she reaches for my T-shirt. When she pulls it over my head, I feel her eyes on me.

Her hands are warm as she places them on my torso and takes a deep breath. "You work out?"

I nod. "Box mostly, but sometimes weights."

"It works."

I grasp her chin and pull her gaze to mine. "Touch me as much as you want."

She smiles as she explores my skin with her fingers before dropping them to my jeans. After she fumbles with the button, I suck in a breath, and she drops the zip and pushes my pants down.

"Mia," I whisper.

She keeps her gaze on me as she pushes at my underpants and grips my cock. It's so fucking hard, and I hold my breath for a moment, fearful that I'm going to come from her touch.

"I want this, James Campbell. It's crazy and a bigger risk than I've ever taken before, but I can't fight it."

"I don't want you to fight it."

She lets go of me when I kiss her.

"Bed," I say.

"Should I take off my skirt?"

I shake my head. "Lie down. I'll take care of that."

She pulls back the duvet and top sheet while I climb out of my jeans and underpants. When she turns, her eyes widen and she lies down.

Her skirt has an elastic waist, and I climb onto the bed, grabbing the fabric and pulling it off in one move. Dragging her panties down her legs, I take in the sight of her naked.

"Shaved."

She smiles. "I like it like that."

"I'm not complaining." I lie down beside her, pulling her into my arms.

"Can I tell you something personal?" she asks, her eyes searching mine.

"You're in my arms, and you're naked. I'll listen to anything." I laugh.

"I touched myself thinking about you."

Wow. My eyebrows rise. "Really?"

"What just happened on the couch. Well, I did it solo the night after you kissed me." She blushes, burying her face in my chest. "It was much better when you did it."

I'm already hard, but the thought of her touching herself with me in mind? Holy shit. "Can I tell you something personal?"

Her lips twitch. "What?"

"I want to taste you so bad. It's all I've been thinking about."

Her eyes widen. "Really?"

I chuckle. "Yes, really. Do you think you were the only one with indecent thoughts? Thinking of you helped make the nights we didn't see each other go faster."

She sighs when I drop my hand to her breast. She's perfect.

I suck one of her nipples into my mouth, caressing her other breast.

She lets out a long breath, as if she's been holding it for ages. "James."

Dragging her nipple gently through my teeth, I raise my head. "Mia."

Her chest rises and falls rapidly as we look into each other's eyes. There's so much need in her expression.

"You're so fucking beautiful."

She blinks rapidly again, as if she's trying to process what I've said.

"Are you okay?" I smile.

"I never … no one's said anything like that to me before. That's the second time you've said it."

"You've got to be kidding."

She shakes her head. "My ex wasn't good at compliments."

"I can't understand that. You're a goddess."

Her eyebrows creep up. Maybe that was taking it a bit too far.

I shrug. "I'm not going to apologise for how I feel."

She searches my expression. I'm not sure what she's looking for. Maybe she still thinks it's an empty platitude. But this is a beautiful woman who needs to be told that she's beautiful. And I'm only too happy to oblige.

I run my hand down her thigh, and she shivers when I

move it back up to her pussy. Her breaths grow deeper. "Are you okay?"

She nods. "I'm fine."

Caressing her clit with my fingers, I study her face. Her eyelids flutter at the contact.

"I thought I'd be kissing you a lot, but this isn't how I pictured spending my weekend." I grin.

"Me either." She laughs. "I feel ..."

"What?" I slip a finger into her, and she sucks in a breath.

"Well, your finger, but it's so screwed up. I've never done anything bad in my life."

I grin. "And this is bad?"

"No, it's good. But you know what I mean."

Her mouth falls open when I slip in a second finger, my thumb rubbing over her clit.

She widens her legs, giving me more access, and I return my attentions to her breasts.

Her nipples pebble as I lick them one by one. I circle the closest nipple with my tongue, and she lets out a moan. When I suck it gently into my mouth, she bucks.

"James."

I sit back up, looking into her eyes. She seems to be fighting the urge to close them. She's so beautiful when she comes.

My hand's covered in her wetness, and as much as I want to be inside her, I could spend hours just watching her as she gives into pleasure.

"Interesting," She whispers.

I laugh. "What is?"

"What happened on the couch isn't a fluke."

"What do you mean?" I plant a kiss just under her breast.

"Coming with you is different. I mean, I don't have much to compare it to, but …"

After running my tongue up and over her breast, I find her mouth with mine. She sighs as I kiss her.

"You are working with a very narrow field of experience here."

She nods. "I'm sorry."

"Stop apologising. I think it's amazing. And I love that I can bring this out in you."

She tilts her head. "How'd you get to be so great? You're sweet, and caring, and when you touch me I feel things I've never felt before. And I'm nearly twice your age."

I shrug. "I was the quiet one in my family. I've got four older brothers who would have slapped the snot out of me if I wasn't respectful. And then there was the mother factor I already told you about."

Mia laughs. "My parents were like that. They were so strict. I guess they were worried I'd embarrass them. Then they disowned me when I ended up with Garrett."

"What? I can't imagine any parent disowning their child."

She shrugs. "I think they saw what he was like years before I did. They warned me, and told me to keep away, but all it did was make me dig my heels in. We were married as soon as I could do it without their permission."

"I'm so sorry."

"I still haven't been in touch with them since I left him. I'm not sure how to."

"I'm not sure why we're talking when I could be making you come again."

Her lips spread into a smile. "I don't know either. I did say you were easy to talk to."

"So are you, but I'd rather be doing something else with my mouth right now."

Mia's eyebrows creep up. "Like what?"

I move down between her legs, pushing back the sheet. Her eyes widen. "Oh."

Laughing, I nod. "Oh."

I feast on her. Her breathy gasps spur me on as I tongue her clit. She lifts off the bed when I suck it gently into my mouth. If I thought she liked my fingers, she loves my tongue. And I love going down on her. "You taste so fucking good."

Mia runs her fingers through my hair, gripping it and pulling me closer. I love how quickly she's become so uninhibited, how she's not afraid to show me what she wants.

I lick up both sides of her pussy, and suck gently on the flesh. I'm consumed by her, and I just want Mia to have the best sexual experience of her life. I'm not cocky enough to think I'm anything amazing, but all that matters is that she enjoys herself.

When I move back to her clit, her breathing falls apart, and she lets out a moan as she thrusts toward me. Her body shudders.

I run my tongue over her, licking up her juices. She lets out puffy breaths as she recovers.

I plant kisses on her thighs, and she squeezes them together. Laughing, I look up. "Are you okay?"

"Very okay." She sighs a contented sigh. "Why did you stop?"

"You squeezed me out." I laugh.

"I want you inside me."

I don't need to be told twice.

"I've got a condom in my wallet. One second." I lean over and pick up my pants from the floor.

"I don't have any. You can probably tell I didn't plan for this." She laughs.

"Me either. It's probably expired." I joke.

"What?"

When I pluck the condom out of my wallet and sit back up, she stares at me.

"I'm kidding. Check it yourself if you want to." I wave the foil packet in the air.

She snatches it from my hand and examines it.

"I can't believe you checked."

"I can't believe you joked about it."

I take it back from her. "I'd never do anything to hurt you, Mia."

She sighs. "That was a dick move."

"I'm sorry." I search her expression. "Are we still okay?"

She nods, pointing at my cock. "As if I'm gonna waste *that* now."

I chuckle, tearing open the condom wrapper.

She watches as I roll the condom on. Even her watching me is hot.

"Ready?" I ask.

"Yes."

"Are you sure about this?"

She nods. "Are you trying to talk me out of it?"

"I would never do that."

Her smile lights up the room as she palms my cheek. I lean forward, claiming her mouth with mine, our bodies pressed together.

"I want you so fucking much," I murmur.

"Then take me." She guides me with her hand, and I slide into her. Fuck, if this isn't heaven, I don't know what is.

"Mia," I meet her gaze. Her eyelids flutter as I move inside her.

She lets out a long breath, and her lips stay parted. Everything she does makes me harder. She's so beautiful.

We maintain eye contact as I thrust. Sex has never been like this before. It was always emotional, and I'm not a guy who has it for the sake of it, but this is different. There's a connection between us that I've never felt with anyone else.

God, how I hope she feels it too.

Her chest rises and falls underneath me as her breathing grows strained.

"It feels so good." She moans.

I run my tongue up her neck until I reach her ear. "What feels good?"

"You do. You feel so good."

I search her expression, but the emotions she has on display leave me feeling overwhelmed. "You feel amazing." I lick my lips. "You are amazing."

Her heels hit the back of my thighs as she pulls me in deeper. "You're pretty amazing too."

"I'm sure I can do better than pretty amazing."

Mia's lips curl into a smile. "Fine. You're incredible. Is that better?"

"It must be. I ..." Waves of pleasure wash over me as I come. My body jerks as if I'm not in control of it, and I thrust hard twice before coming to a stop.

"Now you're the one not finishing sentences." She laughs softly as I roll to her side.

I pull her into my arms. "It's difficult to find the words when you're so overwhelmed."

"I know."

She sighs, running her finger down my chest. "If I was being responsible, I'd tell you we shouldn't do this again," she says.

"I know."

"We shouldn't have done it this time." She lets out a laugh, and buries her face in my chest. "This is so not like me."

"Me either." I chuckle.

"I've been in one relationship in my life, and it was with Garrett."

I shrug. "I've had one serious girlfriend. There have been a couple of hook-ups, but nothing like this."

"Like what?"

I turn my head. Her eyes are full of emotion. I feel it too. "I can't answer that. It's just different with you."

She smiles. "You're too young to know that."

I shake my head. "I'm old enough."

Mia slaps her hand to her face. "I just had sex with a … how old are you?"

"Twenty-two."

She groans.

"Why? How old are you again?"

"Thirty-nine."

"Woah. That is old."

Her mouth falls open.

"I'm kidding. I don't care. You're gorgeous, and I was already enamoured with your brain."

When she laughs, I smile. If her marriage was that bad,

how long has it been since she's just enjoyed herself? Since that laughter was free and uninhibited?

I shrug. "It could always be worse. At least I'm not in your class."

"But you will be next year."

I sigh. "Then you're right. We won't do this again."

"We shouldn't." A smile spreads across her lips.

I lick my lips. "I'll buy a box of condoms for next time."

Mia laughs again, and I press my mouth to hers. However long this lasts, I intend to make the most of it.

And from the way she responds, so does she.

7

———

JAMES

IT'S A LONG WAIT to the following weekend. I spent Friday and Saturday night with Mia, coming home on Sunday to prepare for uni the following day.

To be honest, I needed a good night's sleep after our time together.

We text each other throughout the week, and talk on the phone every night, but it's not the same as seeing her.

Friday is the longest day ever, and all I want to do is get to my car and get away from uni.

"Are you coming to the pub?" Sara asks as we walk through the doors to exit the lecture hall.

I shake my head. "Not tonight."

She places her hand on my arm. We're outside the lecture hall, and I'm so close to getting away. I'm off for a shower and change of clothes at home before heading over to Mia's.

"Please, James. Come out with us."

Her grip tightens. Damn it. I tried to let her down gently,

but I obviously wasn't clear enough. "I've got other plans. I'm sorry, Sara. You guys go and have some fun."

She licks her lips. "I thought maybe you and I could hang out together."

"Sara. I'm sorry if I ever gave you the wrong idea, but …"

She turns on that doe-eyed look. Another time, another place, it might have worked, but the woman I think I'm falling for is waiting for me. "Come on, James. It'll be fun."

I pull my arm away gently. "I'm going home. Enjoy yourself."

I walk away without looking back. It's not until I reach my car that I turn again. Sara's right behind me.

"Take me with you, then."

I shake my head. "Are you always this pushy?"

"Only when I really like a guy. And I really like you." She's breathless, and if I was still unattached maybe I'd make a stupid decision and take her home. But I'm not.

"I like you too. As a friend. I'm not looking for anything else."

Her face falls. "It's *her*, isn't it?"

I swallow hard. Am I that transparent?

"Ashley. You still have a thing for her."

I shake my head. "No, it's not Ashley. That was over ages ago." Letting out a breath, I take her by the arms. "You're really nice, Sara. And I'm sorry if I'm not feeling it, but I'm not interested in you in that way."

She pulls away. "Okay. Have fun by yourself."

"Do you want a lift to the pub? Seeing as you've walked all the way to my car."

Her cheeks are flushed. I understand it. I've had my share of rejection, but she's handling it okay. "I'd appreciate it."

"I'm heading that way, anyway."

Opening the passenger door, I wait until she's in before closing it again. When I round the car, I look up as I open the driver's door.

Mia's at the edge of the car park next to her car.

Our eyes meet, and I don't have to see her face to know she's curious about what's going on. From where she's standing, it can't look good.

I pull my phone out of my pocket before I get into the car.

I'm just dropping Sara at the pub. Will be over to see you once I've showered and changed. I take a breath. *Can't wait to get you alone.*

I hope that's enough as I start the car and pull into the street.

Mia's in her living room when I get there, and when she sees me, she picks up the remote to close the garage door.

"Hey, beautiful." I lean over and kiss her.

She kisses me back, but withdraws, and I round the couch and sit beside her.

"You okay?"

"I saw you with your friend. It seemed pretty intense. What's going on with you two?"

"Nothing. I dropped her off at the pub." I lean back. "She likes me, and I guess I was too subtle for her to get that I wasn't interested. I made it clear."

Mia drops her gaze. "Okay."

I grasp her chin, pulling her face up until I meet her eyes.

"I'm not lying to you, Mia. She followed me to the car, and I was straight up with her. The pub was on my way, so I gave her a lift. And then I went home, showered, changed, and came back here."

"I believe you."

"Why does your body language say otherwise?"

She flicks her gaze to the ceiling and back again. "I just don't want to be hurt. She's your age, and she's pretty. I could understand if you wanted something with her."

"I had the chance before us, and I didn't take it then. I'm not going to screw up whatever this is with you for someone who's not even really a friend."

"What is this?" she asks.

I drop my hand. "I don't know. Do we have to define it yet? All I know is that I like spending time with you. And I'm not talking about studies or science. I like being with Mia, not Doctor Scott."

She laughs. "We're the same person, you know."

"I know, but I don't want you because of your academic prowess. That was just the reason for both of us being at the university."

Her smile turns into a grin. My heart thuds at the sight. I want her to be this happy all of the time.

"I love your smile."

Her lips twitch, and she leans forward, meeting my lips with hers. Her kiss is tender and sweet when all I want to do is devour her.

When she pulls back, she sucks her bottom lip through her teeth. "I thought maybe I could make us some dinner. Maybe some cheese toasties. And then we could go to bed."

She swallows hard when she finishes her sentence. I'm not sure if she's ever been this forward before.

"That sounds like a really good plan to me."

"I like being with you, James. I'm so scared of screwing this up."

I study her expression. "I like being with you too. There's no way you could screw this up. You know this isn't all about the sex, right? I'm happy just being with you. We can watch movies all night if you like."

She nods, her cheeks flushing pink. "I just really enjoyed sex with you."

"I enjoyed it with you too." I cock my head. "Ohhh, you just want more of the James Campbell loving. I hear it's pretty good."

Mia's mouth falls open. "Don't you be getting an ego on you."

"Oh, it's *way* too late for that." I hold up one palm. "I'm happy to sign an autograph afterward."

She laughs, shoving my bicep. "Stop it."

I wrap my arm around her, pulling her close. "We'll find our way, Mia. To where, I don't know, but you are welcome to help yourself to whatever you want of this." I wave my other hand over my chest.

"You're terrible."

"Only with you."

8

———

MIA

I'm forty.

How the hell did that happen?

I mean, I know how it happened, but waking up and knowing it makes me feel old. And James is on my mind.

There are seventeen years between us.

When we're together, it feels like nothing. When we're apart, it seems like a massive gap we'll never overcome.

All I know is that when I'm in his arms, our age difference is meaningless. He's tender, loving, and everything I should have in my life.

I feel like I wasted so many years before meeting James.

It's the middle of the week and he's working, so I didn't get to see him last night. It's been eight weeks of this routine so far. I'm not sure if I'll see him tonight. But we'll have the weekend together at least.

I'm lost in thought when I open my office door and the blended scent of so many different types of flowers hits me.

My office is full of colour. There's no one flower that dominates. It looks like someone's bought an entire florist and transferred it to my office.

And there's only one person I know who's romantic enough to do this.

James.

I shake my head. He can't afford this. His dad is paying his rent, and his job barely covers his other bills.

My heart swells at the thought, but at the same time I know we are going to have words. He can't do anything this public.

"Do you like them?"

A voice comes from behind, and my stomach twists because it's not the person I want to ask me that question.

I turn. "Garrett. What can I do for you?"

His lips twitch. "Happy birthday, Mia. I hope you like my gift."

"You did this?"

"Who else would? I managed to persuade the cleaners to leave your office unlocked for a special delivery." He chuckles, and my heart sinks. Of course it's not James. James is the type to buy me flowers, but this is too much for him. But then, Garrett never bought me flowers. Ever.

My mouth goes dry. *Who else would?* I can't let him suspect anything's up. "I don't know. I thought the faculty might have."

He snorts. "No. I bought my wife flowers for her birthday, and I'd like to take her out for lunch. Maybe spend some time at home with her."

"No."

His eyes narrow. "Are you busy?"

"No, I just don't want to have lunch with you."

"Not even for your birthday?"

I walk back toward the door. "Not even for my birthday. I've got work to do, Garrett."

After closing the door on him, I walk back to my desk, looking around the office. I was happy a few minutes ago. His act has sucked all the joy out of the day. I'm surrounded by reminders of my previous, shitty relationship.

I bury myself in work, but the scent of the flowers keeps reminding me that they're there. I wish to God this was a heavy lecture day, but it's not.

By lunchtime, I resolve to just leave and do what I can from home, but a gentle tap on the door knocks me out of my thoughts.

James steps into my office, closing the door behind him. He's got a big smile on his face, but it drops when he sees the flowers. "What the hell?"

I lick my lips. "Guess who?"

"Garrett did this?"

I nod.

His mouth straightens, as if he's trying to hide his feelings.

"I was happy and excited when I thought it was you. Knowing it's him, not so much."

The corners of his mouth curl into a smile. "I wish I could do this for you."

"I know you do, and I love that you would do it." I sigh. "I think I'll book myself into a hotel for the night."

"Why?"

"Garrett was put out that I wouldn't have lunch with him. It wouldn't surprise me if he turned up."

James frowns. "I wish he would just leave you alone."

"So do I, but there's not much I can do about it. I think it takes a lot more than buying me flowers to be considered harassment."

He huffs out a breath. I understand his frustration. He just wants to know I'm safe, and he doesn't trust Garrett. With good reason.

"Well, I came here to tell you that I've got tonight off. The boss wasn't too happy, but I told him it was a family emergency. Can you lock your office door from the inside?"

My eyebrows pop up. "What are you suggesting?"

"What do you think I'm suggesting?" He grins.

"The door locks. You just have to turn the knob."

He turns back to the door, turning the lock until it clicks and trying the handle. "Sorted."

"I don't know about this."

He chuckles. "I was going to wait until tonight, but seeing these flowers changed my mind."

I stand, walking around my desk. "What did you have in mind?"

James pulls me hard against him. His kiss is deep, filled with meaning. "Turn around."

"James, we can't. Not here."

"I'll be quick. Promise." He grins.

"Now's the only time I want to hear that." I laugh softly. It doesn't make this any less of a thrill. If we get caught, I can't imagine the hell that would rain down on me. But it's my birthday, and I want James.

I turn and he bends me over the desk, pushing my skirt up and dragging my panties down my legs.

My heart thuds when he stands close behind me and

reaches around to stroke my clit. My body's so tense, it doesn't take much to get me to the point of orgasm.

"Mia," he whispers. Him saying my name is enough to finish me off.

He pauses to take a condom from his pocket.

I whimper when he pushes his cock into me. This beats the flowers and the unwanted gesture from Garrett hands down. James is hard, really hard, and it's all for me.

"Fuck," he murmurs as he slams into me over and over again. "It's so hard to keep quiet."

I laugh softly. "No kidding."

"I want to hear you when you come."

"You will tonight." I thrust my hips back, and he lets out a deep moan. It almost seems sacrilegious having sex in the midst of all these flowers from another man, but I welcome it.

"Mia, I'm going to come." He leans over and bites my shoulder to muffle his moan.

This is what I want. The raw passion of James. The aching need we have for each other. Nothing else matters right now but us.

He slows, and I let out a loud breath.

"You okay?" he asks.

"Very okay."

"Happy birthday."

I laugh softly, and he pulls out of me. Wrapping the used condom in a piece of paper from my printer, he drops it in the bin before zipping up and kissing me tenderly.

"I'll get us a hotel room for the night. We won't have to worry about anyone finding us, or anyone interrupting us, and it'll just be you and me," I say.

He strokes my face. "I like that idea."

"I'll text you the details."

James gives me a tender kiss on the lips. "I wish I could afford to do more for your birthday."

"You just gave me an orgasm in my office, and I'm counting on you to give me more tonight."

He grins. "Whatever you want. Happy birthday, Mia. I love you."

My heart stops.

We were heading in this direction, and I knew it, but the words make this real. Make *us* real.

"I'm not expecting you to say it back if you're not ready. But I wanted to make sure you knew."

I throw my arms around his neck. "This is the best birthday ever."

"It's not over yet."

"I do love you, James."

After kissing my cheek, he steps back. "Are you sure?"

"I've never been more sure of anything in my life."

JAMES HOLDS me in his arms, his bare skin against mine. I don't think he's stopped kissing me in one way or another since we ended up in bed.

His lips graze up my neck, and I sigh.

"What are you thinking about?" he asks.

"How happy I am."

James smiles. "Me too. I hope you had a good birthday."

"It started out a bit shaky, but it ended up kind of amazing."

His eyebrows dip. "Only kind of amazing? Clearly I haven't been doing my duty."

I laugh. "You. The *you* bits of my birthday have been amazing. Donating all those flowers to the hospital felt good too."

James's mouth falls open. "You did what?"

"Donna and I loaded all the flowers into her van, and we took them to the hospital to be given out on the wards. Cleaned my office and did a good deed."

He grins. "That's my girl."

"I am, aren't I?" His expression is so full of love. It has been for a while, but I recognise it now. I've never felt so loved in all of my life.

"Yes, you are." He plants a kiss on my temple. "I love you, Mia, and I'm never going to get sick of saying it."

"I hope not. Because I rather love hearing it."

He chuckles. After running his hand down my spine, he rests it on my arse, pulling me closer.

"We should go somewhere. Maybe to a tropical island," I say.

"You want to run away?"

"Just for a week maybe? Somewhere we can walk down the road holding hands, and not have to worry about anyone seeing us."

He nuzzles my ear. "Like a resort?"

"That's it. We can order room service and live like this for a whole week."

"You know there's a good chance we'd never leave the room."

I turn to look into his eyes. There's mischief written all over his face, and I can't help but smile.

"Well, we'd have so much sex that you wouldn't be able to walk, so there's that." He shrugs.

I laugh. "I wouldn't be surprised."

"Do you have to work tomorrow?" He laughs against my cheek.

"I have lectures tomorrow. And you have work." I look up at the ceiling. "You know, booking into a hotel room for the night with a much younger man makes me feel like a cougar."

He laughs. "No, not a cougar. I chased you."

"You didn't have to chase me far."

James nuzzles my neck again. "If I hadn't come to your office that day to tell you I couldn't stop thinking about you, would you have come to me?"

I shrug, but I know the answer. I would have written off his kiss as a one-off, never thinking he could be interested in more with me.

"No, not a cougar. More like a … not a MILF, because you're not a mother. Maybe a TILF?"

"What on earth are you talking about?" I laugh.

"Teacher I'd like to fuck."

I give him a gentle slap on the arm. "James Campbell."

"But it's so much more than that, isn't it? For both of us. I can't believe my life right now."

"In what way?"

"I got the woman of my dreams, in my arms, in bed."

My heart leaps. God, how I love this man.

"And I get to spend her birthday with her. A very important birthday."

"It's not that important. It just makes me feel old."

The words hang over us for a minute, until James raises

his hand behind my head and pulls my forehead to his. "Age doesn't matter between us. You got that? You're everything I ever wanted, and I'll be damned if I'll ever be made to feel bad about that. We belong together, Mia."

I grin, and when he kisses me, I sigh and lose myself to it.

Best birthday ever.

9

JAMES

It's Friday, and Mia's our guest lecturer today.

I knew our academic worlds were going to collide, but I wasn't quite ready for this.

She handles it like a pro.

She speaks and answers questions, and when the lecture finishes, she disappears toward the staff room for lunch while I head out to my car. I don't have any other lectures today, and I need to catch up on sleep after working the past three nights.

My phone buzzes as I place it on the passenger seat, and I pick it up and smile.

See you tonight?

God, I love this woman. She wants to be with me as much as I want to be with her.

You mean you haven't had enough of me over the weekend?

Never enough. Love you. Call you later.

I jump at the rapping on my car window, swallowing hard when I see who it is. I wind the window down.

"James, isn't it?"

Garrett Scott stands beside my car. One of his eyebrows is raised. My heart thuds. I can only hope he hasn't found out about us, for Mia's sake.

"That's right."

"James Campbell?"

I nod.

He hands me a text book. "You left this behind in Doctor Scott's class."

Anger builds inside me. He's a control freak that Mia took years to get strong enough to leave. What the hell would he be doing inside the lecture hall she'd just vacated? At lunchtime?

"Thanks."

"Mia's had her eye on your studies for a while now. She seems to think you'll go far. Are you staying on to do your master's degree?"

I try my best to keep my face neutral. I've been studying Biological Sciences with my interest in plants and conservation, and my plan was originally to keep studying. Now, all I want is to take this guy's former wife and disappear with her. "That was the plan."

"It takes a lot to impress Mia. Believe me." He gives me a small smile, and turns, walking away. Is this his way of telling me he suspects something's going on? I can't see Mia discussing me with him, or any of her other students for that matter.

I watch him until he's back in the building. He's spent

years degrading Mia, telling her how worthless she is compared to him.

I'm so proud that she found the strength to leave.

I'll never do anything like that to her.

I DRIVE AROUND for a while before heading to her place. There are no cars on the street outside, and I pull out the garage remote she gave me last time I was here, opening the garage from the road.

Her car is there.

With a sigh of relief, I drive straight in and close the door behind me.

After walking the short distance from the garage to the house, I find the kitchen door unlocked.

"Mia," I call.

She appears in the doorway leading to the living room. Her face lights up. "I was about to make some lunch. It took you long enough to get here."

I let out a long breath. "We need to talk about that."

"What's happened?" She crosses the room and takes my hands in hers.

"I left a book behind. Garrett kindly delivered it to my car."

Her mouth falls open. "What was he doing with your book?"

I shrug. "I guess he went looking for you. He had some advice for me."

"What did he say?"

"That I should stay on and do my master's because you think a lot of me. And that it takes a lot to impress you."

She pales. "He must suspect something."

"How?"

"I don't know. Your visits to my office?"

"They're few and far between."

Mia swallows hard. "I think you should do your master's. And I don't want to be the barrier between you going onto bigger things and not."

I give her hands a gentle squeeze. "None of it means anything if I don't have you too."

She gives me a small smile. "Maybe we should cool things off for a while. The last thing I need is Garrett finding out."

"You want to break up?"

Mia drops her gaze.

"Really?"

Jealousy wells in me. Not once have I felt that way until now, because I knew where I stood with Mia and how she felt about me. And I knew how she felt about Garrett and the end of their relationship.

But now she's telling me what she's thinking, and she wants to take a break. Maybe there's another reason she never wanted anyone to find out about us.

"Is it Garrett? Are you thinking about getting back together with him?" My voice cracks, and pain rips through me.

When Ashley left me, I was a mess for a while. But losing Mia would destroy me. She's the best thing that's ever happened to me.

Her eyes widen. "No. There's no way that will ever happen." She raises her right hand and runs her finger along my jawline. "I love *you*, James Campbell. No one else. I just think maybe it'd be less stressful if we weren't having to hide for a while."

"By staying apart?"

She nods. *"For a while."*

I close my eyes as she presses her lips to mine.

I love Mia, with everything I have. She's it for me. "Are you really sure about this?"

She shakes her head. "No, but I don't know what else to do. If Garrett suspects, he'll make my life hell before we're divorced, and we both know he'll do the same to you." Tears appear in her eyes. "I'm just trying to protect you."

I could tell her that I don't care, but I know she won't listen. She's too sweet. I could tell her anything he does I'll protect her from, but I don't, because I know she's made up her mind.

Instead, I let her walk away and hope she'll come back.

And with that, it's over.

10

JAMES

WHEN ASHLEY LEFT, I fell apart.

I let myself and my home become a mess before Drew showed up and sorted me out.

This time's so much worse.

But I'm not going to let myself fall apart again.

I'm angry this time.

Was any of it real? I fell in love with Mia, and I thought she loved me back, but what if this was really a game to her?

I can't stand the thought of her being with Garrett. What if they get back together?

It's easier to keep away from people and throw myself into my study. While I haven't neglected it since the start of this relationship, it's been tough to cram my uni work into less hours. My weekends belonged to Mia and me.

I sit at home and pore over my books to the point that even Cody notices something. And he's not the most observant person at the best of times.

Two weeks after our breakup, I'm trying my best to just get on with things. And I'm snappy as hell.

He sits beside me at a table in the quad. I pick at my food. I've been working out more than usual, and haven't been eating as much as I should. I glance up just as my old biochemistry lecturer crosses the quad, and I hate that I checked to even see who it was. I shouldn't hang around here between lectures. It's just making things worse.

"Are you going to finish those chips?" Cody asks.

"I'm sure your main aim in life is to harass me into giving you my food," I mumble.

"Dude. They're long cold. You're not eating them."

"Help yourself." I push the plate toward him.

"What's up your nose?" he asks, picking up three fries and dangling them above his open mouth.

"Nothing."

He wolfs down a bunch of chips and smiles. "Wanna know what I think?"

"Not really, but I'm sure you're going to tell me anyway."

"You need to get laid."

I laugh. "No. I really don't."

He nods. "Sure you do. Your sexual frustration is written all over your face."

If only you knew the truth. Sure, I miss sex with Mia. But what I miss more is the intimacy and the closeness we had. She wasn't just my lover; she was rapidly becoming my best friend. The person I could confide in, and the person I could laugh with. *My* person.

Cody's probably the closest friend I have in Auckland, but I don't feel that I can confide in him. Not about this.

"I just need this year to be finished with so I can have a break."

He nods. "Me too. It's pretty intense."

Behind him, I spot Mia. She's coming out of a café, a takeaway coffee in her hands. For just a moment our eyes meet, and my heart skips a beat. She looks how I feel: tired and sad.

All I can do is to give her time and hope she comes to her senses.

11

MIA

I HAVE SO many regrets in my life.

All of them right now are about James. Not being with him is the hardest thing I've ever had to do. Even harder than leaving Garrett. And that's saying something.

James is unhappy, I'm unhappy, and Garrett's sniffing around me like a dog in heat. I think he senses that I'm down, but of course he assumes it's because of him.

It's been a month since I spent any time with James. I've seen him around the university, and his eyes are so dead. I did that. It's my fault.

I can barely think of anything else but him. Still, I know this is the right thing to do. I need to get my independence back all on my own.

Garrett sits at the same table as I do in the staff room. I would move, but the other tables are full, and I just want to eat my lunch and get back to work.

"We haven't had lunch together for a long time." He smiles, and my stomach flips. Not in a good way.

"There's a reason for that."

"You look tired." Garrett reaches to stroke my face and I pull away.

"Don't. I'm fine."

"I'm not sleeping either." He takes a sip of his coffee. "I miss you."

"I told you, I'm fine. I'm just busy."

He nods. "Sure. I still miss you."

I take a deep breath. "I want to sell the house."

Garrett makes a huffing sound. "We talked about this."

"I want out now. Not at the end of next year."

His gaze fixes on mine. And for the first time in a long time, I don't look away. I can't give in. "Then pay me out."

"You know I can't do that. Let's sell the house and split it like we agreed."

He nods. "We agreed you would have the house to live in until the divorce was final. The only way out is to buy me out."

Tears form in my eyes, but I blink them away. "This is exactly why it doesn't matter if you miss me or not. We're not together, but you're still controlling everything."

"Not controlling. I'm trying to guide you back to the path you should be on. The one you deviated from. You belong with me, Mia."

I shake my head. "No. I don't."

Standing, I pick up my rubbish and walk away. He won't make a scene in public; he never does. Nothing to take away from that calm image that he has.

But I know he'll be angry inside.

I've got a lecture next, and then I can go home, but there's only one place I want to be. Where I always need to be.

With James.

Garrett won't intimidate me anymore.

I STAND in front of the apartment building and look up. I've only been here once before. There are other students living here.

But my agitation overrides my common sense, and I find myself in the elevator on my way to his apartment.

When I reach it, I pause, chewing on my lips before I raise my fist and knock on the door. It takes a moment, but it opens, and I suck in a breath.

He answers in a pair of sweat pants. The ones I like that sit low on his hips. Sweat drips down his chest, his face reddened with what I assume is effort from exercising.

His eyes widen. "Get in here."

I step into the room, and he closes the door behind him.

"What are you doing here?" His tone is angry. He's never been angry with me before. In the corner of a room, the punching bag still swings.

"I needed to see you."

"You made your feelings clear last time we saw each other."

I nod, and take a step toward him. "I hurt you."

"Yeah, you did."

When I meet his gaze, he scans my face. "What's wrong?"

"Maybe I made a mistake coming."

His expression softens. "No. I'm not sure how wise it is, but I'm glad you're here."

"Me too." I pause. "I miss you."

Tears prick my eyes, and he pulls me into his arms. I ignore the sweat, and close my eyes as he embraces me. Being in his embrace feels so right. This is where I'm meant to be.

"I've missed you too." He sighs. "What's going on, Mia?"

"Garrett pushed me to get back together, and …"

James lets go. "He what?"

"He tried to pressure me. But all it did was make me miss you more. I'll declare the relationship, and deal with any fallout from him."

James shakes his head. "No. You won't. I won't let you make yourself a target for him."

"We have to, James. I can't do this anymore, and I won't give you up."

He bites down on his bottom lip. "Why don't we wait until the end of the year and see how we feel? All I want to do is protect you."

For the first time all day, my heart warms. Garrett always does that to me—makes me feel like I'm frozen as he pushes and pushes for what he wants.

I'll never go back to that.

I nod. "I like that idea."

He smiles. "So … does this mean we're back together?"

His eyes shine with happiness, and I nod again. "I can't live my life without you."

"Woah. You are strong, lady. Stronger than you know. I wasn't even around when you left that dickhead. You don't *need* me."

I laugh. "I want you."

"That's what I want to hear." He grins.

"But I do need you in other ways."

"What kind of ways?" He places his hand on his heart, and gives me that oh-so-innocent look of his.

"I could show you, but ..." I screw up my nose. "You stink."

James makes a show of sniffing his armpits while I laugh. "Must be shower time, then."

I sigh. "It must be."

He holds out his hand. "Care to join me?"

My heart leaps, and I slide my hand into his. "Thought you'd never ask."

His bathroom's small, and the shower's seen better days.

He turns on the water, and drops his clothing to the floor. I drop my skirt, pulling off the rest of my clothes while he steps into the shower.

"I'm sorry." I follow him and close the door.

He wraps his arms around me. "I know. It's okay."

"No, it's not."

"You got scared. I understand. Didn't like it, but I got why. Turn around."

"Why?"

"I'm going to wash your back."

I grin as I turn, bunching my hair in my hand and pulling it forward over my shoulder.

His gentle hands massage my back as he washes me with the shower gel. He runs them up until he's grasping my shoulders, squeezing them as I relax. "Maybe I should just give you a massage."

"I wouldn't say no. It's been a tough week."

"It's been a tough month."

He wraps his arms around my waist, pulling me in tight as he nuzzles my neck. I gasp as he presses his erection against the cleft of my arse.

"Tell me how much you missed me," he murmurs.

"I missed you a lot."

"You can feel how much I missed you."

I laugh, turning in his arms. His eyes are so full of love, just as they usually are, and any anger from before is gone.

James loves me.

I love him.

And I am never going to let fear separate us again.

WHEN WE'RE out of the shower and dried off, he leads me into his bedroom.

I love just looking at him.

He's tall, and his well-built frame with defined abs makes my legs turn to jelly. There's nothing better than his strong arms wrapped around me. I've missed them and him so much.

He lies back on the bed and beckons me forward. I grin, joining him as I slide into his bed beside him.

"You're lucky. I changed the sheets earlier. They're clean."

I laugh. "I'm glad to hear it."

"I must have known you'd show up." He reaches for me, cupping one breast in his hand, his thumb grazing my nipple. I suck in a breath. "I can't believe you're here."

"I'm so sorry, James."

"It's okay. You're with me, and that's all that matters.

Stop apologising." His mouth closes over mine, and I sink into the familiarity of his kiss. He sighs. "I could kiss you all night."

"I would let you kiss me, but I want more."

"So do I." He lowers his head to my breast and sucks my nipple into his mouth. His tongue rolls across it, and I gasp at the sensation I've missed so much.

I shiver as he runs a hand down my stomach and between my legs. But he doesn't go for my clit straight away. Instead, he takes his time, stroking my spread thighs.

"You're a tease."

He raises his head and grins. "I'm just enjoying my lady being back with me. What's the rush?"

"The rush is that I need you inside me. I've gone a whole month without you."

I gasp again when he slips one finger into me, followed by another.

"Really? How much do you need me?" His thumb hovers over my clit, and I push my hips up to meet it. "That much, huh?"

He circles my clit with his thumb. To be honest, it doesn't matter what he does—I just want him touching me. I need him that much. I've missed him.

When he gently presses on my clit, I nearly go through the roof. "Stop teasing me."

He laughs as I push him onto his back, and straddle his hips.

"Top drawer of the side cabinet," he says.

I lean over to pick up the condom, and roll it on before lowering myself onto his cock. I moan at him filling me.

"Happy now?" he asks.

"You make me happy." I lean over and kiss him, rolling my hips.

"I'm gonna last about five seconds if you keep that up."

I shrug. "Personal experience tells me that if that happens, I can get you hard again pretty quickly."

"You have such a dirty mouth, Mia Scott."

"You love it, James Campbell." I push myself back up, riding his cock like it's the only time I'll ever have it in me again. How did I ever think I could last until the end of next year? Sex with James is sweet and sexy and everything I ever wanted. *He's* everything I ever wanted.

My heart is full again. It always is with James. What I have with him is so different than anything I've ever had before.

"Mia," he moans as I grind hard against him. I want him to come. I don't care if this isn't a marathon. All I want is to give him what he gives me—complete and total satisfaction.

"I love you," he says.

"I love you too," I whisper. I press my hands to his pecs, and he grasps my arms.

Forcing my eyes to stay open when all I want to do is close them, I meet his gaze. He does love me. I know I hurt him when I pulled away, and there's no way I'm doing that again. This is it. We belong together. If I didn't know it before, I know it now.

His body tenses under me, and I know he's close when his thrusts grow harder and slower. He lets out a long groan, pushing his hips up and holding me in place. His expression is strained, and I lean over, peppering his face with kisses.

James laughs.

"I can't stay away from you," I whisper.

"I don't want you to." He rolls us to one side, and we lie there for a moment while he softens inside me. His mouth finds mine, and I'm lost in a tangle of lips and tongues, our bodies still pressed together.

When we finally break apart, he caresses my cheek, and I close my eyes.

"Where's your car parked?" he asked.

"At home. I caught a taxi."

He smiles.

"There's no parking anyway."

James laughs. "No." He strokes my hair. "Are you staying over? I'll sleep much better tonight with you here."

"I can stay. I'll just leave early. And I'll sleep better too."

He plants a soft kiss on my lips. "My beautiful Mia."

It doesn't take long for him to fall asleep. He looks so peaceful.

When we were together before, I spent my time terrified that someone would find out about us. While I worried, he was my calm.

I'm in love with James Campbell.

Maybe I'm not quite so terrified anymore.

At the start I felt self-conscious about our age gap. I didn't want him to see the dimples in my thighs, and that my stomach's not as flat as it was when I was his age.

But he loves me. And he loves the way I look.

Every day he teaches me just how shitty my relationship with Garrett was. My ex never failed to tell me of my flaws.

James embraces them.

How did I ever think I could stay away?

12

―――――

JAMES

WE WAKE before dawn and make love again before Mia dresses and leaves for work. I doze, and I'm not sure how much time passes before I hear a knock.

It makes me smile.

I tug on a pair of boxer shorts and head out to answer it.

"Did you forget something?" I laugh as I pull open the door.

It's not Mia.

Ashley's been crying. Black tracks down her face, and her red-rimmed eyes tell me that. I hold up my arms when she throws herself at me, burying her face in my chest.

"Ashley? What's wrong?"

She sobs, and I don't know what else to do. I wrap my arms around her waist and hold her. Her body trembles, and I guide her to the couch to take a seat. But she won't let go.

"Ashley. What's going on?"

"I didn't know who else to go to. I'm sorry."

"It's okay. Just tell me what's wrong." I pull back, unhooking her arms from around my neck. Looking at her closer, I see she's exhausted on top of the crying. It's not just the mascara under her eyes. She looks like she hasn't slept for a week.

"I made such a big mistake." She sniffs. "I thought Alex loved me, but the whole time we've been together, he's been screwing someone else."

I'm not sure what she wants from me. She left me for Alex, so what am I supposed to do? "Well, I'm sorry to hear that."

"Can I stay here for a while?"

I exhale through my mouth, unsure of what to stay. Not that long ago, I would have let her, but now I have Mia in my life and she's the real deal. "I'm not sure—"

"I need some help to get my things from Alex's flat. We sold my car, so I don't have one right now. After my mid-year exams are over, I'll go home, so it won't be forever."

I close my eyes, trying to absorb what she's saying. Part of me wants to tell her to leave and turn my back on her, but I know I'm probably the closest friend she has in Auckland. Or rather, I used to be. I doubt she has anyone else who would do everything she's asking.

I'll have to explain it to Mia. Maybe I can stay with her while Ashley stays here. If we slot back into our previous routine, I'll be spending the weekends with her anyway. There's got to be some way to help Ashley even though she's not my problem. And at least it's only for a short time. "Hang on a minute. You're dropping out?"

Ashley shrugs. "I've done half my honours year. Maybe

I'll come back and finish it later. I just don't have the heart right now."

I sigh. "Tell you what. We'll go and get your stuff, and you can stay here until exams are over. Then I'll take you home to Copper Creek. How does that sound?"

"Thank you." She sniffs again.

"I should go and see Mum anyway. She's not getting any better."

Her face falls. "I'm so sorry, James."

I shrug. "I think the treatment she got before gave her more time with us. I'm not sure she'll be around much longer. I haven't been home for ages, and exams will be over soon."

Ashley nods.

"You can take the bed. I'll take the couch if I'm here."

"Are you seeing someone?" Her mouth falls open. "Oh God, I didn't even ask."

"It's complicated. But yeah, there is someone. I'll talk to her and explain about you and maybe I can stay a few nights with her."

"I'm so sorry, James. I don't want to put you out. I just didn't know where else to turn."

I nod, sighing when she wraps her arms around my waist and pulls herself in.

"I knew I'd be safe here. I'm sorry for what I did to you. Now I know how much it hurts."

"Yeah, it really did."

She lets out a sigh. "I just want to go home now."

"How many exams have you got left?"

She leans back. "Two. You?"

"One. We'll go home once we're both all done."

Ashley nods again. "Thank you. You're such a good guy. I appreciate it."

"It's no problem."

Or is it?

"SHE'S *WHAT*?" Mia stares at me. I didn't want to tell her at uni, but it was something I needed to say face to face. I popped into her office to let her know about Ashley. The last thing I need is for anyone to gossip and for it to get back to her without me telling her.

"She's going to stay with me for a couple of weeks, and then I'll take her home to Copper Creek. We're going to pick up her stuff from his flat tonight and get her out of there."

Mia's pacing. I've never seen her so worked up. "And she needed your help. No one else's."

"I'm the person she trusts more than anyone." I cross the room to meet her and grasp her arms. "You don't have to worry about her, Mia. I love *you*."

She nods. "I know. It's just that you wouldn't be happy if I let Garrett move in under the same circumstances."

"I'd fucking kill him."

Mia laughs. "There you go."

"So, I'm proposing that for the next couple of weeks, I stay with you."

Her eyes widen. "Really?"

"I'll leave my car in the park at the apartment, and catch the bus."

"Are you going to tell Ashley about us?"

I shake my head. "I've told her I'm seeing someone, but she doesn't need to know the details. It's just for two weeks, and then I'll take her home and visit Mum for a bit."

"How is she doing?"

"It's all downhill from here." My heart hurts over that. Mum doesn't deserve what's happening to her, and I haven't been home in forever with the various dramas in my life. My focus has been on uni and Mia—not much else.

"I'm sorry. I wish I could do something to help."

I slip my arms around her waist. "You are helping. You're here for me, and I love you for it. That's all that matters."

"I like the thought of you being with me for a couple of weeks. We'll just have to be wary of Garrett."

"Maybe we can think of it as a test run for the future."

She smiles. "I like that idea."

"I promise I'll cook dinner and clean up after myself."

"Damn right you will."

I gape at her. "Such tough talk."

"Wait until you're living with me." She laughs, but I know she's a million miles away from where she was in her former relationship. I'm privileged to be watching the evolution of Mia Scott. She's becoming more comfortable in her own skin.

"I'm just looking forward to spending more quality time with you. Between work and uni, it never feels like we have enough. We know we're sexually compatible, but I think we could strengthen all the other parts of our relationship."

Mia nods. "I feel the same way."

"We already have a lot of interests in common as far as

study goes. Let's see what else we can find." I peck her on the lips. "See you tonight at home?"

She grins. "Sounds good. I love you."

"Love you too."

13

JAMES

Ashley's things fill my car.

I guess I don't have much more than she does, but it's kind of sad that four years of someone's life fits into such a small space.

But I help her load it all in, and then unload it into my place.

"Where are you staying if I need anything?" she asks.

"Just send me a text."

She scowls. "You're not going to tell me anything, are you?"

I chuckle. "No. You're not entitled to know."

Ashley shrugs. "Fair enough. I do appreciate you letting me stay here."

"I'm not about to make you sleep on the street."

She grasps my arm. "Thank you, James. You're such a good person. I'm sorry I hurt you."

I'm not sure how to respond. Do I thank her for saying it? Or do I ignore it?

Shrugging it off, I hand her the spare key from the side table by the door. "Here. Let me know if you need anything."

She nods. "Okay. Thanks again. I can't wait to go home."

"I bet. Are you okay? Do you need anything before I go?" I point toward the kitchen. "There's a bit of food in the fridge, and tea and coffee."

Ashley smiles. "I know where it all is. I did used to live here."

"I know, it's just … I want to make sure you're okay. Until I can deliver you home, I feel kinda responsible for you."

"That's really sweet, and I appreciate it. But I'm thinking I might just order some Uber Eats and fall asleep on the couch watching television."

I laugh. "Some things never change then. I should get going and leave you to it."

She slips her arms around my waist and snuggles in. It doesn't feel familiar at all; it just feels weird, and all I want is to get to Mia. "Thanks, James. I hope this means that we can be friends."

"Of course we can."

Ashley lets go of me. "I'll talk to you during the week."

I nod. "You bet. And call me any time if you need anything."

Walking away feels freeing, and I smile all the way to the elevator. I've got a backpack with some clothes in it, and that's all I'm taking to Mia's. I'll leave the car parked in the building and catch the bus. If Garrett turns up, then there's less chance we'll be caught that way.

I can't wait to see her.

———

I TAKE a deep breath as I step inside Mia's kitchen. She's been cooking, and with two hours to go until I start work, I get to have dinner with my lady before my night shift.

"You're just in time." She walks in from the living room and wraps her arms around my waist. This is what feels right now. She plants a tender kiss on my lips.

"Something smells good. I can smell you've been cooking too." I laugh.

"I thought I'd make an effort for our first night. I made some chicken cordon bleu, mashed potato, and some fresh vegetables." Her eyes search mine as if she's looking for approval.

"Sounds amazing."

"Are you sure? I can make something else if …"

I grasp her arms. "Completely sure. Anything you've made will be amazing, I'm sure. Where's the doubt coming from?"

She shrugs. "I know you'll be coming and going with work, but this is kind of a trial run for living together."

"And you can't be yourself if you're forever seeking my approval. Babe, I'm not Garrett. Stop doubting yourself around me."

She laughs when I lean in and press a kiss to her neck. "I should know that by now, shouldn't I?"

"Yes, you should. You don't doubt yourself at work. And you don't need to do it at home anymore. I'll never be that guy who picks holes for the sake of it. And I'm pretty sure that's what he's like."

She nods. "You're right."

"I've got two hours, so let's eat and then make out on the couch before I go."

From the kiss I get in return, and her laughter, I know she agrees.

14

JAMES

THE FIRST WEEK IS EASY.

We settle into a routine that is one of us cooking dinner, me going to work, and then me crawling into bed with Mia a little after four when I finish. That's when I miss my car, but there's usually an Uber around to get me back to her.

By Friday, I'm more than ready for a break. I just have study to do before the last of my exams, and I'll make Mia dinner tonight.

Mia's warm body against mine, her soft kisses on my cheek before she leaves for work.

It's a little after eleven when a crash in the kitchen jolts me awake.

Someone's in the house.

Mia's usually home around one on a Friday. She'll be in a lecture right now.

I grit my teeth. There's only one other person it could be, unless there's a burglar.

I climb out of bed, and peek out of the bedroom door.

No one's in the hallway.

A familiar voice comes from the kitchen.

"Damn it. Where did she put those plates?"

Garrett.

I know better than to confront him. But Mia has to know he's here.

Tiptoeing back to the bedroom, I close the door as quietly as I can. My phone's on the bedside cabinet, and I quickly type out a message.

Me: Garrett's in the house

It only takes a few moments.

Mia: What? I'll come home

Me: Want me to get dressed and sneak out?

Mia: I won't be far away. I'll excuse myself and be there soon.

I could always climb out the window, but I'll only do that if I have to. The last thing I want is him to spot me doing a runner.

The longer I wait, the angrier I get. How dare he do this to her? And how many times has he been in her house when she's not here?

The distinctive sound of Mia's Subaru comes from outside. I place my hand on the handle of the door in case she needs any help. It sucks. I should be out there with her, but I know Garrett will try his best to destroy everything she's worked for if he finds out about me.

A door slams.

"What the hell are you doing here?" she asks.

"I bought lunch. Thought you might like some."

I close my eyes.

"Well, I don't, and you're not supposed to be here. You know that."

"It's still my house, Mia."

"That I live in by our agreement. You don't get to come in whenever you feel like it."

He snorts.

"Leave, Garrett. Before I call my lawyer."

I swallow hard. I've not been privy to a conversation between them before, and I'm so proud of her for standing up to him. I hope my presence helps give her strength.

"You don't have to do that. Next time, I won't try do something nice for you."

"I don't want anything nice from you. I don't want *anything* from you."

From the way the door slams, I guess he's stormed off. That, and the way Mia flies into my arms the second she's in the bedroom.

"I'm sorry," she whispers.

"You have nothing to be sorry for. Why the hell does he think it's okay for him to just walk in?"

"I don't know. I just don't want it to affect us."

Grasping her chin, I pull her gaze to mine. "It won't. This isn't your fault, Mia. I hope you know that."

She nods. "I do. He just always manages to knock my confidence."

I give her a tender kiss. "I love you. And I know how strong you are. I'll always be here for you."

"I know."

GARRETT'S VISIT makes her a little cautious in the second week. Her work is winding down for the semester, and she spends more time at home.

It unnerves me.

I know she's trying to protect us, but she shouldn't have to live her life like this. All it does is make me angrier that she still has another year of this crazy behaviour to go.

She withdraws a little from me too. I feel it. And our week is disrupted by me working nights, which doesn't help at all.

By Friday, I'm tired and I just want her. I fall into bed a little after four, and she wraps her arms around me.

"I love coming home to you," I murmur.

"I love you coming home to me."

"Are you going in to work today?"

She snuggles her head against my chest. "No. I've just got some paperwork to finish off at home."

I kiss the top of her head. "Are you worried about a repeat of last week?"

"A little."

"We'll work it out."

She rubs her nose between my pecs, and I chuckle. "I know we will. Can we just stay like this all weekend?"

Chuckling, I run my hand down her spine. "That's fine with me."

15

JAMES

MY CAR IS PACKED solid with Ashley's things when we leave
for Copper Creek.

We're on break now for three weeks before the second
semester starts.

Two weeks of essentially living with Mia was made
harder by Garrett's intrusion, but that last weekend we got
back on track.

We talked late into the night about biotech, and other
scientific areas we both have interest in. We discovered a
mutual love of bad science-fiction movies. And through it
all, when I worked nights, she was there at four in the morning, welcoming me with open arms. It's felt like home.

And at least I'm not leaving town with things being
weird.

Ashley hasn't asked questions. She knows she has no
right to my private life anymore.

It wasn't that long ago that I mourned our lost friendship.

Now I'm happy to move on with the rest of my life because I have a new best friend.

Ashley's a lot happier now than she was two weeks ago when she turned up to my place. Despite our differences, I'm glad she felt that she could come to me. That ex of hers is a real dick.

"I'm so glad to be almost home. I can't wait to go swimming at the cove. Are you sticking around for a while?" she asks.

I nod. "I thought I'd spend some time with Mum before I head back. At least it's nice and quiet to get some studying done."

"I'm not sure if I ever want to go back to complete my studies." She sighs.

"He's not worth throwing away your dreams for."

I flick a glance at her. Her gaze is fixed on me. "I feel so awful, James. I know I was one of the reasons you chose Auckland, and I treated you so badly."

I swallow hard. There's nothing incorrect in what she's saying, and I was deeply hurt. How am I supposed to reply? "Yeah, you did."

"I'm so sorry, James. I never really said that to you before this, and you've been so good to me these past couple of weeks."

"You really hurt me. But I've moved on, and I'm happy now. I hope you find someone who makes you happy."

"Who is she?"

I grip the steering wheel. "I can't tell you. But I'm in love with her, and she loves me. And I know she'll never cheat."

She's staring at me wide-eyed. "Why can't you tell me who it is? I didn't want to pry, but now I'm really curious."

"Because I promised her I wouldn't. She's going through a divorce, and we're keeping it on the down low because her ex is a real dickhead."

Ashley bows her head. "I'm sorry to hear that."

"Honestly, no one should be treated the way she was. And What's-His-Name should never have treated you the way he did."

She lets out a shaky breath. "He only did to me what I did to you. You're such a good guy, James. I hope that you and whoever your lady is are happy. You deserve it."

I nod. "I hope you find some happiness too."

As we take the last turn before hitting town, Ashley beams. "I can't wait to see Mum and Dad. Being home is going to be so good."

"Says the woman who couldn't wait to leave."

She laughs. "I just didn't realise what I had until it was gone."

We travel the distance to her parents' place in silence. I'm sure she has a lot of regret, but my heart is back in Auckland with Mia.

I wish she was with me.

Ashley's father greets us with a smile, and I help him unpack her things.

There's a sense of relief that comes over me as I leave. I'd thought that part of my life was over, and when I drive away, I know for sure that it is.

I turn onto our street and smile.

Home still looks the same.

It's so beautiful here. When I stop the car and get out, I take a long, deep breath of the familiar air. The gardenia and freesias I smell—I'm the one who planted them. So much of this garden is me.

"James." Dad grins as I walk through the backyard. "This is unexpected."

"I brought Ashley home. Figured you might like a visitor for a few days."

"Your mum'll be over the moon to see you."

When I reach him, he embraces me. I haven't been home often since I left, and I can see how much he's aged. The stress of Mum's illness won't have helped at all.

"I'm looking forward to seeing her. How are you two?"

"We've both been better. How's Ashley?"

"She's okay. The guy she cheated on me with cheated on her. So she packed up her stuff and left."

"Are you two …?"

I shake my head. "No. I wouldn't go back there. She really hurt me. But I'm okay. I've got someone, and I'm happy."

He beams. "Glad to hear it. Come in and see your mother."

It's good to be home.

***

MY MOBILE RINGS late morning the following day. I smile when I see that it's Mia.

"Babe." I sit on the bed.

"Hey. I just wanted to hear your voice. How was your trip?"

I swallow. "Good. Ashley's settled in with her parents."

"Missed you last night."

"I miss you too."

"It'll be weird when you come back, not having you sleeping here with me."

I close my eyes. "Tell me about it. I was lonely last night without you."

"I can't wait for you to come home."

Home.

"Is that an invitation to spend more nights at your place?" I ask.

"Always."

My heart bursts with her word. I love Mia, and she loves me. There's no doubt in my mind that we're meant to be together. We just have to work out the tricky parts of her life first. "I really want to … shit. I'm not sure if telling you what I want to do is appropriate given that I'm in my childhood bedroom."

She laughs. "You can tell me whatever you want."

I grin. Fuck I miss her. I wish she was here. "Do you really want to hear what I want to do to you?"

A deep voice comes over my shoulder. "What do you want to do to me, James?"

Shit. My heart leaps as I do. *Corey.* "My brother's here. I'll have to call you back."

Mia's laughter fills my ear as I end the call. I glare at Corey.

He laughs. "I'm sorry. It was just too good an opportunity to pass up."

"I didn't hear you."

"No, you were too busy sexing up whoever that was on

the other end of the phone. Got something to tell me, little brother?"

I shrug. "What are you doing here?"

"I came to visit Mum, and to check in on my baby bro. You know, seeing as he hasn't come to see me in forever. Thought you might want to go for a beer."

Glancing at my phone, I nod. "Sure, that sounds good."

"You're old enough to drink now, right?"

I roll my eyes. "I'll just send a quick text and I'll be ready."

He nods. "Say hello to her for me."

Corey just turned up and wants to go for a beer. I'm sorry. Talk to you later? I love you.

"Come on, let's go. We'll take my truck, and I'll drop you off before I head home," Corey says.

"Sounds like a plan."

My phone buzzes. *It's okay. I thought it was funny. I can't wait to meet your family. Love you.*

I follow my brother outside, grinning as I climb into Corey's ute. "I thought you might have traded this thing in by now."

"And get what? She's never skipped a beat."

I nod. "I guess. Suppose it helps that Adam's around now to fix her when she does break down."

"Is this a diversion tactic to make me forget about that phone call?" He starts up the car and backs down the driveway, then turns onto the road.

I laugh. "I guess it's not working."

"Memory like an elephant. You should know that."

As we drive into town, the conversation shifts to Corey's love life. Thankfully. I never saw him as the settling-down type. He loves his solitude, living alone on McKenzie's

Mountain. Well, alone but for that weird commune-type place on the property next to his. Now he's fallen for one of its former occupants. I'm looking forward to meeting her.

I've heard stories of when they were a bit more outgoing, and used to come down the mountain to shop. But for as long as I can remember they've been closed off and secretive. Every time I went to Corey's place, I'd go past the massive corrugated-iron fence that surrounded the property.

Every time, it would give me the shivers.

I'm glad she got out.

And that Corey's smitten.

WHEN COREY DROPS ME OFF, I head inside to see Mum. She's in her bed now, and rarely gets out. Dad's her nurse, and it breaks my heart to see them both like this.

She smiles when I walk into the room. "Did you see Corey?"

"We went into town for a beer. I just got back."

She shakes her head. "You boys and your beer."

"It was one, Mum. And we're all old enough to drink."

Her smile's faint. "I love all of you so much."

"I know you do. And we love you. How are you feeling?"

She sighs. "Tired. Just very tired. I want to sleep, but I feel like I've been sleeping for hours."

"Can I tell you a secret?" I ask.

"I'll take it to my grave." She laughs softly, and it hurts, but I know she's still trying to look tough. Mum's always been good at that.

"I met someone, Mum. And I think she's the one I'm meant to be with."

"You should have brought her to meet me."

I nod. "I know, but we have to keep things on the down low for a few reasons, and I'm trying to protect her."

She gives me that faint smile again. "You must love her."

"More than anything. I also know you wouldn't approve."

"Pfft. Life's too short for that. I already caused enough damage in Adam's relationship. And poor Hayley got the worst of me." She takes in a breath, and pauses as if she's catching up. "Just be happy, James. If she has your love, she's the luckiest woman in the world. As long as she appreciates that and loves you back, I'm happy for you."

I fight back tears. This is all I ever wanted. We all love Mum, but she never thought anyone was good enough for any of us. It's hard that it's taken this to get her acceptance. "Thanks, Mum."

"Tell me all about her."

I let out a long breath. "Well, she's a lecturer at the university."

"An older woman."

I nod. "But she's spent most of her adult life with a man who didn't appreciate what he had. They were separated well before I was on the scene, but he's still an unwanted part of her life until the divorce is final."

"I'm sorry to hear that. She must be special for you to love her."

"She is."

Mum sighs. "As are Lily, Hayley, and Ginny. I'm sure Corey's lady is special too. Your brothers all found the right women for them. I have confidence that you know what's best for you."

"I never thought I'd hear those words."

"Well, if she doesn't treat you well, I'll haunt her."

I laugh despite myself, and lean over to kiss her on the cheek. "Love you, Mum."

"I love you too. So much. Now, I need to sleep, but will you stay with me a while longer?"

"Of course."

As I sit there, she drifts back off to sleep. I hate this. I wish I could conjure up a miracle that would let her live. But the reality is that every day she creeps closer to death. It's so unfair.

But I'm glad I told her about Mia.

***

LATER, in my room, I lie on the bed where I can keep an eye on the door and dial Mia.

It's been a good day. Mum's worse than I thought she would be, but I enjoyed catching up with Corey. It's left me feeling homesick when I'm already here. I miss this town and its people. I miss the peace and quiet. I miss my family.

And right now, there's someone else I miss.

"Hey." Mia's voice makes me warm.

I close my eyes. "I just wanted to call to say sorry about earlier and hear your voice. I really miss you."

"I miss you too. How was Corey?"

"Curious about you." I laugh.

"You didn't tell him?"

I swallow hard. "I thought it was better if I didn't. The

fewer people who know about us, the better until we can tell everyone." I smile. "And when we can, I'll be singing it from the rooftops."

Her soft laugh warms my heart. "I love you."

"I love you too. I'll be back in a couple of days."

"I'll be looking forward to it. Not much is happening here. How's your mother?"

I pause. Seeing Mum is hard. We don't always agree, but watching her waste away has to be the most painful thing I've been through. "She's dying. I'm glad I'm here to see her."

"I'm so sorry. If there's anything you need, let me know."

"Just be there when I come back."

"That I can do." Her tone is so warm and loving. What did I ever do to deserve Mia? I'm the luckiest man alive.

"I can't wait to see you."

16

———

JAMES

I'M NOT BACK in Auckland long when I get the call I've been dreading.

We're in semester two, but I have to walk away from everything for a few days.

This is it.

My mother's got hours to go.

I've just finished a lecture when I get the phone call, and there's not much time. It's a long drive home, and I need to leave straight away.

I don't hesitate.

When I get to my car, I flick Mia a text.

I'm just leaving town. Mum's close to death.

It only takes a few seconds.

I'm so sorry. Have a safe trip. I love you.

I love you too.

This whole situation sucks. Mum fought so hard the first

time around, but this second time she decided to let nature take its course.

Nature can be so cruel.

I take a deep breath, and start the car.

My phone buzzes. *Text or call me if you need anything. I can drop everything. Xxx*

I love her. She's everything I ever wanted, and I'll wait as long as I have to for her to be free. My love for Mia helps build my strength to face this.

EVERYONE'S there when I pull into the backyard.

Corey's a bit worse for wear. His girlfriend dumped him a couple of weeks ago, returning to that community, or cult, or wherever it is she came from. He's morose, and he's been drinking.

"Should have seen him when he got here. Drew was purple from him chatting up Hayley," Owen says.

I laugh. "I've never seen him drunk."

"Ava didn't want to go near him at first. She was already freaked out at him shaving his beard off."

"He did what?"

"Corey went to get his hair cut, and decided to shave, ready for Adam and Lily's wedding."

"Isn't that months away?" I shake my head, laughing.

"James." Dad stands in the doorway. "Come on."

Swallowing hard, I walk toward him. As much as I need to see her, I don't want to see her like this. I hate the thought of a final goodbye.

She's asleep, and Dad nudges my arm. "She can hear you. Get closer and talk to her."

I nod, and I step forward to speak to her. "Mum, it's James."

Her eyes stay closed, and more than anything I wish they'd open just for a few minutes. But I know that's not going to happen.

"I came as soon as I heard. I'm sorry I haven't been here more often. But I'm here now."

The room's silent but for the faint sound of her breathing. It'll stop soon, and the strong, vibrant woman who raised me will be no more.

I hate this.

"I wish Mia was here. You'd love her." While I have no regrets about hiding our relationship, I do wish I'd brought Mia to meet Mum. "She loves me so much, and I haven't told her yet but when she's divorced, I'm going to marry her."

Mum's breathing is slow and steady, but I'm not sure for how much longer.

"Love you, Mum. It'll be hard when you're not around anymore." I lean over and kiss her on the cheek. *I can't imagine this world without you.*

I stand and make my way to the door. When I open it, Dad's on the other side. He folds me into his embrace, and I cling to him like I'm a child again.

"It's okay. She'll be free of pain soon," Dad says.

"How are you coping?"

He shrugs, and when he lets me go he looks at me with so much pride. "I'm not sure that I am. But I have all my sons under my roof when I need them the most. When she needs them. That's all parents can ask for."

I blink back tears.

"I'm so glad you made it in time."

"So am I," I whisper.

THE ONLY PLACE I can get peace and quiet is my room.

I sit on the bed and close my eyes. Mum's death has been coming for a long time, but now it's here, it seems surreal.

I check the time. It's late afternoon. Despite the break, Mia still has work preparing for next semester. If I can't get hold of her, at least I can leave her a message.

She answers on the third ring.

"Hey." Her tone is so full of affection.

"Hi."

"What's up?"

Tears prick my eyes. "I just wanted to call to tell you how much I love you."

"I love you too. How are things with your mum?"

I catch my breath. "It's just a matter of time. We've all said our goodbyes, and now Dad's in there with Drew."

"Oh, James. I'm so sorry."

"I'll be okay. I spoke to her. The doctor told Dad she could hear us."

"I wish I was there."

Sighing, I nod. "I wish you were too. But I'm glad to hear your voice."

"Me too."

I lie on the bed with the phone to my ear. "I just really want to hold you right now."

"I'd love to be there." She pauses. "I'll be thinking about you."

"I hate that I can't share us with the world."

Mia lets out a breath. "So do I. I just want to leave that old life completely behind and start fresh somewhere else with you. I don't care where, as long as we're together."

My heart, which has been hurting so badly all day, feels a little less broken. Mia's right—nothing matters but us. Once all her shit is resolved, nothing and no one will be able to cause us any problems.

We'll be together.

***

WE'RE ALL in the living room when the time comes.

Drew comes out first, but he doesn't say a word. Instead, when he gets to the hallway door, he just gives us all a nod.

Hayley goes straight to him, wrapping her arms around her husband as he buries his face in her hair. Lily holds Adam; Ginny holds Owen. There's just Corey and me left, and he lets out a sigh and stands, walking toward me.

He pulls me into a bear hug, and I'm so grateful for him.

"I'm glad you're here, little brother."

"Me too."

"Fuck, these past couple of weeks have been hard."

I nod. "I heard about Constance. I'm so sorry."

"It sucks. Mum's death, I understand, but I don't get why she'd leave." He pauses. "I bet you wish your lady was here too."

"Yep."

He chuckles in my ear. "You'll have to put up with hugs from your big brother."

"There are worse things in life."

Corey lets go of me and looks down. I grin when I see Ava tugging on his shirt.

"What's up, sweet pea?" He picks her up and cradles her on his hip.

"Daddy wanted me to make sure you're okay."

"I will be. Especially now I have you here."

Ava looks at me. "Are you okay?"

I can't help but smile. "I'll be fine. Thanks, Ava."

She leans her head on Corey's shoulder. This kid is so damn cute. It was a surprise when she came into this family, but now it's like she's always been here.

Mum's death has hit us all hard.

But we'll emerge as a stronger family for it.

17

———

JAMES

Today's so hard.

There's a big turnout for the funeral. Big by Copper Creek standards.

We're sat down the front ready to begin when the last people walk in. I run my gaze across the room, and take a breath when I see her. Down the back in a black dress, her dark hair down, and a pair of dark glasses perched on her head, is Mia. She gives me a reassuring smile and nods.

I want to go and get her. I want to claim her and sit her with my family. But my urge to protect her is stronger. I know Ashley's here somewhere; I saw her before. All I can do is hope she hasn't seen Mia, or if she has that she doesn't recognise her.

"James."

I turn to Owen.

"You okay?"

I nod. "It's a big turnout."

"Who knew she had so many friends?"

"I think most of them are here to be nosey. Isn't that what happens at funerals around here?"

He laughs. "You're probably right."

Owen nudges my leg with his. "You okay?"

"I will be when today's over and done with."

"As will we all."

Mia doesn't follow me to the wake, and none of us want to be here long. We all want to withdraw and do our own thing as a family that doesn't involve so many people.

Owen catered, and that's a drawcard for people who don't really know us that well to attend. It's cynical, but true.

I sit in the corner, watching everyone, when Ashley walks over to me.

"Shove over."

I move to my right on the bench seat.

"I'm glad she's here." Ashley meets my gaze.

"Who?"

She slaps my arm. "I saw Doctor Scott. That's who you're with now, right? I tried to work out why she'd show up, and it's the only conclusion I can come to."

"Maybe you're the one who should have been a scientist." I laugh.

"I won't tell anyone. If she makes you happy, then I'm glad. But don't let anyone find out."

I sigh. "That's the plan. I didn't know she'd be here today."

"She clearly cares a lot about you."

I nod, kicking my toe into the carpet. "I love her."

"I'm happy for you." She wraps her arms around my neck and plants a kiss on my cheek. "What happened between us was all my fault. And it was my loss. I threw away someone who loved and respected me for nothing."

"Thanks, Ashley."

"I'm so sorry about your mum."

I nod. "I appreciate you being here."

"How could I not be? Besides, Owen's sausage rolls are to die for." Her eyes widen. "Oh my god, I never meant that to come out the way it did."

Laughing, I roll my eyes. "It's okay. It was funny."

"It wasn't meant to be a joke."

"Not what you said. The look on your face when you said it."

She blushes. "Well, I'm going to go and see if I can steal a plate of sausage rolls and get out of here."

"I'm sure Owen won't mind. See you another time."

Ashley nods. She grabs a paper plate and fills it with as many sausage rolls as she can fit on it before walking away.

I laugh.

Owen walks toward me. "Was that Ashley taking all those sausage rolls?"

"She's addicted."

"Well, she can bloody pay for them next time." He laughs. "It was kind of funny."

"I think she's your biggest fan right now." I pull out my phone and send Mia a text as Adam approaches.

Where are you?

"Let's go to the pub for dinner. I doubt anyone can be bothered cooking," Adam says.

When I don't hear from her, I follow my family to the pub. A beer seems like a nice end to the day.

It doesn't take long for everyone to get a drink. I smile at Corey policing the kids' table like he's the parent of all of them.

When silence falls over the group, I look around to see what's caused it and spot Ash Harris walk through the door. He's the leader of that weird community next door to Corey. Nearly two years ago, he drugged Hayley to assault her and brainwash her into joining them, and Drew ushers her behind him.

"Ash," Drew says.

Ash nods. "Drew. Hayley."

Drew stares him down as Corey steps up to the conversation. I join Owen to the right of Corey. Ash scans the room. We're united, and he'd be a fool to start anything.

But no one ever said he was smart.

"I just wanted to pass on my condolences. I never met your mother, but I know how painful it is to lose someone so close."

"Get the fuck out of here, Harris. We don't want your sympathy." Corey fists his hands. He's got a lot of height on Ash, not to mention what looks to be a longer reach. Ash would be toast if he started a fight.

Ash straightens up. "Constance sends her regards. She regrets she can't invite you to her wedding."

Adam stands, stepping in front of Corey. "Corey told you to leave."

For a moment, Ash looks at us all as if weighing up his chances. There are none. If Corey gets hold of him, Corey will kill him. It's as simple as that.

He opens his mouth as if to say something more, then looks away, closing it again. With a quick nod, he's gone, and I turn to Corey.

I'm not sure I've ever seen him so angry.

He's holding himself together, and it's probably because we're somewhere public, and the kids are here with us. If that wasn't the case, I wouldn't want to be Ash Harris.

The tension has eased, but I'm still relieved when my phone buzzes in my pocket.

Copper Creek Motor Inn. Room 4.

The inn's just out of town. It's not far to drive.

I catch Corey's gaze. He's in so much pain right now. It bleeds through that tough exterior, and it's on display for the whole world to see.

I hate this.

"Are you okay?" Corey asks.

"I should ask the same of you."

He shrugs. "Apart from wanting to kill that motherfucker Ash Harris?"

"I'm so sorry, Corey. I can't understand what you're going through."

"How could she do it, James? How could she go back to that place?" He's full of anguish, and my heart breaks seeing him like this. As if we haven't already been through enough.

"I don't know. He's such a piece of shit trying to wind you up today of all days."

"Well, it worked." He huffs.

"Go home. Or have a few more drinks and go home later with Dad. I've got somewhere I need to be."

His eyebrows rise. "Where?"

"Just somewhere."

"Is she here?" He looks around.

"No. Yes. Kind of?" I shrug.

My big brother shakes his head. "You are so lucky that there are other things distracting me right now." He grins. "Go get her."

"You're not going to follow me or anything?" I tease.

"James. Go and be happy. I'm not going to remember this in the morning by the time I'm finished."

I laugh. "Have a good night."

I've had one beer, thankfully, and that was a while ago, so I'm good to drive. It doesn't take long to pull into the car park. Stopping my vehicle beside Mia's car, I climb out and head straight to the door.

I tap gently. The door opens.

My heart leaps at the sight of her. I knew she was on the other side, but laying eyes on her fills me with more emotion than I can handle.

"Mia," I whisper.

Her eyes are full of sorrow as she closes the door behind me, and opens her arms. "Come here." She wraps her arms around my waist, burying her face in my chest, and I breathe her in. She grounds me.

"I'm so happy to see you." I swallow down tears. Today's been emotional, and this is the best reward. I want to spend my life with Mia.

"I had to be here."

"Ashley saw you."

Mia pulls away. "Shit."

"It's okay. She's the only one who knew who you were, and she promised not to tell anyone. She just wants me to be careful."

Mia leans back into my chest. "Can we trust her?"

"She's not going to uni next year. We're good, Mia."

"Okay. If you trust her, I trust her. Have you had anything to eat?" she asks.

"I'm fine. I just came from the pub. My brothers are still there. I slipped away. But not without Corey knowing you're here."

She laughs. "He knows too? Maybe we should tell the rest of your family."

"He knows my lady is here. And that's all. I think he's about to have a really messy night and forget anyway."

Mia turns up her face to meet my gaze. I bend a little, pressing my lips to hers. "Have you eaten?"

"I grabbed a takeaway pizza. The rest is in the fridge if you want it."

"What I want is to curl up with you and sleep."

Mia strokes my face. "You look exhausted."

"I've slept, but I don't feel like I have. What I needed was you."

"Come to bed."

We lie down, still fully clothed. It doesn't matter. We don't need to be naked or have sex to share intimacy.

I'm the big spoon, she's the little, and I curl up around her as if I'm protecting her.

And I'll always do that.

She's all I ever need.

I WAKE with a face full of Mia's hair, but I don't mind. Having her here is everything.

It's still quite dark, and I reach for my phone on the bedside cabinet. It's a little before five, and I put the phone back and gently shake her. "Mia, get up."

She rolls onto her back, slowly opening her eyes. "James? What's wrong?"

"Nothing. There's something I want to show you. Let's go."

I grab a blanket from the bed as she wakes herself and stands up.

"It's still dark."

"Not for much longer. Come on."

She follows me out to my car, yawning as she climbs in. "Where are we going?"

"Somewhere special. Just trust me."

Leaning on my arm, she smiles. "Always."

It's not too far to the cove, and I escort a still sleepy Mia down to sit on the sand.

"Come here." I pull her closer, wrapping the blanket around both of us.

"What are we doing? It's freezing." She shivers, snuggling into my side.

"Just give it a few minutes."

We sit in silence. I hold her close, losing myself in the feel of her being with me.

She gasps.

I look up to see what we came for. The sun peeks over the mountain, slowly filling the cove with golden light.

"It's beautiful." Mia leans her head against mine.

"I used to do this sometimes when I lived here: sneak out of the house early and come down here to see the sunrise. When Mum first became ill, this was my favourite spot to get away from it all. And this early, no one's around."

"I want to live here."

I pull away from her, scanning her expression. She seems sincere. "Really?"

"Let's buy a place out here, James. I can write text books, and you can find something to do. It's magical."

"I'd love that."

"Once next year's out of the way and the divorce is final, I'll have enough to do what we want. Let's do it."

I grin, leaning closer again to kiss her. But I don't make it when she places her hand on my groin. "Are you after something, Doctor Scott?"

"We need to go back to the motel room." She nuzzles my ear.

"You are insatiable."

"Only with you." Mia laughs. "Besides, it's still cold."

"I'll take you back *and* warm you up."

Her smile is enough to warm me. The love that's written all over her face takes my breath away. "That sounds like a great deal."

***

PERSUADING Mia to stay another night is easy.

We spend the morning in bed, and I venture out at lunchtime for food and to grab my things from Dad's.

What I need right now is to be with my girl and shut out the rest of the world. Room four at the Copper Creek Motor Inn will do just fine for one more night.

I pull into the driveway. Corey's ute is still there, and I chuckle to myself. I'm sure he has one hell of a hangover.

He's sitting on the back deck wearing sunglasses, sipping from a beer.

"Hey." I grin.

"Hair of the dog. Want one?"

I shake my head. "I'm just here to grab my things and get out of here. You okay?"

"I don't know if I'll ever be okay." He sighs. "Mum died; my girlfriend dumped me. I need to get my shit together though. I know that much."

"Yeah, you do."

"I'm just gonna have this and then I'll make a coffee. I'll stay here again tonight rather than drive home."

"Good idea. Dad probably needs the company anyway."

He laughs. "Have a good night?"

"I slept better than I have in days. Yesterday was tough."

"It sure was."

"You're still not going to give me shit, are you?" I laugh.

He shakes his head. "I don't have the energy. Besides, one of us has to get a happy ending, right?"

My heart hurts for Corey. I didn't get to meet Constance, but I've never seen him so down over a woman. She was the real deal for him. If anything, it leaves me wanting to protect Mia all the more.

"Take care, Corey. I hope you guys work things out," I say.

"She's marrying someone else. There's nothing to work out."

I'm not sure what else to say. Instead, I nod and head inside.

Dad's standing at the kitchen bench.

"Where did you disappear to last night?" Dad's expression is bemused.

"I didn't think you'd notice."

"Corey was a big distraction. He came back here and drank a bottle of something, but I still missed my youngest son."

I nod. "I'm not surprised."

He laughs. "I just hope you're happy, James. Whatever you're doing. Life's too short for anything else."

"I am happy. And she was here when I needed her, Dad. That's got to count too, right?"

"Bring her round. I won't bite."

I shrug. "I'm not worried about you."

"Whatever you're protecting her from—she's safe here, son."

I take a deep breath. "I know. It's just hard to drop the habit. I'll bring her here when we're ready."

He nods. "I trust your judgement."

"That means a lot."

Dad grips my shoulder. "I'm so proud of you."

"I won't be home tonight either. I just came to get my stuff. I'm heading back to Auckland in the morning."

"So, this is goodbye."

I smile. "For a while. I'll be back soon. I'm not sure if I'll be home for Christmas, though."

He frowns.

"She doesn't have anyone, Dad. Just me. You'll have the others and their kids with you."

"Can't you bring her?"

"I'd like to, but she's going to be one of my lecturers next year. We're going to have to be even more careful. I don't want to risk it. All the students will be home for Christmas and if we're seen together it could blow everything."

He reaches for my arm. "James, you're safe when you're home."

I shrug. "Ashley recognised her at the funeral. I can't have that happen with anyone else."

Dad nods. "I understand. Be careful. I guess that means she's older than you."

"Don't you dare have a problem with it. Corey was twelve years older than Constance."

He lets me go. "I don't have a problem with it." He smiles. "No matter what, I'm on your side, James. Don't push people away who want to care."

I sigh. "Sorry, Dad. I'm just really protective of her."

"I can see that. Tell me if there's anything I can do."

"I will."

18

MIA

UNTIL TODAY, the secretive community based in Copper Creek has sat behind a large iron fence. It was only erected a few years ago, when Ash Harris inherited the leadership of the community from his father, Robert.

I stare at the screen. James told me all about this place. It's on the mountain located right next to where Corey lives. It's where Constance came from, and where she went back to, breaking Corey's heart.

"James," I call.

"What's up?" He appears in the doorway leading to the kitchen. He's making dinner tonight while I put my feet up. I don't usually watch the six o'clock news, but I'm really glad I am tonight.

"It's about that place where Constance lives."

"What?"

Tonight the gates are open, and the inhabitants are free. Police raided the community this morning, resulting in a hostage situa-

tion that was resolved earlier this afternoon when Harris was shot by a police sniper.

"What the fuck?" James sits on the couch next to me.

Also uncovered was one of the biggest methamphetamine labs that police have ever seen. There's no further comment from them about exactly how big, or what led to the shooting of Ash Harris, but there will be a press conference tomorrow at midday to announce their findings.

James picks up his phone from the coffee table and starts franticly tapping. "I wonder if Constance is okay. Corey'll be going nuts."

When there's no immediate response, he puts his phone back down. I reach over and rub his shoulders. "The only death they reported was that Ash guy. I'm sure she'll be fine."

"She'd better be. For Corey's sake. I don't know what drove her to go back, but if he was broken over her leaving him, he'll be shattered if she's been killed. He's still so in love with her."

Tears well in my eyes. The thought of losing James kills me inside.

We've been through so many stages of our relationship. Initial attraction. So much sex. Now we have companionship, and if Corey and Constance had even a tiny percentage of what James and I do, Corey must be a mess.

There's nothing more on the news, but I flick channels to see if there are updates anywhere else.

"What are you doing?" James asks.

"Trying to see if there's more news. There has to be. Surely."

He shrugs. "I guess we'll find out when they have their press conference."

"Call Corey. I want to know he's okay."

James's lips twitch. "You're such a big softy. You know that, don't you?"

"He's family. I'm allowed to worry."

I squeal as he pushes me back on the couch and covers my face with kisses. "I'm so lucky to have you."

"Why?" I laugh.

"You care so much. I think you're going to fit into my family just fine." He links his fingers with mine. "I need to go and finish cooking dinner. Tell me if you find any updates."

"I will."

With another peck to my lips, he gets up and walks to the kitchen. I sigh, watching him leave. I love that man.

***

WE WAKE in the morning to a message from Corey.

Constance is home.

"Did he say anything else?" I ask.

"There's a bunch of very happy emojis. I didn't think Corey knew how to do that on his phone." James laughs. "I'll get the full story out of him when he's ready. I'm sure they're busy."

I grin. "I'm sure they are too."

"As long as he's happy."

19

JAMES

THIS IS the first Christmas I've ever been away from home.

I thought long and hard about it, as it'll be Dad's first Christmas without Mum. But then he'll have everyone else around him.

Adam, Drew, Owen, and Corey will all be there. And with them come their wives and partners, not to mention all the kids. The thought of Dad with Ava, Rose, and the twins running rings around him makes me smile.

Mia and I decided to take that tropical holiday, and flew to Samoa on Christmas Eve.

Well, Mia decided. I was happy to be with her wherever we were. Her paying for everything leaves me self-conscious, but it makes me more determined than ever to make sure she has the best trip ever.

At least we don't have to worry about hiding here. While there's always a chance we'll run into someone, it's a lot less likely on an island far from home. Especially at this time of year.

On the flight, I hold her hand. She looks nervous, her eyes darting from one side of the plane to the other.

"I'm right here." I catch her gaze.

She shoots me a nervous smile. "I guess I should have told you that I hate flying."

I shrug. "It's just one of many things I'm sure I have to learn about you."

When the seatbelt sign goes off, we stay in our belts, but raise the arm between us. She snuggles in against me.

"Thank you for coming with me," she says.

"There's nowhere else I'd rather be."

"Your family are going to miss you."

I nod. I've got no doubt that's true, and I'll miss them. But I plan on spending next Christmas with them *and* Mia. My heart warms at the thought of her making friends with Lily, Hayley, and Ginny.

I have yet to meet Constance, but Corey adores her, and that's good enough for me. Both Constance and Ginny are pregnant, so next Christmas there'll be two more Campbells in the fold.

"I'll call them on Christmas Day. They'll be fine." I press a kiss to her temple. "Why don't you watch a movie and try and take your mind off us flying?"

"I might just do that."

I FEEL FREE.

Once we land and get to the resort, it's like a weight's

lifted from my shoulders. I'm sure Mia feels the same way. Though, I think a lot of it is that she's just glad we're on the ground again.

On the way to our room, we walk down a pathway lined with plants and frangipani flowers. The scent coming from them is heavenly.

"This is so beautiful," Mia says, linking her arm in mine. "And just what we needed."

"I think so too."

When we get to the room and the door's closed, I take her in my arms.

"I want to go out and explore, but I'm so tired after flying," she says.

"Me too. Why don't we have a nap first?"

She runs her fingers up my chest. "Just a nap?"

I chuckle. "What else did you have in mind?"

"Well, I thought we could kick things off with a shower because that drive from the airport made me hot and sticky." She gives me a sly smile.

"Hot and sticky, huh? I think we can take care of that." I grin.

Her expression softens. "I'm glad we're here. Leaving the rest of the world behind is the perfect Christmas present."

"I agree. I get to spend the whole week showing you just how much I love you, and not caring who sees."

I kiss her softly, but with Mia it's so easy to get carried away. I skim my tongue over hers, and she relaxes in my embrace.

"Forget the shower. Let's do that after." She's breathless.

"After what?"

Taking me by the hand, she leads me to the bed.

I nod. "Ohhh after *that*."

"Are you complaining?" She climbs onto the white linen and scoots across to the other side, beckoning me with her index finger.

"Never."

It's mid-morning the following day when I call Dad. Mia's still in bed.

We emerged from our room last night for dinner before returning and spending the night in each other's arms. The air con is a lifesaver.

"Hello?" Dad answers.

"Dad, it's James."

"James." I love the warmth in his voice. I've no doubt he misses me.

"I just wanted to call and say Merry Christmas."

"And the same to you. I hope you had a good trip."

I smile. "Long flight, but it's warm, and we'll go and get some sun today."

"Grandad." Ava's voice is in the background, and I find myself grinning. How excited will she be today? She'll be spoiled rotten if I know Owen.

"Just a minute, Ava. Uncle James is on the phone. Do you want to talk to him?"

There's a clatter, like Dad's dropped the phone, and I laugh.

"James. Where are you?" Ava asks.

"I'm in Samoa, sweetheart. Are you having a good Christmas?"

"Daddy bought me a bike with training wheels."

"Did he?" I turn my head as Mia places her hand on my shoulder. Her eyes are so full of love and happiness, and I peck her on the lips.

"Yes." She starts listing the things she got, and my heart's so full. Next year, we'll all be together.

I swear.

20

JAMES

MONDAYS SUCK.

Not only in the general sense, but somehow I managed to draw the eight a.m. lecture for this class. At least I'm not the only one having to deal with it. It's our first morning back at uni for our master's year.

"Have you seen what Mia Scott is wearing today?" Cody asks.

I look up. "No. Why?" When I left her place this morning, she was in the shower.

"Over there."

It's her legs I notice first. Those long, slim legs that wrap around me just perfectly. She's wearing a tight white skirt that comes to about halfway down her thighs. Over her white shirt, she's wearing a black jacket. She looks professional, and hot as all hell.

My cock twitches at the thought of sliding between her red-painted lips.

I can't do this while I'm here.

"Jesus, she's hot," Cody says.

I nod, and return my attention to my book. Only it's hard to concentrate now because I know what it's like to be buried inside her. Roll on the end of the year, when Mia and I can move on.

"I would fuck her in a heartbeat."

"Dude."

He shrugs. "She can't hear me."

"But I can, and it's not appropriate." Even if she wasn't mine, I still wouldn't talk out loud about a woman like that.

"Good morning, everyone." Mia's voice rings out over the top of all the talking. "Take a seat and we'll begin."

Her eyes meet mine, and the warmth that was in them this morning is there, but held back. She's so good at putting a mask on.

When everyone's quiet, she smiles. "With today being our first day, I'll start with introducing myself, and then we'll quickly go around and you can tell me who you are."

Cody puts his arm up, and she points at him. "Yes?"

"That could take all morning, Doctor Scott."

She nods. "It could do, but the class isn't too big, and I doubt any of you are going to concentrate on anything serious with this being your first lecture of the year. Especially at this time of the morning."

Laughter crosses the room, and she smiles. "My name is Doctor Mia Scott. I have a doctorate in biotechnology, and I know some of you will have read various papers of mine. At least, I hope so, if you're pursuing a career in biotech. I'm a self-confessed geek, and I love science fiction." She scans the room. "Now, who wants to go first?"

I chuckle as Cody puts his hand up again. Mia knows who he is. I've told her all about him. And she's aware of some of the higher-achieving students in the class too. Biotech is her baby, and she loves the idea of people moving into the field.

Mia smiles and nods at my friend "Okay. You go first."

"My name is Cody Johnson. I got into biotech because I wanted to study genomes and work with DNA. To be honest, it's a miracle I got this far as my interests also include girls and partying. But I'm here."

I bury my face in my hands.

Mia laughs. "Okay. Who's next?"

I look up to see her gaze fixed on me. I guess it makes sense, with me sitting next to Cody.

Taking a deep breath, I start. "I'm James Campbell. It was a toss-up between botany and biotech. But I'm really glad I chose biotech because I think it's going to lead to something in the future for me."

She licks her lips. This year is going to be so tough. She knows I'm not talking about the science.

"And are you like Mr Johnson as far as your interests go?"

I shrug. "I'm not big on partying. I'd much rather have a quiet life."

Mia smiles. "I know what you mean."

She moves onto the next person, but there's such a big part of me that wants to just abandon all pretence and show the world she's mine.

At first, we didn't tell anyone because we didn't want her douchebag ex to know. And now, I'm in her class. We just have to get through this year, and we'll be free. I'll graduate, she'll have her divorce, and the two of us can go away together and start a new life.

For now, I listen to her lecture, make notes, and try desperately to ignore the fact that there are several male students looking at my girlfriend as if they want do the dirty things I do with her.

We're stuck, and it's so fucking awkward.

21

COREY

Six months later

"Push."

Constance glares at me. It's nearly midnight, and she's been pushing for an hour. The tension's obvious on the midwife Margaret's face. Con's exhausted, and Margaret's worried about her and the baby.

"Come on, sweetness. You can do it." I say.

Tears appear in Con's eyes as she bears down. "I'm so tired, Corey."

"I know you are. I wish I could take it all away."

Her face is red with effort, and I take the wet washcloth and wipe her cheeks.

"You're so close, Constance. Keep going." Margaret sounds as if she's trying to keep her tone neutral, but we both know what could happen if this goes wrong. We're remote, and it's a long way to the nearest hospital.

I should have booked her into Tauranga, or even asked Drew if she could deliver in Hamilton. But it's too late, and she has to get through this.

"I love you," she whispers.

"I love you too, sweetness. Let's get that baby out."

"It's easy for you to say." Despite her pain, she laughs before her face distorts again.

She lets out a moan.

"That's it. The head's crowning. Push down as hard as you can." Margaret's voice is so full of hope, and I exchange a relieved look with her.

"I can't do this." Constance's tears are back, and I squeeze her hand.

"You're so strong. You have no idea."

It's times like this when I can still picture her in Ash's grip. His hand had been wrapped around her throat, and he'd had a gun against her temple. I nearly lost her then. I will not lose her now.

She nods, her features contorting as she bears down hard again.

I turn my head in time to see our son slip out of her. It's the most incredible thing I've ever seen.

He's covered in blood and mucus, but he's pink, and he's perfect from what I can see.

"Con." I turn back. Her eyelashes flutter, and I wipe her forehead tenderly with the washcloth before I kiss her. Her lips are soft, and there's no sign of the tension that held her in its grasp just a few seconds ago. "He's beautiful, Con."

"He is," Margaret says. "And very healthy."

She places him on Constance's bare chest. He squawks, then settles, his head resting over his mother's heart.

My heart's about to explode.

———

WHILE CONSTANCE SHOWERS, I hold my son for the first time.

How can something that small be so difficult to get out? Constance is amazing.

"He's a lovely baby," Margaret says.

"He's perfect. Will Constance be okay?"

She nods. "She needs a lot of rest, but I think you'll help her with that. Do you have a name for him?"

"Eli."

Margaret smiles. "It's a nice name."

"Con and I spent hours going through a baby name book, and it was one of the few we both liked."

"It's lovely."

Eli stares at me. He's got a shock of dark hair, just like both his mother and me. His eyes are grey, just like Constance's, though they could change colour later on.

"I was so scared, little man. I was really worried about you and your mum. But now you're here, and I'm going to pamper your mother more than usual."

Margaret pats my arm. "I'll be back later today to check on her. It was a difficult labour."

"Thanks. You were fantastic. But I still wish we'd gone to a hospital."

She nods. "I can understand that. But they're both okay now."

"That's so much better." Constance walks into the

bedroom. We set up the spare room as the birthing room, so we can sleep in our own bed now. Her smile is faint, and her exhaustion still clear, but she's looking so much better than she was half an hour ago.

"Hey." She reaches for Eli, and I hand him over. "You two look good together."

She smiles at our son, cradling him in one arm while she holds his tiny hand. "Were you having cuddles with Daddy?"

Daddy.

I'm a father.

"I guess I should text everyone."

She nods. "We'll never be forgiven if we don't let them all know."

"I'll take care of that. You go and get into bed with Eli." I lean over, giving her a tender kiss on the lips.

"I'll just finish cleaning up here, and I'll see you later on after we've all had a sleep." Margaret smiles.

Constance nods. "Thank you for everything."

"You're welcome. You have my number. Call me if you need anything, and don't worry about the time. It's what I'm here for."

Con disappears back out to the living room, and I turn to Margaret. "Don't worry about the rest. I'll sort it out later on."

"The bed's remade and I've got all the rubbish in a bag. There's not much left to do."

"Thanks, Margaret."

She smiles. "I'm so happy for you two. Give my love to Hayley if you're talking to her."

"Will do."

When she's gone, I sit with my phone and compose a

message to the family. Max set up groups on my phone to make this easier for me, and I just send out a mass text to the lot to tell them Eli's been born and attach a photo. I even remember to include his length and birth weight because I know Hayley, Lily, and Ginny will all want to know.

When I get to the bedroom, Constance lies in bed, Eli at her breast. It's a breathtaking sight. The earlier struggles of this evening are forgotten as he feeds in peace.

I'm sure the quiet won't last for long, but for now we enjoy it.

22

JAMES

My phone buzzes beside the bed.

"Ignore it. Let's go to sleep." Mia's voice is tinged with tiredness. It's been a long week for both of us, and spending all of Friday evening in bed hasn't helped. Not a lot of sleep has gone on so far.

"I should check. As far as I know, Constance is still in labour."

She nods, and I grab my phone, grinning as I see what's come through.

"Check this out." I hand my phone over to her, and a smile lights up her face.

"What a beautiful baby."

"That's my new nephew, Eli. Born about an hour ago. Ginny and Owen's baby is only a few weeks away too."

"That's so sweet. The two cousins will be able to grow up together."

I nod. It's times like this that make me homesick. Having Mia in my life distracts me from missing home.

Seeing Eli tugs at my heartstrings.

I miss Copper Creek. I miss my family.

"You should go and see him."

I meet her gaze. She knows me inside and out. No one's ever read me the way Mia can. "I wish I could take you with me."

She smiles. "One day."

"Soon." I put the phone back, and reach for her, running my fingers through her thick, dark hair.

She sighs. "We're not going to sleep yet, are we?"

"Nope." I bury my face in her neck, gently sucking at her collarbone. She lets out a moan that tells me exactly what she thinks of that.

"I'm so tired." She laughs.

"I'll do all the work." When I pull away, she looks at me with so much love. God, I love this woman so much. I hate that we have to hide it from everyone. "We can spend tomorrow in bed."

"That works for me." She sighs. "Love you."

"I love you too."

I'M NOT EVEN sure what time I fall asleep, but I know it's daylight from the sun peeping through the curtains.

But that's not what wakes me.

I roll my eyes at the sound of plates being moved in the kitchen, and nudge Mia.

"I think you have a visitor."

"What?" She turns, her eyes still hazy with sleep.

"Garrett's here." It's been ages since he's randomly shown up.

Her eyes widen. "Shit. He can't find you here."

"I know. Want me to climb out the window?"

"Why would I want you to do that?" She laughs softly. I hate this. Hate that we have to keep *us* secret. But it's not for much longer, and it's for a good purpose. "I'll get rid of him."

"Last time you said that, he invited himself for breakfast."

"He's not the easiest person to get rid of."

"Can you at least save me something to eat?"

Mia grins, and presses her lips to mine. "I've got plenty for you to eat."

"Are you being dirty, Mia Scott?"

She shakes her head. "Just a little accidental innuendo."

"There's nothing accidental about it."

With another kiss, she climbs out of bed, drags on her jeans and a shirt, and disappears out the door, closing it behind her.

I lie back in bed, my hands behind my head. Mia's my whole world.

I feel like I've been waiting my whole life for her.

"James."

Mia shakes me gently awake, and I roll over.

"Sorry. I guess I must have nodded off. Is Garrett gone?"

She nods. "It took a little while, and about a million questions about why I'd changed the key to the garage. He obviously hasn't tried that door for months."

I grin, reaching up to twist a lock of her dark hair around my index finger. "What did you tell him?"

"I told him it was to hide my lover's car. What do you think I told him? I lost the key." She grins. "Of course then he pointed out he has a key, but I told him that I didn't need him to solve my problems."

"Does he want access?"

She shrugs. "I kicked him out before he could ask."

"You kicked him out?"

Mia snuggles into the bed beside me. "He brought breakfast. I asked him to leave. He left, but the food's still here."

"He's probably gone to get a locksmith."

Laughing, she plants a kiss on my chest. "Maybe."

"Maybe it's time to come clean. Deal with the consequences."

Her face falls. "I want to, James. But we both know what happens if we do." If he gets nasty, he'll drag out the settlement for as long as possible, inserting himself in Mia's life even longer. Not to mention the damage he could do to her at work.

I nod. "I just want to wipe that smug smile off his face."

"Next year, we'll get out of here and leave all this behind."

I sigh, and take a deep breath in her hair. "I can't wait for that."

"Me either."

23

COREY

I hate being away.

I'd told Constance that I wouldn't be far from her and Eli for at least six weeks after he was born. But four weeks in, a job came up from a new client promising to pay a lot more than my other clients usually do. I never would have done it if Constance hadn't agreed. The client was desperate.

Now I'm the desperate one. Even one night is too long to be away from my family, and it's been three.

The money for this job will go into the nest egg we're accumulating toward our future. It's nice to be so much further ahead of where we'd planned to be.

It would have been easy to stay another night and travel home in the morning. But my arms long to hold Con and Eli again, and once I'm home I think I'll sleep for a week.

Constance sits in her favourite chair with Eli in her arms when I walk in.

"Hey, sweetness. It's so good to be home. I'm starving." I

drop my bag by the door. It can wait. Constance and Eli come first.

She sniffs, and I walk closer. Her eyes are rimmed with red; she's so tired. She's rocking the baby in her arms, tears rolling down her cheeks.

"Con? What's wrong?"

She shakes her head. "I'm useless. There's no dinner. I can't—"

"You're not useless." I bend, planting a lingering kiss on her head. "It's still early days. I'm sorry I had to leave. You know I hate being away from you." I squat in front of the chair. "Tell me everything."

"The baby won't stay asleep. I can't get anything done."

I rub her arm. "It's okay. I'm back now, and I'll help."

"It's like the second you walked out the door, everything went wrong." She sniffs again.

Squeezing her knee, I stand. "Here. Give me him and you go and have a sleep."

She shakes her head. "I need to cook dinner."

"You don't need to do anything. I'll pop him in the ute and we'll go into town and bring back something to eat."

Constance pouts. "I said I'd take care of both of you."

"You do. Just by being you, you do. But sometimes, we have to look after you." I reach down, and she sighs as she hands the small bundle to me. "You have a nap. When you wake up, *we* are having a bath."

She gives me a small smile.

"Have you seen anyone while I've been gone? Lily or Ginny?"

Shaking her head, she stands. "No, it's just been me and …"

"Not even your mother?"

She shrugs. "It's not exactly the easiest walk to see her."

"We'll keep going with your driving lessons, and we'll get a car." I lean over and brush her lips with mine. "I should have made sure you had help while I was gone."

"Then people will think I can't manage." Panic flashes in her eyes. It's no shame to need help, but her upbringing wasn't exactly normal and I think she still has concerns about being judged outside the compound.

I shift the baby to one side, and slip my other arm around her waist. "They won't think that at all. You have a big family now, and they'll all love to help."

"I don't want to be a burden."

"Sweetness, you're not. Trust me. If I'm ever away and you need anything, give Lily a call. Maybe next time we can organise you going to stay with her. Or with your mother." I bristle at that last suggestion. As much as I like Constance's parents, the thought of her and my son staying on that property overnight grates. Ash might be dead, but the memory of him lingers.

"Do you think Lily would mind?"

"Adam and Lily have room. And I bet anything Lily would love to get her hands on this little one for a while. If you hadn't noticed, you and Ginny both being pregnant made Lily pretty clucky."

She snuggles into my side, and I lean my head on hers. "I hate you being away."

"I hate being away. I'd much rather be here with you two." After planting a kiss on her head, I pull back. "Now, go get some sleep. I'll take care of him, and when you wake up there'll be something to eat."

"He'll be hungry soon."

"Is there any expressed milk in the fridge?"

She nods.

"Well, his dinner's sorted too, then."

Tears well in her eyes again. "I'm so glad you're home."

"Me too."

IT TAKES minutes for Constance to fall asleep. She's so tired. And I feel like shit for being away while she struggled.

I'm glad for the time I can spend with my son.

I pull up outside the fish and chip shop, and step out of the truck. After opening the back door, I unclip the capsule from the base and head inside.

Owen's standing in the queue. The queue that's much longer than I'd expected. I scowl.

"Dude. About time you got here." He signals for me to join him, and I get a couple of dirty looks when I jump the queue. "Took you long enough." He lowers his voice. "It's good to see you. Glad I could help you move up the line."

"You are a prince among men."

He grins. "I'm just doing this for Eli. How's he going?"

"Great. Want to see?" As I switch the capsule from one hand to the other, Owen makes the front of the queue.

"I've got two orders," he says.

The man serving him nods.

I look down at Eli while Owen places his order. My heart's so full of love when I look at him. I never knew the human body had so much capacity for it. Constance is everything, and this little guy? He's the cream on the top.

Owen nudges me.

"Oh. Can you hold him?" I pass the capsule to Owen.

"With pleasure. Come on, little man."

I step up to order as Owen takes a seat. "Can I please order the twenty-dollar deal, and can you throw in half a dozen scallops. No, make that a dozen. I'm starving." I grin.

After paying, I make my way over to Owen. He's already extracted Eli from the capsule, and he's pulling faces at my son.

"Getting practice?" I ask, sitting next to him.

"I can't wait. How are things going with you guys?"

I shrug. "Today's a bit shit. I've been away for three nights, and come back to this one not sleeping and Constance exhausted. She wants to take care of everything when none of it matters but her and Eli."

"I thought you weren't going away for a while?"

"That was what we decided, and then an opportunity came up that was too good to ignore. But it doesn't matter how much money the job's worth. Constance is more important."

Owen nods. "Too right. I feel the same way about Ginny."

"Mate, I'm so happy for you two. In a few weeks, you'll know all about the sleepless nights like us." I chuckle.

"I can't wait." His smile's distant. "I'll always regret what I missed with Ava. And I'm so glad it's Ginny I'm doing this with."

Eli grizzles. Owen hands him over to me. I place Eli back in the capsule to rock him.

Owen leans over. "Hey, little fella. Are you going to be like your mum or your dad? Please take after your mother. The world's not big enough for two Coreys."

I laugh. "I hope he takes after his mother too. She's so patient and kind. Not at all like me."

"I'm not sure about that. You were always so good with Max when he was little. And that kid needed a lot of patience."

Grinning, I look down at Eli. "I'm sure you'll get into everything. Just like Max did. I hope you listen to your mother like he listens to his."

"Where's Constance? Didn't she want to come for a drive?"

"Fast asleep. I ordered a heap of food, but I'm starving so hopefully there's some left for her."

He nods. "Ginny's at home with her feet up. She's finished work now, so the baby can come at any time."

"I hope for her sake that's soon. Constance was so over it by the time Eli arrived."

Owen laughs. "Listen to us."

I shrug. "It's nice to have people to love who we want to talk about. I can't imagine life without my two special people in it anymore."

"Me either."

WHEN I GET HOME, I drop the fish and chip package on the coffee table and poke my head into the bedroom. Constance is still asleep, and her expression is so peaceful. There's a part of me that wants to crawl into bed, wrap my arms around her, and fall asleep myself. But Eli's awake and my stomach grumbles.

Returning to the couch, I open the fish and chip package

and take a deep breath. Eli grizzles again, and I unbuckle him, lifting him gently out of the capsule.

Cradling him in one arm, I pick up a hot chip.

"One day, you'll eat this, mate." I grin. "You'll love it."

His grey eyes just stare at me as I take a bite.

"Now, when I'm not here, you need to be good to your mum. She loves you so much." I bite down the rest of the chip, and raise my free hand to his face, running my index finger over his cheek. "So do I. And you and your mum are the best things that ever happened to me. We all need to take care of each other."

He waves his arms excitedly, and I chuckle. "You know what I'm saying."

I love this kid with everything I've got.

I place him down on the couch so I can eat. My stomach grumbles. "I can't wait to introduce you to this kind of thing, mate. Your mum's not a fan of scallops, but she loves fish. And we can go fishing at the cove and catch them really fresh."

I wolf down half the scallops as Eli looks around. He screws up his face.

"Oh, buddy. Are you getting hungry?"

He lets out a whimper, and I pick up another scallop.

The whimper turns into a wail.

"Okay. Let's go get you sorted."

I pick him up and carry him into the kitchen. There's a bottle of milk in the fridge, and I boil some water to warm it up. It won't take too long.

He lets out a lusty cry, and I rock him. "Hey, buddy. It'll be ready soon. I'll check your nappy."

I grab a nappy, wipes, and the change mat, and settle him

on the floor. He doesn't smell, but I blow out a breath at the sight of a mini poo explosion.

"Dude. No wonder you're pissed. At least the nappy covered the bit up your back."

It takes a few wipes, but I clean him off and slip a clean nappy on.

I pop him in his bouncer, then I wash my hands and return. "Is that better, my little man?"

He screws up his face and lets out another cry. I hold my finger to my lips. "I'll just check that milk. Don't wake your mother."

The milk has warmed, and I scoop him up in one arm. Sitting back on the couch, I offer him the bottle. He sucks on it with gusto, gulping it as fast as the bottle will let him.

"Dude. I know you do that feeding from Mum, but ease up." I shake my head.

As if on cue, my stomach gurgles, and I look down at the food on the table. *Soon.*

Eli swallows the milk, and I lift him over my shoulder, gently rubbing his back. I laugh when he lets out an almighty burp.

"You're worse than me, kid."

With two smaller burps, he settles back into my arms and I rock him gently. He yawns, and I can't take my eyes from him. *My son.*

It takes a few minutes, but his eyes close, and I smile. At least Constance won't have to worry about him for a while once she wakes up. Although, she was so tired she could probably sleep longer than he does.

I sit with him a while longer, watching Eli sleep peacefully, and knowing that if he's not sound asleep, he'll be awake again as soon as I put him in the bassinet.

My heart is so full. How did I survive even three days away from him and from Constance?

When I place him in the bassinet, he lets out what sounds like a sigh. I hold my breath, fully expecting his eyes to open and for him to roar for his mother.

Instead, he surprises me with sleep, and I stroke his head.

Time to finish this feed and wait for Constance.

AFTER DEMOLISHING MORE of the food and putting the leftovers in the fridge, I settle back onto the couch and flick on the TV. About half an hour later, Constance emerges from the bedroom.

She runs her fingers through her hair and yawns. "Where's Eli?"

I reach for her hands. "Fast asleep. He had a bottle, and I changed his nappy, and with a bit of rocking, he was out like a light."

She pouts. "Why won't he do that for me?"

"You smell so good, he can't resist." I grin. "Seriously, I read that babies can smell their mother's milk. You're a source of food and distraction for him."

She smiles, and it fills my heart. "I guess that makes sense."

When she sits beside me, I wrap my arms around her and pull her in tight. "I understand it. You're a huge distraction for me. And I'm not the breastfed baby."

Constance laughs, burying her face in my chest.

"I love you. And if Gary wants me to go back anytime soon, I'll say no."

She shakes her head. "You still need to work."

"I know. But you and Eli come first. And I don't want you to get overwhelmed again."

"I just have to learn to cope."

"We'll work things out. In the meantime, I'm going to heat up some food for you, and then I'm going to run a bath for us."

She leans back. "I'm not sure if that's a good idea. We can't have sex yet."

I run my finger along her jawline. "No, but I just want to be near you. If you're okay with that."

"I'm so okay with that. I've missed you."

"I missed you too. I much prefer your body next to mine in bed than being alone in a sleeping bag on the hard ground."

Constance smiles. "You're so sweet, Corey Campbell."

I shake my head. "It was just a matter of finding the right body to want to be with."

She laughs softly, and for a moment longer, I sit with my eyes closed, my arms around the woman I love.

"You must be hungry," I say.

Constance nods. "Starving. I'm always hungry now I'm breastfeeding."

"Gotta keep up Eli's food. He just gutsed that bottle. It was like he thought it was his last meal."

She grins. "He feeds like that all the time."

"And then he let out a huge burp." I twist my lips. "He really is a lot like me, isn't he?"

When she nods, I laugh and stand. "I'll go and sort that food out."

When I return with a plate laden with food, I watch her eat. She already looks so much more relaxed than she did when I got home, and a warm bath will help even more.

She's been through so much. I tried to make life as relaxing as possible for her when she found out she was pregnant, and she let me after everything she'd been through. But being kidnapped by Ash, and his flagrant disregard for her life, scarred her more deeply than she ever lets on. She's had nightmares for months.

Not that she tells me.

They seemed to stop when Eli was born, but I'm acutely aware that her experience will still be lurking in the back of her mind. It lurks in mine, too.

I thought she'd left me. Then I thought he'd killed her.

Those ideas haunt me, especially when I go away. Even though Ash is long since buried, I'll never forget the sight of him with the gun against her head, his hand tight around her throat, choking her.

She's talked to Victim Support through the police, but maybe now she needs more.

I need to get a real job. One where I can work days and come home to her at night. One where I can be here when she needs me. I've lived a fairly transient life up until now, and it's suited me. I work every few weeks and it pays the bills, but maybe I need to get consistency.

The thought is alien to me.

But I'd do anything for her. For my family.

Dad worked a regular job. We had him there for us at

nights and on weekends. I've just never thought about anyone other than myself because I didn't have to.

Now I do.

THE TUB'S big and deep. It's an old one I bought years ago that came out of a demolished old Victorian house.

It's the best thing about the bathroom. But it takes an age to fill.

Constance is worth it.

I miss being intimate with her. I'd be fooling myself if I didn't acknowledge how addicted I am to sex with my girl. Where I could take or leave physical intimacy before, I have this craving for her that's unparalleled in my life.

The past few weeks have been frustrating, but I also want Constance to take the time to heal and be ready for me. However long that takes.

I flick off the taps when the tub's full.

"Constance," I call.

After tugging my shirt over my head, I throw it to the floor. My jeans and underwear follow, and I step into the tub.

The hot water soothes my muscles. I hadn't realised how tired and sore I was until I got in.

Constance appears in the doorway. "You started without me."

I don't miss the appreciative gaze that she runs over me. It's been a while since we've seen each other naked this way.

Although, she has yet to disrobe.

She takes some steps into the bathroom.

I grin as she stares down at me in the tub. "Come on."

Constance grimaces. "I don't know if …"

"What are you afraid of?"

She shrugs. "I don't want to strip off in front of you."

"I've seen you naked a million times. I like you naked."

"Not since I had a baby."

I swallow hard. I've never given her cause to think I wouldn't find her body attractive. At least, I don't think I have. I watched this powerhouse of a woman give birth to my son, and there's nothing but pride and admiration in my heart for her. "Baby, you're beautiful. Nothing's going to change my mind. Get naked, and get in this tub."

Uncertainty crosses her face, and she takes a deep breath. After raising her nightgown over her head, she throws it to the floor.

I drink in the sight of her.

Her breasts are bigger, but I already knew that from before Eli's birth. Her skin still bears the signs of a baby having been inside her, silvery stretchmarks crossing her tummy which isn't as flat as it once was.

She's so beautiful.

"Corey?"

"You are fucking magnificent. Come here, mother of my child."

With a small smile, she dips her toe in and screws up her nose. "You always make it too hot."

I chuckle. "Give me a moment." Leaning forward, I run the cold tap for a few seconds. "Try that."

Constance nods. "That's much better."

"Get the hell in here."

She laughs as she drops her panties to the floor and steps in, and I let out a low whistle as I get the full sight of her lowering her naked body into the bath from behind.

Her back is creamy and flawless. I know my way around each and every freckle on her back, but it's been a while since I've seen them all.

She leans against me. I pick up the sponge, and soap it up.

"I'm glad you're home."

"Me too. I think we'll sleep well after this."

"Hopefully Eli does too."

I drop my head to her neck, nuzzling her skin. "Night time baby delivery service is here to help now."

Con laughs, and I raise the sponge, swiping it down between her breasts. "You're such a good father, Corey."

"And you're an amazing mother."

"I'm not so sure about that."

"You are. Even if you don't feel it right now." I sigh. "You know, I don't care if the house gets messy, or dinner's not cooked. I can take care of that. Your priority is you and Eli. And my priority is both of you."

She sighs. "I love you, Corey."

"You and Eli are my whole heart. If you hurt, I hurt."

Constance yawns.

I chuckle. "Am I keeping you awake?"

"I'm just so tired."

Running the sponge across her stomach and over her legs, I press a kiss to her neck.

"There'll be none of that yet, Corey Campbell."

I laugh against her skin. "I know that, but I'm still allowed to kiss you."

"My back is pressed against your …"

With another quick kiss, I lean back. I'm rock hard being pressed against her naked body. I can't help it. I have a craving for her that nothing can replace. "I swear my cock has a mind of its own when it comes to you."

She laughs.

"When we get out of the bath, I'll make us both a hot chocolate, and we'll go back to bed together. While I was away, all I could think of was sleeping beside you." I nuzzle her neck again. "I've just gotten reacquainted with my hand again. That's done just fine."

"Reacquainted with your …" She gasps. "Corey."

I shrug. "It's not often I can shock you."

She laughs again. It's such a beautiful thing to hear, especially after the way I found her when I came home.

"I'm just so glad you're here," she says softly.

"Me too. I hate being away nowadays. It used to be easy. Now it's anything but when I know you're in my bed."

"You always know the right thing to say."

"I hope so. I hope I always do. You're the one person in my life I never want to let down." I chuckle. "Except for Eli. I want to always be here for him, Con."

She raises her hand behind her, running her fingers through my beard. "You will be. You are."

"I haven't been these past few nights."

"You were working. And now you can spend lots of time with him until the next job."

When we're out of the bath and dried off, I climb into bed beside her. I'm not sure how long it'll be before Eli wakes, but I'm not letting Constance out of this bed unless I have to. She needs her rest.

I wrap myself around my girl in my arms, and close my eyes.

It's early days. We'll find our feet.

24

COREY

Buzz.

I'm vaguely aware of my phone vibrating on the bedside cabinet.

Buzz.

Maybe I'm dreaming it.

"Corey."

Constance's voice makes me smile. Lord, how I want that woman.

When I force my eyes open, the soft light of the bedroom lamp fills the room. It's sometime in the middle of the night, and her breasts are in my face.

Well, her nightgown with the insanely distracting neckline is in my face.

"Sweetness," I murmur.

She laughs softly as I release a breast from its imprisonment.

"You smell like milk."

"I just fed Eli." She laughs.

"He woke up? I never heard him."

She sighs. "As much as I love your offer to get him in the night, you're impossible to wake sometimes."

I chuckle. "Well, I'm awake now. Kind of."

"Corey, you're—"

I graze her nipple with my lips. A gasp catches in her throat.

After licking up her breast and back down again, I settle on her nipple. Her skin's so sweet from feeding Eli, and I tongue it, leaving her moaning.

"God, Con, I want to eat your pussy so badly. I've missed it so fucking much."

"I'm not going to stop you," she whispers. "I wasn't sure before, but I'm ready."

"Seriously?" Now I'm awake.

"I've missed it too." Her eyes are so full of love. "I've missed you."

She laughs as I roll us over so I'm on top, and runs her fingers through my hair. I reach for the hem of her nightgown and slide it up and over her head. She sighs contentedly when I hook my fingers in the waist of her panties and slide them down.

Mine.

She was mine from the moment I met her, and she always will be. Constance makes me whole. She completes me in a way no one else ever did. My heart, soul, and my body belong to her.

I start slowly. The scent of her is tantalising, and I want to devour her, but she gave birth just over a month ago and the last thing I want to do is to rush her.

But damn it, she tastes like heaven.

I plant kisses on her thighs. She bucks her hips, and I chuckle against her skin. "Patience, sweetness."

"I'm all out of that right now." She reaches down to stroke my hair as I grow closer to my target. All it does is spur me on. I need her touch as much as she needs mine.

I lick up each side of her pussy before running my tongue over her clit. It swells at my attention, and I suck it gently into my mouth.

"Corey."

I look up to see the love in her eyes.

It's all I need.

I tongue her clit while she squirms underneath me. The tension's building in her body, and all I can think about is pleasing her. It's all for her.

"Corey." She cries my name as she comes, bucking her hips. I lick her clean before moving up to kiss her.

She's so soft and warm beneath me.

I love kissing her. We've shared kisses since Eli's birth, but not like this one. It's deep and hot, and only makes me ache even more for her. "Fuck I love you, Con. You're so fucking perfect."

Her eyes search mine. There's so much emotion on her face, she doesn't even need to reply.

"Are you sure?"

She nods.

I let out a moan when I slide into her. Nothing in my whole life has ever felt this good.

She laughs, her pussy pulling me in.

"You should laugh more." I kiss her again.

"Why?"

"Because it feels so fucking good."

I love seeing that warmth and affection in her eyes. It's not that it's been missing, but it's been distant recently.

"I love you." She reaches up and strokes my beard.

I turn my head, kissing her hand. Her body responds to my thrusts, and I close my eyes to enjoy the sensation of her heat surrounding me.

Constance and me, we were always meant to be. I was never a big believer in destiny, but being with her has changed my mind.

This is right.

This is perfect.

This is love.

"Corey." Her voice wavers, and I shift to put pressure on her clit. I want her to come when I do.

Her breathing quickens.

"You undo me, sweetness."

She bucks underneath me, and I soar as my release hits. Everything's right in our world.

I pant when I pull out and roll to her side. "What time is it? It's not like you to wake me in the night for sex."

She laughs. "It's around four-thirty in the morning, and I didn't."

"What did you wake me up for?"

"Your phone kept going off. It was Owen to say Ginny had the baby."

I grin. "Really?"

"A little girl named Violet. They're all well." She nuzzles her nose against mine. "I was leaning over to check your phone when you accosted me."

"Are you sorry I did?"

"Not at all." She smiles, and I take in the sight of her. Her hair's messy, and she's got that 'just fucked' look about her. All it does is make her even hotter.

The phone buzzes again, and this time, I pick it up.

Come and visit us later today. Ginny wants to see Constance.

Will do. Congrats, Dad.

"Ginny wants to see you." I put my phone back on the cabinet and roll toward Constance.

She smiles. "I'd love to see her."

"Let's get some sleep, and we'll go late morning."

"They want us to go today?"

I shrug. "So says Owen. I'm sure it's been a crazy night, and Ginny would appreciate some female company." After reaching over, I run my fingers through her hair. "You two grew close when you were both pregnant. I'm sure she just wants someone to talk to, especially when it was you a month ago."

Constance nods. "If she's ready for visitors, I'll be happy to go." Her smile grows. "I'm so happy for them, Corey. We were so lucky with Eli, and Ginny's been through so much to have her baby."

"I want to have more babies."

She laughs. "Can we just enjoy the one we have first?"

"Sure, but you were so horny when you were pregnant. I liked that." I reach for the lamp, flicking it off to leave the room dark.

Taking a deep breath, I wrap myself around Constance and close my eyes.

OWEN'S EYES ARE BLOODSHOT.

I grin at the sight of them. The night has been exhausting for them, but I bet it was worth it.

"Congratulations." I beam as I walk into the living room with Eli in his capsule. Constance follows.

Owen grins. "I'm so tired, but it's all worth it."

"How's Ginny doing?"

He nods toward the hallway. "Go and see. Ava's in her room playing if you want to see her too."

"Ginny first."

Owen turns toward Constance. "I'm about to put the jug on for another coffee. Want one? I grabbed a bunch of things from the bakery if you want something to eat too."

I place the capsule on the floor.

"I'll go sort it out, Owen. Take a seat. You look so tired," Constance says.

"Thanks, Constance. Violet has a shitty sense of timing. Wait until you see Ginny. She seems as high as a kite after giving birth."

Constance laughs, giving Owen a quick hug. "Sit down with Eli and I'll make some coffee for all of us."

"Ginny will want a hot chocolate."

She nods. "I'll take care of it."

I turn and head up the hallway toward Owen's bedroom, sticking my head around the doorframe. "Hey."

Ginny's radiant. She cradles that baby in her arms as if it's the most precious thing on the planet. And I guess she is. "Corey. Is Constance with you?"

"She's in the kitchen sorting us all out a drink, but she'll be through in a minute." I nod. "You're looking good."

"I'm exhausted, but I appreciate the compliment."

"How did it go?"

She shrugs. "Most of it is a blur. I thought we'd have plenty of time, but it was all very sudden in the middle of the night. I'm glad we didn't have to go anywhere."

I laugh. "I can understand that."

"Want to see your niece?"

Grinning, I take a seat on the bed. "I'd love to."

"This is Violet." She hands the baby over, and I cradle her in my arms.

"Hello, Violet." Her blue eyes stare at me. Will they become green like her mother's? She's got a shock of light hair on her head. So different from Eli. "Ginny, she's beautiful."

"I think so too. But I'm a bit biased." She smiles.

"That's my sister." Ava appears in the doorway.

I nod. "I know. She's as gorgeous as you are."

Ava climbs onto the bed beside me, looping an arm in mine. I lean over and press a kiss to the top of her head. "What do you think of her, Ava?"

She shrugs. "She's a bit useless."

Ginny and I laugh. "She will be for a little while," I say. "But you just wait. She's going to think you're the bee's knees."

Ava rolls her eyes. "Bees don't have knees."

"Are you sure? They're pretty small. Maybe you just can't see them." I lean her way. "You're still my girl. Even if I love your sister too."

She beams. "I saw Eli. He can't do much either."

"I don't know about that. He eats, poops, and sleeps. Same as Violet will for a while."

"I'm just hoping for the sleep." Ginny grins.

"I would too. Eli's not that bad, but we're still looking forward to sleeping the whole night again."

Ginny leans back. "I'm just so glad she's here. Even if she doesn't sleep, she's my little miracle."

I grin. "I'm so happy for you two."

"Three," Ava says.

I laugh. "Sorry. Three of you."

She rolls her eyes, climbing off the bed and disappearing into the living room.

"Ginny." Constance stands in the doorway, a smile on her face a mile wide. "How are you doing?"

"Feeling a lot better now she's here," Ginny says.

"I bet." Constance walks in and places two cups on the bedside cabinet. "Your coffee is in the living room, Corey."

"Is that a hint?" I laugh. Standing, I pass the small bundle that is my niece to Constance. Her mouth falls open as her eyes land on the baby. "She's so precious."

I peck Con on the cheek, and nod at Ginny. "I'll leave you ladies to it."

When I get to the door, I turn and look at the three of them. Constance sits on the bed, cradling Violet. It causes a surge of confusing emotions in me. We literally just had a baby boy, but I want so much to have a baby girl with her too. Maybe fate won't see things the same way, but I'd love one of each. I could teach them both how to live off the land, how to hunt, and how to take care of themselves.

A year and a half ago, I had nothing.

Now I have everything.

I TAKE in the sight of Owen on the couch with Eli.

He's taken him out of the capsule and is rocking him like a pro, Ava watching on. Eli appears to be fascinated with Owen.

"I can't believe we're both here with our children. Whoever thought we'd be like this a couple of years ago?" Owen says.

"Like what?"

"All settled down and having babies."

I chuckle. "It's a beautiful thing."

"Corey, look," Ava says." She holds up a large teddy bear.

Joining Ava on the couch, I smile. "Who's that?"

"Daddy bought it for me. He got Violet the same one, but it's smaller."

"Did he? That's pretty cool."

Owen nods toward us. "We wanted to make sure Ava knew she was just as important to us as the baby. And that she's going to be an awesome big sister."

I stroke her hair. "You'll be great, Ava."

"Can I see Eli?" she asks.

I hold out my arms, and Owen passes him over. "Here he is."

Her lips twist. "He looks a bit like Violet. But his hair is dark."

"Well, they are cousins. I bet Violet looks a little like you do when she's older."

She beams. "Really?"

"You're sisters. There'll be similarities. Are you proud to be a big sister?"

Ava nods. I shift Eli to one arm so I can wrap the other around her. She snuggles in against my side. Eli yawns.

"Is Eli tired?"

I nod. "I think the car ride wore him out."

"Ava, do you want a hot chocolate?" Owen asks as he stands.

She rolls her eyes as if he's asking the dumbest thing in the world. "Yes."

Owen laughs. "Now I'm going to have three girls looking at me like that. Just as well I love you all so much."

"Can I have marshmallows too, Daddy?"

"Of course you can." He bends, giving her a kiss before standing and walking up the hallway.

"Corey?" Ava asks.

"Yes, sweetheart?"

"I think you're a good daddy."

I grin. "That's nice of you to say."

She leans in to take a closer look at Eli. I can't wait until he's old enough to play with his cousins. "When will he be able to walk?"

I shrug. "Maybe a year? It's hard to say."

Owen comes back into the room with a plate of pastries and Ava's hot chocolate.

Ava shakes her head with a dramatic sigh. "I have to wait a whole year."

Owen and I chuckle as she takes her hot chocolate.

"I guess so."

25

JAMES

IN THE PAST YEAR, Mia and I have been through a lot. Falling in love, all while keeping it as secret as we can. The death of my mother. Now, the birth of my niece and nephew.

I've never been so happy or so homesick.

I moved into Mia's place after Christmas. Most of my stuff is in storage in the garage because she had everything. Garrett's occasional flybys are irritating, but we've managed to keep under his radar.

So far.

When he has seen her, he's been quite aggressive about them getting back together. But Mia's strong, and she knows she has me behind her.

We both know we should declare it all. But we're so close to the end and being able to leave Auckland for good.

Now I get her all to myself for the break between semesters, but home's on my mind.

"You're brooding."

It's day two of the holidays, and she's right. I am. "We should go to Copper Creek."

"We?" She joins me on the couch. I want my family to meet her. The only reason they haven't yet is in case anyone in town from uni sees us together.

"I want to visit my family. And I don't want to go without you again."

She plays her bottom lip between her teeth.

When she gives me a small nod, I grin. I place my hands on her arms. "I know you're scared, Mia, but we're so close. My family want to meet you, and we can trust them."

"I know we can." Tears form in her eyes. "It's not just fear. I think we need to declare our relationship when uni starts again."

My mouth falls open. "Are you ready for that?"

"It's all I ever think about, James. We've hidden for so long, and I hate it. Garrett is just proving he's going to be a pain in the arse no matter what, so let's do it."

I lean over, kissing her so hard she pushes me away.

"I can't breathe when you do that." She laughs.

"Sorry. I just want to go and meet Eli and Violet. And show you off to my family. They'll love you, Mia. I promise."

She gives me a timid smile. "I can't wait to meet them."

ON SATURDAY MORNING, we pack her car. It's more economical over a long distance, and I like driving it. It's newer than my Toyota and bigger.

"Are you going to tell anyone we're coming?" she asks.

"I sent a text to my dad earlier in the week. There's a

barbecue at Adam's this afternoon, so we'll go there first and then onto Dad's afterward, if that's okay. It means you get to meet everyone."

"That's a little overwhelming."

"I'll be by your side. I told you they'll love you. It's easier than going to see them all individually."

"I guess." She shrugs.

"Let's get going. Sooner we're on the road, the sooner we're there." Leaning over, I press a tender kiss to her lips.

"Okay."

"It'll be fun. I'm not sure when the last time was that they were all together."

"Any particular reason this time?"

I shrug. "I mean, it could be because I told Dad about you coming to visit."

She laughs. "Great. No expectations whatsoever."

"We'll be fine."

Once we're on the road, she grows more relaxed. Last time we were down this way, we were in separate cars. This is our first road trip.

"I like not having to drive," she says as we make our way out of Hamilton. "It's nice being the passenger."

"We should get out of town more often. It'll be good to see the country together."

"Maybe we can when the year is up."

I grin. "I love that idea. I've seen from Copper Creek to Auckland, and that's about it."

She sighs. "I went to Christchurch for a conference once. And I've been to Australia a few times."

"I've been to Samoa. With you."

"Maybe we should go again to celebrate my divorce." She laughs.

By the time we take the final turn off to Copper Creek, she's fast asleep.

It's good to see her stress-free. There's always a part of her that doesn't turn off, knowing that Garrett can and will still make her life difficult.

I'll be glad when I can take her away from all of that. She'll never have to want for the love and affection from me.

Coming up to the last few twists in the road, I nudge her arm. "Wakey, wakey. We're nearly there."

She blinks a few times, and gives me a hazy smile. "Where?"

"Copper Creek. We'll be at Adam's in just a few minutes."

When she takes a deep breath, I take her hand in mine and rest it on the gear lever. I can't wait for my family to meet her.

26

MIA

I'M NOT sure about this.

James has told his family very little about me.

Not about my pending divorce, or that I'm one of his lecturers. Or that he's twenty-three and I'm forty-one.

My stomach is in knots.

As if he senses it, James reaches across and takes my hand in his. "You okay?"

"Nervous."

He nods. "They'll love you."

"Are you sure? You have this way of making me not feel the age gap, but if they have a problem…"

"Corey and Constance have something like twelve years between them. It's no biggie."

I let out a breath. "That's what you say. Twelve is very different to seventeen."

"Babe, if we're going public, there are going to be people who have an opinion on it. But you know what? I don't care."

He raises my hand to his lips. "As long as I have you, that's all that matters."

I nod. "I love you."

He grins. "Love you too."

We turn into the main road of Copper Creek, and I lean back in the seat and close my eyes. I can't even remember meeting Garrett's family; it's like they just turned up in my life one day. His mother was so lovely, but in hindsight, Garrett took after his father: controlling, demanding, and angry.

I'm looking forward to meeting James's dad. And I'm sad I didn't meet his mother before she died, although from what James has said, in her prime she would have had a problem with our relationship.

"Adam's place is just down here." He slows when we approach a garage. The driveway's full, so James pulls into the yard in front of the main building. "At least we can park the car in the shade here."

He climbs out of the car and comes around to my side while I'm picking up my handbag and sorting myself out. Opening the door, he extends his hand. I grin, taking it and stepping out.

He leads me up the driveway behind the garage. It's love at first sight when I see Adam's house. I'd love a place like it. The verandah running around to the back of it makes me think of my parents' house. I can't wait to see the inside of this place. It's a real mix of old and modern.

"Shit. I left my phone in the car. Stay here and I'll be back in a second," James says.

I smile. "You and your phone."

He shrugs. "Damn millennials."

I laugh as he disappears back around the side of the house.

"You must be Mia."

A crazy-tall man approaches. I can see a passing family resemblance. James is big, but this guy?

"That's right. And you're … Corey?"

He smiles, and his smile is so much like James's. Even if it's hidden behind a thick beard. "That's right. I'm sure James has told you all about us. Where is he?"

I grin. "He left his phone in the car."

He shakes his head. "I swear he's got some attachment issues around that phone. Though the last times I've seen him, it's been because you've been at the other end."

I laugh.

He nods toward the house. "Come this way."

Instead of taking me through the front door, he leads me around the back of the house. He pauses at the corner. "You know, he's been really secretive about your relationship."

I swallow hard.

"But I know he's trying to protect you. I just don't know what from. If there's anything any of us can do, let us know."

For a moment, I just stare. I never had siblings to stick up for me. Is this what it's like?

He smiles. "Are you okay?"

I nod. "I'm just not used to family support."

Corey frowns. "That's no good. You'd better get used to it then."

I can't stop myself. I grin, and he does the same in response.

"Welcome to the family, Mia."

A group of women sit at a table on the deck when we

turn the corner. Nerves churn in my stomach. I've been alone for a long time, except for James and the odd visit with Kelly. It's been a while since I've socialised with a big group of people I don't know.

Corey puts his hand to his mouth and lets out an ear-piercing whistle. So many eyes turn toward us. "This is Mia. Mia, this is everyone."

"Mia." A dark-haired woman smiles. She stands and walks toward me. "Come over here, and I'll introduce you properly. I'm Hayley."

So many faces are looking at me, but the thing I really notice is the children. I turn my head to see a blonde girl, maybe about five, running around. She's closely followed by a smaller blonde girl, and two even smaller children.

"The oldest one is Ava—she's Ginny and Owen's. Then there's Rose, who is Lily and Adam's youngest, and then my two, Amelia and Logan," Hayley says.

Nodding, I look back at her. "I've heard the names. It's just putting faces to everyone."

"Mia, you made your way back here." James walks toward me, a big smile on his face.

"Corey found me. Hayley was just about to introduce me to everyone."

Hayley slips an arm around my shoulder. "I've got her."

"Grab a beer," a blonde woman sitting opposite where Hayley sat says.

"Thanks, Lily." James reaches for the chilly bin. "Want one, Mia?"

"That'd be great."

Hayley steers me toward the table, pointing around. "Mia, this is Lily."

The woman who spoke smiles warmly at me. "It's so good to finally meet you."

"You too."

"And at this end of the table are Ginny and Constance." She points to them both. I smile at the sight of them breast-feeding their babies.

"So, they must be Eli and Violet." I point at the babies. Corey sits beside Constance.

"That's right. Take a seat." Ginny nods at a chair. "How was the drive?"

"Long, but it's so nice to be out of the city."

"Here you go, babe." James places a Tui beer in front of me. "You met Corey. What about the others?"

I shake my head.

"Over by the barbecue, the one holding the tongs is Adam, and standing beside him is Drew. And I can't see Owen."

"He's in the kitchen making us some dessert for after lunch," Ginny says.

James sits in the chair next to me. He takes one of my hands in his and squeezes it.

"James has told me all about Owen's baking. I can't wait to try some."

"Good. Because I made something extra special in your honour."

I turn to look in the direction of the house as Owen makes his way toward us.

"I hope you like it." He holds out his hand. "I'm Owen."

"Mia." I shake his hand. Everyone's so friendly. *I hate that I didn't come here to meet them earlier.*

"James's secret lady. We were all beginning to think you were a figment of his imagination," Owen says.

James laughs. "I don't think I could conjure up anything as wonderful as Mia."

"Wow. You really do have it bad, little brother." Owen laughs. He walks around the table, and bends to give Ginny a tender kiss. She smiles up at him.

"Need me to do anything?" he asks.

She shakes her head. "Violet's nearly asleep."

"She does have that milk-drunk look about her." He peeks over at Constance. "So does Eli. They make a great pair."

Constance laughs. "I'm hoping he's taking his cue from his cousin. He's not usually this easy to get to sleep." She turns to Corey, on the other side of her. "Let's hope he emulates Violet tonight too."

"Amen to that." He holds out his arms, and Constance passes the baby over. His face tells a story. He's a man completely besotted by his son. It makes my heart ache a little for what James and I can never have. Not that I'll ever admit it.

"They're such lovely babies." I grin.

"They're a lot quieter than usual. You arrived at a good time." Constance laughs.

"We're in for a lot of trouble once they can run around," Ginny says.

"I'm sure they'll just follow Ava. If we have her under control, the others will fall into line. Won't you, little guy?" Corey takes Eli's hand in his. His fist looks huge in comparison to the baby's, and it makes me smile even more.

"I hope you guys are hungry. There's a ton of food." Adam

approaches. He smiles at me. "Hi, you must be Mia. James has told us nothing about you."

I laugh. "Well, he's told me about you at least."

"You've got us all at a disadvantage then." Drew walks up behind Adam and sends James a pointed look. "This guy's been keeping you all to himself."

"Anyway, we're just going to grab some trays to bring the cooked food to the table, and we'll be ready to eat." Adam passes me, brushing my shoulder with his hand. "It's good to finally meet you."

"You too," I call as he disappears into the house.

"Where's Dad?" James asks.

"He's on his way," Lily says. "I called him a couple of times earlier. He was in the garden and lost track of time, so he was showering and then coming over."

James reaches for my hand and squeezes it. "You okay?"

I nod.

"Of course she is, James. We won't break her." Lily laughs.

"I'm just checking. I'm sure Mia was nervous about meeting all you lot at once."

"What are you trying to say?" Lily asks

He shrugs. "Nothing. It's just a change for her. Mia's family isn't that big."

"Neither was ours, once upon a time." Lily cocks her head.

"It was. We just weren't very united." Owen nudges her.

I love this. I love their closeness, and even though I might not get all their references to each other, I want to be a part of this. I'm not sure why I was so nervous. They know so little about me, but don't press me for details.

James nudges me. "Here's Dad."

I turn. James's father walks toward me, a huge smile on his face. Despite our differences, I miss my own father. It's been so long since we've seen each other.

Standing, I smile as James's dad opens his arms to me and hugs me tight. "I'm pleased to finally meet you, Mia. You make my son so happy."

I can't stop the grin on my face as he lets me go. James slots his fingers in mine. We should have come here a long time ago.

I just belong.

27

JAMES

Today is going even better than I'd thought it would.

I knew my family would welcome Mia with open arms, but they've even exceeded my expectations.

The women are all in the living room now the meal is over. Mia and Lily are deep in conversation, and it's such a wonderful sight.

Ginny and Constance sit together on the couch, holding each other's babies. Dad sits with them. It's funny how different my nieces and nephews are, yet they all come from the same gene pool. Already, Eli and Violet have very different personalities.

Ava tugs on my sleeve, and I smile at her. "Hey. What are you up to?"

She gives me a little wave, her cheeks flushing.

"Did you eat your dessert? Your dad makes amazing cakes."

She nods. "And he made me a gingerbread man."

"I hear you're a gingerbread addict."

She laughs as she runs back outside.

Corey comes out of the kitchen and hands me a beer. "Let's leave them to it and go sit outside."

I follow him out. Adam, Drew, and Owen have taken over the table, and we join them.

"Your lady's nice. I don't know why you kept her hidden for so long." Corey takes a swig of his beer. "None of us care that she's older than you."

"That's not the reason I didn't tell you, guys. We haven't told anyone."

He frowns.

"She's one of my lecturers at uni."

His mouth falls open, and as I look around the table, I fight a laugh when my brothers all react the same.

"Dude. Have you declared the relationship?" Drew asks.

I shake my head.

"Why not? It'll save you a whole world of hurt if you do."

"It's complicated. Her husband works at the uni too."

His eyes widen. "She's married?"

I shake my head. "Soon-to-be ex-husband. He's a real dick, and he's made things difficult enough for Mia as it is without knowing about me."

Drew nods. "That's a shitty situation to be in."

"It's not been easy, that's for sure. But we're so close to getting out."

"You could have told us. We wouldn't have said anything," Corey says.

I shrug. "It was just easier not to tell. The last thing I wanted was to burden anyone else with our secret."

"So why are you telling us now?"

"Because I'm sick of hiding it from the people I love. And Mia feels ready to declare our relationship when we get back."

"That could impact your studies," Drew says. "The university might want to re-mark some of your work."

I nod. "I know. But I'm confident it stands up, and even if there are issues, I've got Mia. I win either way."

He grins. "As long as you're okay."

"I've just been in her class this year, not previous ones. Even if I have to do over, it's not the end of the world." I take a deep breath. "We were thinking about coming back here next year. Mia's been asked to write a text book, and I can find a job. We could rent a place near the cove."

"You're always welcome at the garage. There's plenty of work there," Adam says.

I nod. "I hoped you might say that."

He grins. "It'll be good to have you around. I know I pushed you to go to uni in the first place, but we've all missed you."

"Once the divorce is final, the house will be sold, and Mia gets half the proceeds. Then we can move here."

Adam puts a finger to his chin. "I've been thinking a lot about something lately that might help."

"What's that?"

"The house Lily grew up in. It never sold, but if it was cleared, it'd be a good central location to build. It'd be cheap as to buy."

"That's a good idea," Owen says. "In the meantime, you could use my flat too. By the time you two move here, we'll be in the new house. We can lock off the entrance to the bakery to give you privacy."

"Really?"

"You wouldn't need to pay rent." He shrugs. "I was going to leave it empty unless Mel wanted to use it. But you're family, so help yourself. It'd mean you were close to the garage too."

My heart swells. My brothers seem to work together to make things happen for me.

I just wonder what Mia will think about it all.

28

————

MIA

The Campbells are wonderful.

They're a close-knit family, but it takes next to no time to feel like I fit in. Maybe it's because James has told me so much about each of them.

I don't talk a lot—the others more than make up for me. I'm enjoying just sitting and listening.

It makes me think of Mum and Dad. They didn't like Garrett. They saw through him. But I was young and in love, and no one could have talked me out of our relationship.

I love watching the kids play. It's clear that Ava is the leader, and the younger ones hang on to her every word.

"Ava's so bossy." Ginny laughs, and I shift my gaze to her.

"I was just thinking how she's definitely in charge." I smile.

"Max was the one who used to lead them around, but he's much older and so over it," Lily says. "He's staying with a friend tonight, but if you're still around tomorrow you'll meet him."

"Max is your oldest, right?"

She grimaces. "Fifteen going on twenty-five."

"That must be fun."

She nods. "At times. He's just discovered girls."

"Oh." I laugh. "There's trouble."

Lily nods. "He's a sweet boy. I'm sure he'll be okay, but it still scares the hell out of me."

"He'll be fine," Adam says, walking through the living room. "I met the love of my life at fourteen. Maybe he'll be that lucky too."

He walks to her chair and bends to give Lily a kiss. She cups his face, and for a second they seem to get lost in each other.

"Are you okay, Mia? Need another drink?" Adam asks, turning his head. "Is James taking care of you?"

"James always takes care of me." I laugh. "He's a sweet boy too."

I turn and see James in the doorway. He shakes his head.

"Make sure you keep it that way," Adam says.

AFTER LUNCH, we drive to James's father's house.

It's lovely. His home is off the road, surrounded by greenery. I sigh as James pulls into the back yard.

"You okay?" he asks.

"It's just so beautiful here."

"Now you see why I love this place so much." He smiles. "Let's get our bags inside, and I'll show you around."

Inside, the house is just as beautiful. The living room is littered with pictures of the different Campbell boys at various stages of their lives. Their parents were obviously very proud of them.

It makes me think of my parents' house. When I stuck to their rules, Mum and Dad took so much pride in everything I did.

Until I met Garrett.

It took a while for me to regret not listening to them, but they were right. He was never the man for me. James is.

"This way." James leads me up the hallway to a room at the very end.

He pushes open the door and we walk in. This room is very teenage boy. But I guess he was when he lived here.

Against one wall is a double bed. It's smaller than I'm used to, but James and I spoon at night so we'll fit. There are bookshelves with sport magazines, and I smile at a pile of scientific journals.

The posters on the wall make me laugh. James likes rock music. I already know that. What I'm not ready is for the members of AC/DC to be staring at me from every direction.

"I'll take the posters down," he says as if reading my mind.

I shrug. "They're fine."

"I haven't been here for any real length of time since I left for uni. It's probably time."

On his desk is a photo of him with a woman I don't recognise. When I pick it up, he runs over, snatching it from my hand.

"Shit. Sorry. I meant to get rid of that last time I was here."

"Is that …"

He looks at the photo. "Ashley. I kept our relationship secret from Mum for ages because she was such a pain in the arse when it came to my brother's girlfriends. It wasn't until I came back from uni the first time that I put that photo on the desk."

I nod. "After she approved?"

"Yes. My mum never thought anyone was good enough for her boys. She would have had kittens over our relationship when she was well. But the last time we spoke, she told me that she approved of us as long as I was happy."

Despite myself, I laugh.

"But once she got to know you, she would have known how good you are for me anyway." He throws the photo toward the bin, and it lands inside with a loud clang. "And I'd tell her just how much I love you." He wraps his arms around me.

"Your family is great."

"I thought it went well. They all like you." James nuzzles my neck.

I pull away.

"What's wrong?"

I let out a long breath. "Watching them with their children. That's not going to be us, James. You know that, don't you?"

He nods. "I'd never put pressure on you to have a child with me, Mia."

"But do you want one?"

James shrugs. "I haven't given it that much thought."

"Maybe you should."

He places his hands on my arms. "Babe. Nothing else

matters but us. If I'm destined to be an uncle and not a father, then it is what it is. I don't want anyone else, Mia."

"I don't want you missing out if it becomes important." I search his expression, but all I see is the love in his eyes. "You're all I want."

"Then there's no issue." He smiles. "The way my brothers are breeding, there'll be no end to nieces and nephews to spend time with."

I laugh. "I'm not sure if they'd appreciate you talking about them that way."

"Probably not, but I'm glad you're smiling. Did you enjoy today?"

I nod. "I really did. Everyone's so lovely. I can see where you get it from."

He flutters his eyelashes, and I giggle at the sight. "Is that right?"

"You're such a flirt, James Campbell."

"I try my best."

29

JAMES

Dad arrives home shortly afterward.

I can't get over how relaxed he looks. I'm sure the time spent looking after Mum took its toll on his own health. "Hey, Dad."

He rubs his stomach. "As much as I love my family, I'm glad we're home. I think I need to rest for a week after eating all that."

I laugh. "I know what you mean."

He looks around. "Where's Mia? How's she settling in?" he asks.

"She's in the shower. And she's settling in really well. It's good to be here."

He beams. "It's wonderful to have you home."

"I guess this place is still weird without Mum."

He tilts his head. "It's very quiet."

"I miss her. She was such a pain in the butt at times, but she loved us."

He chuckles. "Yes, she did." He sits in his chair. "I didn't do right by her all the time, and I will always feel guilty about that, but there was also a lot of love."

"You mean your affair with Lily's mother?"

His mouth falls open. "How did you …?"

"Something Mum said once. It was vague, but I put two and two together."

He licks his lips. "James, we were in a bad place. We moved here at your mother's insistence, and I gave up a job I loved to do what she thought was the right thing for Corey. There was a period of time when we barely spoke to one another."

"You don't have to justify yourself to me, Dad. You two were still together even after we all left home, so there must have been love still there."

He nods. "There was a lot. We got all you five out of it." His expression grows distant. "You were her pride and joy. All of you. She'd have defended you to the last. Even if she made mistakes along the way."

His eyebrows knit. I know that look. He's thinking about Max—the grandson he didn't get to know. Not when Max was small, anyway.

"Well, I think that's all water under the bridge now. I wish she was here to meet Mia."

He grins. "I do too. And I think it's wonderful. You're clearly happy and must love each other very much to have reached the point you're at now."

"I'm just so happy, Dad. And once we can go public, I can just be with her. No more hiding from anyone. Including you."

He nods. "She's a lovely woman, James, and I'm so proud of you."

"Ahem."

I look up to see Mia standing in the doorway. She's wearing pyjama bottoms and a dark tank top, and I smile. *I get to take her to bed.*

"I hope I'm not interrupting anything," she says.

"Not at all." Dad beams. This is the happiest I've seen him in a long while. It does my heart good.

"Was the shower okay?" I ask.

"It was great. Just what I needed." She smiles, and makes her way to the couch. When she sits, I wrap an arm around her and plant a kiss on her shoulder.

"Glad to hear it. Do you two want a hot chocolate?" Dad asks. "I think that'll go down well after today."

"I'd love one," Mia says, snuggling against me.

Dad disappears into the kitchen while I bury my face in Mia's hair.

"I'm glad you had a good day."

"It went better than I thought it would."

I laugh. "They don't bite."

"I dunno. Corey's so tall. I bet he can be pretty intimidating"

"Only on the outside. He's a giant marshmallow on the inside."

She nods. "He obviously adores Constance. And that baby of theirs is so sweet."

Dad yawns when he comes back in, carrying three steaming mugs. "Here you two go. It's nice to have some company."

"I was so sorry about your wife," Mia says, taking a cup from him.

He nods. "It was a long time coming, which was hard on her. But she's in a much better place now. What about your parents, Mia?"

She sighs. "I still have both my mum and dad, but we're estranged. I never had any siblings."

"And now you're part of this ever-expanding family." He laughs.

I take the cup he offers me, and he settles back into his chair.

"I'm so glad we came and I got to meet everyone," Mia says.

Dad smiles. "I'm happy to meet you. All I knew about you was that you've made my youngest son very happy."

Mia smiles. "I hope so."

I lean my head against hers and take a sip from my cup.

Her estrangement from her parents bugs me. I know it's between her and them, but I'm glad that I can provide her with the loving family that it seems she never had.

She'll never want for anything in that regard from now on.

AFTER THE HOT CHOCOLATE, I nudge Mia's arm. "Come out for a walk in the garden."

"I'm in my pyjamas." She laughs.

"No one will see you. I want to show you the things I planted when I was here. If they're still growing."

Her smile lights up the room. "Then I'd love to."

"Grab a jacket. It's chilly out there. You'll be fine."

Dad nods. "Go on, love. It's lovely out there at sunset."

Mia disappears up the hallway to get her jacket, and Dad nods at me. "She's a sweet girl. I think she fits in well with our lot."

"Me too."

"I heard something about you coming back here next year. Is it true?"

I nod. "That's the plan. Adam and Owen have offered to help us out too, which will make it easier. We had half an idea, but now I think we can really make it work."

"I'm glad. I'm looking forward to you moving back."

Mia appears in the doorway, and I nod at Dad. "Me too."

Standing, I take her hand in mine and lead her out the back door.

The garden's full of golden trees, some missing leaves. The autumn air has a chill to it, but it's not too cold.

I wish it was spring so I could show her just how beautiful it is at that time of year too. I'll have to bring her back.

She holds my hand as I lead her around the garden.

"When we moved here, the section had been emptied to build the house. There were a few trees and ferns, but we all filled in the gaps."

Mia nods. "It's so peaceful."

"And then later on when I was in my early teens, I realised I had a bit of a green thumb. I planted the flowers and made a bit of a vegetable garden, which Dad still uses."

"I love it here."

"Still want to move to Copper Creek next year?"

Mia stops, turning and draping her arms over my shoulders. "More than anything. I want to be a part of this, James.

I want to hang out with your brothers and their wives and girlfriends. I want to live here with you."

I brush her lips with mine. "I'm glad to hear it. We've got somewhere to live when we move here if we want it, too."

Her mouth falls open. "Really? Where?"

"Owen and Ginny are building a house. It'll be finished by the end of the year, and then their flat will be available. Owen says we can have it rent-free."

"That's so kind."

"It's two bedrooms, and right behind the bakery. So, central but back from the main road. It's not huge, but we don't need that much space. If we need storage, Dad's got a huge shed that's perfect for it right over there." I point at the shed and lick my lips. "And Adam said I can work at the garage."

Mia grins. "That's wonderful. Then maybe you can finally teach me about starter motors."

I laugh, wrapping my arms around her waist. "I can. We can get some outdoor furniture for the deck and you can sit in the sun and write your text books."

"I love that idea."

"We'll make it work, Mia."

She nods. "I'm so tired of hiding. I can't wait to not have to worry about it anymore."

I can't help the grin on my face. "I'm ready when you are."

"You've been so patient, James."

"You're worth the wait." I let go of her and cup her face, gazing into her eyes. Everything I ever wanted is right in front of me. Whatever she wants, I'll support her.

And I'll be proud on the day we tell the world about us.

30

———

COREY

I HESITATE when I get the next hunting job, but Constance talks me into it.

"It's just one night. I can cope with one night."

Her words ring in my ears all day.

This one's not a night job, but it's a fair distance from home. It'd be easier to stay, but my bed calls, and Constance is in it. It's the easiest decision in the world to make.

The thought of her and Eli makes the drive go quickly. It's late when I get in, and Constance seems to be asleep.

After a quick shower, I climb into bed and drape my arm over her.

"Corey?"

"It's me, sweetness." I plant a kiss on her bare shoulder. She rolls onto her back and opens her eyes, giving me a hazy smile.

"I didn't know if you'd be back."

"There's no way I'm spending the night away from you. It was a long drive, but I'm glad to be home."

My hand touches something solid beside her—something that wriggles.

"What the hell?"

Cassius's cold nose brushes my palm.

"Con, please tell me the dog's not in the bed."

"On the bed. Not in it."

I sigh. "He's not supposed to be on the bed."

The smile in her voice is obvious. "I feel safe with him here."

"I'm sure you do, but he needs to know that it's not okay to sit on the bed."

"He's not exactly sitting."

"Stop being a smartarse." I laugh, switching on the bedside lamp.

"You love it."

I sigh, but she's right. I do love it. Shifting my gaze to Cassius, I stare him down. He's still a little skittish at times, so I don't raise my hand. "Out."

Cassius makes those big eyes at me, and if I wasn't trying to prove a point, I'd probably cave and let him stay in the room at least.

"Cassius. Down."

He jumps off the bed, and I lead him out to the living room. There's a dog bed by the fireplace, and it's still warm out here, so I don't feel bad making him sleep where he's supposed to.

Curling up, he lets out a whimper before placing his head on his paws.

"Dude. I know you want to be near her. But it's my turn.

And you are not supposed to be sleeping on the bed." I scratch behind his ears and he gives me a hopeful look. "See you in the morning."

He settles down, and I shake my head as I turn back to the bedroom.

Constance waves her arms when I shut the door behind me.

"Eli's in his cot tonight. What about him? I won't hear him if he wakes up."

"I'll open the door when I'm finished."

She raises her chin, still the defiant woman I met a year ago. Maybe she's been down lately, but I know she's about to let loose on me. "Finished what?"

I smirk, and go to my bedside cabinet, plucking out a small box.

Rounding the bed, I drop to one knee.

That irritated expression falls from her face, and her mouth hangs open. "Corey Campbell, what are you doing?"

"I told you that I'd do this when we were both ready. I'm over waiting, Con. You've been through so much, and I know you're still struggling. But the one thing I never want you to be unsure about is how much I love you."

Tears form in her eyes, and I take her hand in mine.

"You're the one I want to spend my life with. The only one I can imagine waking up to in the morning. I'm so glad we found each other, and so proud to be Eli's father. Marry me?" I let go of her hand and open the ring box.

"Corey," she whispers.

"This was my mother's. I saw Dad a while ago and told him I was planning this, and he said that this is what Mum would have wanted. If you don't like it—"

I'm silenced by her kiss as she throws herself almost off the bed, her arms around my shoulders.

I chuckle against her mouth. "I'm guessing that means you like it?"

Tears roll down her cheeks. "I love it."

I stand slowly, pushing her back onto the bed. I sit beside her and pluck the ring from the box. It's not over the top; it's a gold band with diamonds embedded in it. I knew it was *Constance* the minute Dad offered it to me.

I slide it on her; it's not a bad fit. She has long, slim fingers like my mother did. "If it's not quite right, we can get it adjusted."

"It feels okay. Might have to leave it on for a few days to try it out."

I grin. "I hope you'll leave it on for more than a few days."

Constance laughs as I push her back on the bed, pulling her into my arms.

"You know, you never said yes."

Her eyes glisten, and it's been weeks since I've seen her this happy. "Yes. Yes. A million times yes."

"Are you sure?"

She slaps my chest. "Corey …"

"Let's make it soon. I don't want to wait much longer."

"Neither do I."

"Wanna celebrate?" I shoot her a sly smile, expecting her to melt in my arms. All she does is laugh. "What?"

"I would love to celebrate with you. That look on your face is hilarious."

I place my hand on my chest. "What are you saying?"

We've been intimate a few times since the night Violet was born. Constance has done everything she can to hide from me. I know she still feels self-conscious about the changes in her body.

"Want to know something?"

Her lips curl into a smile. "Tell me."

"Even if you gave birth a dozen times, I'd still want to fuck you until you couldn't walk."

"You want a dozen babies?"

"Is that really what you want to take from that sentence?"

She laughs. "I love you, Corey Campbell."

"I love you too. Have I proved my point yet?"

Constance nods. Her eyes shine with happiness, and her smile lights my heart. "Yes. Yes you have."

"Is this where I should strip you out of that nightgown and kiss you all over?"

She licks her lips. "Maybe."

"I can think of better uses for that tongue."

She shoves my shoulder. "You're terrible."

"Sometimes. But as long as I put a smile on your face, I'll keep on being that way."

Constance leans her head on my shoulder. "Do you want to know something that's not terrible?"

I laugh. "What?"

"The way you look at me. All I ever see is love in your eyes."

"Because that's all I feel when I'm with you. I love you so fucking much, Con."

"I know you do. And you know I feel the same way."

She laughs against my mouth as I kiss her again, sweeping my tongue over hers.

I kiss her so hard, she pants when she comes up for breath. "I love the way you kiss me."

I've got my hands on the hem of her nightgown, and with her help, I pull it over her head.

"I love kissing you. You're mine, and I like showing you that." I reach for the elastic of her panties and slide them down her legs. "I want to worship my woman's pussy. And the rest of her. But right now, this."

She laughs softly as I plunge my tongue into her. This is what I miss when I'm not with her. I've always been a man who liked going down on a woman, but doing it with Constance is on a whole other level. I love her familiar smell, her taste, and I also know I'm the only one who's given her this kind of pleasure before—and I love that this pleasure is all mine. I'll be the only one to ever do it.

Constance rakes her fingers through my hair. *God, that feels good.* It still makes me laugh how much she hated it when I shaved my beard off. It must tickle and scratch her legs, but she seems to prefer it to my cleanshaven look.

I'll do anything to make her happy.

"Corey."

I love the sound of my name rolling off her tongue. It makes me all the more determined to give her as much pleasure as I can.

She lifts off the bed as she comes, pushing her pussy toward me. I lap up everything she offers before moving over the top of her. Her eyes are closed, and she takes a deep breath as if composing herself.

"Sweetness," I whisper. Being between her legs is like being home. I let out a contented sigh as I slide into her. *Oh no.* I freeze.

"Shit."

"What?" she asks, alarm in her eyes.

"Do we need a condom? I remember Margaret saying something about not relying on breastfeeding."

"You didn't think of that the last few times we had sex?" Constance laughs, slapping me on the chest. "Doctor Paton fitted me with an IUD last time I saw him."

I shrug. "Obviously sex with you was so distracting, I haven't been paying attention."

She rolls her eyes. "Well, at least one of us is being responsible."

"Maybe I'm not concerned about getting you pregnant again."

Her mouth falls open. "Can we get past the sleepless-night stage first?" She runs her finger down my arm. "Unless you want to be the stay-at-home dad while I go out to hunt."

I capture her mouth with mine, sucking on her bottom lip as I pull away. "Last time we practiced, you were a lousy shot. You'd need another occupation."

She laughs, and it's music to my ears. Constance hasn't laughed much lately, and I need to fix that. I need to make things better.

She gives me a slow smile as I thrust. Each movement is matched by Constance lifting her hips to meet me. We're a perfect match.

"I want more babies," I say.

She smiles. "Me too."

I grin, speeding up my hips as I lean over to kiss her. Covering her mouth with mine, I swallow her moans, and my groan as I come lets go into hers.

I slow, and when I pull out, I roll to her side. Eli's cry pierces the quiet.

"That's our boy." I lean my head against hers.

"He's certainly as loud as you are." She laughs.

I press a kiss to her temple. "I'll go and get him."

"He'll probably stop crying when you pick him up. Baby whisperer."

I laugh, pulling back the blanket and stepping out of the bed. "I'm not sure about that. He's bound to want a feed, and I can't do that."

"You could try," she calls as I leave the room and head across the hallway.

Eli lets out another scream as I walk in the door, and I pick him up, cradling him in my arms. "Settle down. Daddy's here."

Those words still grip my heart. I never thought I'd be anyone's daddy. And in my arms is this small child I helped create.

"Come on, little man. Let's go get some food."

I carry him through to the bedroom and murmur some appreciation over the sight of Constance sitting up in bed.

She's still naked, and I love the sight of it.

I pass Eli to her, and in an instant, he's latched on and feeding.

This is a moment I want to burn into my brain forever. Constance strokes Eli's cheek, talking to him the whole time. Seeing them together is magical.

"Corey, come back to bed."

I climb in beside her and watch over her shoulder. Eli's completely at peace right now, and it warms my heart. The bond between him and Constance is so strong.

"This is what makes it all worth it," she whispers.

I kiss her bare shoulder, and she shifts her focus from Eli to me. "You and Eli are my life. I know I've been tired and struggling at times, but you and he are everything."

"I love both of you so much." I murmur, pressing my lips just behind her ear.

She sighs, and it's a contented sigh, not the exasperated one that seems to be common for her lately.

"Tomorrow, you stay in bed. I'll take care of everything."

"Corey, you don't—"

I silence her with a kiss. This woman is the love of my life, the one I spent so many years waiting for.

"I do and I will. I'm not saying you have to spend the whole day in bed, but put your feet up. I'll bring Eli to you when he needs a feed, and I'll do all the housework."

She smiles. "You're so good to me."

"It's the least you deserve. You do all the hard work around here." I grip her hand. "What I don't want is for you to feel alone. I'm here, babe. Even when I'm not in this house, I'm still with you."

She snuggles into my chest, and I run my fingers down her spine.

Eli pulls off her breast, and stares up at her. I know how he feels. I like staring at her too.

"I'll change his nappy." I let her go and hold out my arms.

She rocks our boy. "Leave him for a moment. He's happy."

"I'd be happy too if I was snuggled that close to you."

Constance laughs. "Mummy and Daddy are getting married, Eli. How do you feel about that?"

"I'm sure he's over the moon about it."

"I am. I'm so happy that Daddy's making good on that promise he made my daddy."

I chuckle. "What are you trying to say?"

"Nothing. Nothing at all."

31

COREY

I'm nervous.

It's not my usual state, and it pisses me off. But I finally decided that it was time to do something about the work situation. Now I have Constance and Eli, I need to get a stable job and one that means I can spend all my nights at home.

Constance will probably have a shit-fit over it. She didn't want anything to disrupt our life the way it was, but Eli was a happy disruption. I'm doing this for them.

As I pull up to the construction site, I take a deep breath. I've never applied for a job before. Not that I've put in any kind of application. I'm hoping that showing up and being enthusiastic is enough.

After climbing out of the car, I walk up to the site office, and grin when I see who's on the way out. *Tim Barker.* I went to school with him back in the day.

He smiles. "Corey Campbell, as I live and breathe. What brings you down here?"

I give him a sharp nod. "Actually, I'm looking for work."

He grins. "We're always on the hunt for labourers. Are you sure? I thought you had some hunting gig."

"I do, but my fiancée and I just had a baby, and I'd rather work days than nights. At least for a while."

He nods. "I'd be really happy to have you. This project is scheduled to go until the end of the year, and I've usually got work going on in the Carlstown area. I appreciate it'd be a bit of a commute, but if things work out here there's always an opportunity for a building apprenticeship."

I smile. "Sounds good. We'll see how it goes."

Tim extends his hand. "That works for me."

I shake it, and take a deep breath. I'm not sure what Constance will think. As much as she'll love me being at home, I know she's going to think this is me giving up what I love for her. I love the outdoors, camping, hunting and tracking—but it'll all still be there whenever I want to return. As long as my family is happy and healthy. "Thanks, Tim."

"You're welcome. Always happy to help an old friend." He smiles. "Besides, there's a fair bit of heavy lifting, and you look like you'd be capable of shifting a ton or two."

"Sounds perfect, then."

"Don't you want to know how much it pays?"

I laugh. "I suppose I'd better find out."

"Come up to the site office, and we'll have a chat."

CONSTANCE IS READING a book in the living room when I get home. The house is quiet.

"Eli sleeping?" I ask as I sit beside her on the couch.

She nods. "He just went down. If he keeps to his routine of the past week, he'll be out for a few hours.

"I have something I need to tell you."

She puts down her book and turns toward me. "Should I be worried?"

"Why?"

"You sound so serious."

I take a close look at her. My whole life changed when I met Constance. And it's all been for the better. "I got a new job."

She seems to force a smile. "When? How long will you be away for?"

"I won't be. It's not a hunting job."

Her eyes widen. "What will you be doing?"

"There's a construction project going on at the cove to add units to the caravan park. It's just for a few months, but it's steady, and I won't have to work nights."

Con's expression softens. "Corey, you don't have to do that. You love your work."

"Not as much as I love you and Eli. It might lead into something more permanent, or I'll see if I can find something else when it's finished, but for the moment it means I can come home every night to you."

Her eyes mist over.

"Hey. It'll be fine. We'll have a steady income for a while, and I can always go back to pest control. But I think it's important right now that I'm here."

She says nothing, and just wraps her arms around my

neck, her head resting against my chest. I always thought if I got a normal job, it'd be a last resort, impinging on the freedom that I had. But that's the opposite of how I feel right now. This feels like the right thing to do.

"You won't have the uncertainty of not knowing when I'll be here or not. And we'll get weekends together."

"I love you," she whispers.

"And I love you. More than anything else in the whole world. I'll do whatever I have to if it means you and Eli have everything you need. And I have a feeling that what you need most of all right now is me."

"Corey." She sobs on my chest, and for a moment, I just hold her tight and close my eyes. She puts up a brave front, but Constance has been through the wringer. We had some months of peace while she was pregnant, but with all she's had to deal with in the last couple of years, it's not surprising that her emotions are now catching up.

"I thought maybe during the week too, if you want to spend time with your mum and dad, I can drop you off in the morning and pick you up on the way home. Until you're driving for yourself."

She nods. "I'd like that."

"We'll make things better. There's got to be something better than being sad all the time."

She raises her head. "You know I'm happy, right? This is just a thing I need to get through."

"We. *We'll* get through it together." I grip her chin and tilt it to me, planting a soft kiss on her lips. "It's you and me, Con. Besides, we have a wedding to plan."

Her brows twitch. "You really want to do that soon?"

"The sooner the better, as far as I'm concerned. I'd take

you to the courthouse and marry you tomorrow if I could, but I want you to have the day you want. I want all our friends and family to celebrate with us."

"Me too."

I kiss her again, this time using my tongue to explore her mouth. She's breathless, and I recall her words about Eli's nap.

We've got enough time.

"Bedroom. Now."

She laughs this gorgeous throaty laugh that does things to my nether regions. "Now?"

"Let's go before the baby wakes up. We're on borrowed time, woman." I stand, taking her hand in mine and pulling her to her feet. When she doesn't move for the first few seconds, I scoop her up and into my arms.

"What are you doing?"

"Man no hunt. Man need love."

Constance shakes her head. "Corey Campbell, you are such a caveman."

"Only for you, sweetness. Only for you."

32

MIA

I GATHER ALL my strength and tap on the door right under the gold sign saying *Human Resources*. Here goes nothing.

"Come in." Heather's voice rings out.

I push open the door and take a deep breath as she looks up.

"Mia." She smiles. "What can I do for you?"

"I need to declare a relationship with a student." I sit in front of her desk.

Heather meets my gaze. "Okay."

"What do I need to do?"

"I'll take the details and process it." She studies me. "Are you alright?"

"Just nervous. I'm not sure how well this is going to go down." I lick my lips. "It's a student in my class."

She nods slowly. "I understand. Does Garrett know?"

I shake my head.

"He'll know by the end of the day. Are you okay with that?"

I shrug. "I can't help it. I'm not going to hide from him."

Her lips twitch. "You shouldn't have to. I just needed to make sure that you were aware. It can't be easy with your ex working here." She smiles. "Now. Let me know the details. Who's the student?"

"James Campbell."

She types it into the computer, and I take a breath. "If you ever need to talk, you know where I am."

I smile. "Thank you, Heather."

"Do you want me to update your emergency contact details to James too? They're still set as Garrett."

"Yes, please."

She taps on the keyboard. "I'm excited for you. You deserve to be happy."

My smile grows to a grin. I can't help it. And now I can be open about our relationship. "I'm very happy. James is so sweet."

"Not like Garrett? He's a bit of a prickly person."

I nod. "Couldn't be further apart. James gets me in a way Garrett never did, and I'm not made to feel inferior to him."

"That's great. For what it's worth, I'm glad you declared it. It's not an ideal situation, but he's close to graduating, and then you two won't have to worry about a thing."

"What else do I need to do?"

Heather smiles. "That's it."

"Really?"

"If there are any questions about it, I'll come and talk to you, but it's not the first time I've dealt with this, and I doubt it'll be the last."

I let out a long breath. "That was easier than I thought it would be."

She nods. "It's really just registering a conflict of interest for you. From here on in, you continue as normal, but his work will be marked by someone else." She pauses. "And James will be offered counselling."

"He will?"

"He doesn't have to do it. It's in place more for the type of situation where you might have a fifty-year-old professor grooming an eighteen-year-old."

My mouth falls open of its own volition.

"But that's not you. If James is in your class, he's what, twenty-two or twenty-three? He's a grown man. And I know you well enough to know that Garrett starting here disturbed you, and you wouldn't go public if it wasn't something serious between you and James."

I nod. "I really love him."

"Good for you. I'm glad to see you happy."

As I leave her office, I pull out my phone and shoot off a quick text.

All done. Relationship declared. Love you xx

JAMES HAS OTHER LECTURES TODAY, but I know word has leaked by the time I hit my second class of the afternoon.

The noise that usually fills the hall is gone, replaced by whispers.

I ignore them. I have to. And for the first time in a long time, every single eye in the room is on me. I'm used to background chatter, and people tapping away on their keyboards.

I know they're not always paying attention, and instead using social media.

No one has their laptop open.

It makes a refreshing change. Maybe I should have done this a long time ago.

Best of all, I haven't seen Garrett all day. Although, I know at some point there'll be a confrontation.

Despite my protests, he's always been convinced that we'll get back together. I hope this will be the final nail in that particular coffin for him. Instead of feeling weak and scared, I'm confident and strong. At the end of the day, I'll go home to James and live my life.

After class, the room empties pretty quickly, and when I leave, there are little groups of people chatting outside. I guess this kind of announcement doesn't happen often.

Making my way to my car, I think about dinner. Drew's in town, and James is going to meet up with him this afternoon, so I'll stop at the supermarket and grab something light to cook. And maybe something bubbly to celebrate.

Today has lifted a huge weight from my shoulders that I'd stopped being conscious of months ago. James was worth it. Being happy is worth it.

Living my life the way I want? Well, that's the best feeling in the world.

My only regret is waiting so long to make the changes in my life that led to my being this content.

But better late than never.

33

JAMES

Word's out.

I know Mia had her appointment this morning, and she sent me a text to say it was done, but I haven't spoken to her. But a secret that's no longer a secret soon gets out in the world. I'm not sure how it was spread, but from the whispers and looks I get in my early afternoon lecture, I know our news is public knowledge.

When I leave the lecture room, Cody's waiting for me outside.

"Is there something you have to tell me?" he asks, tapping his foot on the concrete.

"No, why?"

"Not even that you're fucking Mia Scott?"

I glare at him. "Don't say that."

"Why not? I hear she declared a relationship with you."

"Word spreads fast." I lick my lips. "Then you'd know it's a bit more than what you were suggesting."

A sly grin spreads across his face. "You dirty bastard."

"I just said … oh, forget it. It's not really any of your business."

"That woman is fucking hot. Who knew she'd be a cougar? Maybe when you're finished—"

I grab him by the collar of his shirt. "What the actual fuck, Cody? Don't talk about her like that."

He shrugs. "If she'll fuck you, she'll fuck—"

My fist slams into his face before I even think about it.

Not my Mia.

I know her.

I love her.

"What the fuck, dude?" he cries.

"Don't you ever talk about her that way. Ever. She's worth so much more than that."

He holds up his hands. "Okay. Okay. I'm sorry."

"What the hell is going on?"

I don't even have to look to know who that is. The prick who preyed on Mia's self-esteem for years, the man who thought he could treat her like that and she'd come running back.

Garrett.

"Nothing. Nothing's going on." Cody meets my gaze. "We were just mucking around."

"Really? If you'd like to press charges, I'd be happy to be a witness."

I turn and lock eyes with the piece of shit who used to be married to Mia. "This has nothing to do with you, Garrett."

His eyes flash with anger. "I think it has everything to do with me."

"Believe me, you're not currently occupying my thoughts."

"But my wife is."

I straighten up. "Soon to be ex. She's my girlfriend."

He snorts.

"If you ask me, it's him you should punch," Cody mutters.

"He's not worth it. I've got to be elsewhere. I'm meeting my brother."

Cody holds up his hands, and for a moment Garrett's forgotten. "I'm sorry for what I said. I was temporarily blinded by your girlfriend's hotness."

I roll my eyes. "Dude. I know you like her, but if you ever talk about her like that again …"

"I'd much rather save my friendship with you than be on the receiving end of that right hook again." He looks at Garrett, standing a couple of metres away. "Your friend over there should know about that. It fucking hurt."

Garrett glares at Cody. "If you need a witness …"

"I don't need shit from you."

I bite down a laugh.

Garrett straightens himself up. Cody and I are both taller than him, and it gives me so much satisfaction to look down on him.

"If you change your mind, I'm in the admin building."

Cody and I look at each other while he walks away before bursting out laughing. He claps his hand with mine and pulls me into a man-hug.

"Dude, I'm happy for you. I'm sorry for what I said before."

"Just don't say that shit about her again."

He nods. "I won't. Promise. But you are one lucky son-of-a-bitch."

I grin.

Because I am.

————

DREW ALREADY HAS a beer on the counter of the bar when I walk in. He grins, holding his hand out and pulling me into a hug. It seems to be a day for it. "I thought you'd be here about fifteen minutes ago."

"There was a little distraction."

"What was that?"

"Mia declared our relationship this morning. This afternoon, everyone knows."

His eyes widen. "Shit. I'm assuming that's not good, given what you said about her ex."

I nod. "He's definitely not impressed. So, I'm not staying long."

"I'm happy to do whatever you want, little bro. If you guys want to get out of town for the evening, we'll skip the beer and you can head to my in-laws' place with me. They said you were welcome to join us."

"I'll see what Mia says, but that sounds like a good idea."

"Honestly, they've got some chef cooking for us tonight. Make the most of it."

I laugh. "I like that plan."

He nods. "They certainly know how to spoil their daughter. I'm just along for the ride. Besides, Logan and Amelia would love to see you."

I grin. Drew's kids are so cute. I love spending time with them.

"Okay. Drink up, and we'll go and get Mia."

34

MIA

WHEN I PULL into the driveway, I'm so glad to be home. It might not have taken long for word to spread, but I'm so glad I did it.

My relationship with James is out in the open, and my heart is full. We don't have to hide anymore.

I head toward the house.

My phone buzzes.

Don't worry about dinner. Drew's in-laws have invited us over. I'll finish my drink and swing by to pick you up. Hope you had a good day. Love you.

I grin at the text.

Sounds great. I bought some things, but we can use them for dinner tomorrow. Love you too.

I pull out my key and slide it into the door lock. It doesn't turn. My stomach flips as I push on the handle, and the door swings open.

It's not locked.

The kitchen's a mess. Every cupboard is open, contents all over the floor. Bits of broken crockery litter the lino.

Someone's in my house. At a guess, it's Garrett, but I can't take that risk.

I drop the grocery bags on the floor and pull my phone back out of my bag to call the police.

"Mia."

I look back up to see Garrett in the doorway to the living room. "What are you doing here?"

He grits his teeth. "I came to see my wife. The one who declared a relationship with a student today."

I nod. My fingernails scrape my palms so hard, I'll be surprised if I don't see blood later. "That's right."

"When were you going to tell me?"

"It's none of your business." I walk past him into the dining room and drop my bag on a chair.

"I'm your husband."

I turn. "We're separated, and our divorce is pending. Get out of my house, Garrett."

"*Our* house."

"Fine. Get the fuck out of *our* house, Garrett," I yell.

Pain rips through the right side of my head and I stagger back, tripping over my own two feet. I blink. Everything's a blur, but I can still make out his hand, fisted and raised above me.

My head hurts. I raise my hand to rub my temple.

When my vision clears, I fix my gaze on Garrett. He's standing over me, his arms crossed. "Bastard."

"Now you're not hysterical, perhaps you'd like to explain to me why you're fucking a student when you're married to me."

Shit. I scan the room for anything I can use to defend myself. How far away is James?

"We're separated. We were separated for a long time before—"

"Enough," he roars.

"My relationship is none of your business."

"You're my wife. Of course it's my business."

"We're getting divorced."

He shakes his head. "No, we're not."

"Yes. We are. We were before I fell in love with James, and we are now." I push myself to my feet.

"You love him?" He shakes his head. "Unbelievable."

"Why? He's loving and kind. Not nasty and cruel like you are. You just hit me."

His face falls. "That was a momentary slip."

"You can't even say you're sorry."

"Mia, I …"

"No, Garrett. You don't get to do this again. You don't get to tell me what to do." My hands shake with anger and fear.

"Mia, you need to listen to me."

"I don't *need* to do anything with you. Get out of my house."

He takes a deep breath. "It's *our* house."

"Well, you don't live here anymore." I raise my hand to my face where he hit me. It's tender and sore, and I can't let him get away with it.

We both start at the clap of the door closing.

James walks into the kitchen, looking around before fixing his gaze on Garrett. "What the fuck happened here?" He shifts his focus to me, his eyes narrowing. "Mia? What the hell. He hit you?"

"Yes," I whisper.

Anger flashes across his face, and he storms toward Garrett. Before he can get to him, I grab hold of James's arm. "He's not worth it."

"He hurt you." He runs his thumb down my cheek with all his gentleness. His eyes are full of hurt. This is what love is. Not the twisted mess that I had with Garrett.

"Mia." Drew Campbell's right behind his brother. "Let me take a look. James, call the police."

"We don't need the police," Garrett says.

"Yeah, we do." Drew seems to be taking over the situation while James pulls his phone out of his pocket.

Garrett's mouth opens and closes like a fish. He's not used to people ignoring his wishes.

"You're lucky I'm here." Drew says, flashing me a smile that I'm sure charms his patients. I'm so glad he's here too as he examines my aching face. He studies me intently for a few moments, his fingers brushing over the skin. "That's gonna hurt for a while."

"The cops are on their way," James says.

Garrett just stands there, staring.

"Good." Drew catches my gaze. "Ready to press charges? That's going to be an impressive bruise. He hit you with some real force."

"It wasn't like that," Garrett says. His voice is so quiet.

James takes my hand, and I'm pulled into his arms.

"Just be careful of her face," Drew says.

"Are you okay?" James brushes my cheek with his lips, and I close my eyes, breathing in the earthy smell of *him*.

"I am now."

"I can't imagine ever thinking it's okay to hit a woman." Drew glares at Garrett.

Garrett swallows hard, his Adam's apple bobbing, but he says nothing. For the first time in, well, ever, he doesn't look confident.

It's almost like time stands still. I don't even notice what's going on around me until a police officer appears at the door.

James shows him through to the dining room. The man I love takes one look at me, and his chest moves like he's taking a deep breath. "This is Mia."

"Hi, Mia. I'm Constable Jenkins, and my partner is Constable Peters. We got a call about a man assaulting a woman."

Garrett snorts.

Drew's eyebrows rise. "That's right." He points at Garrett. "He punched her."

"That's not what happened," Garrett says.

"Her bruises are gonna say otherwise, buddy."

"Thank you." Officer Jenkins addresses me, "Are you okay?"

I shake my head. "I came home to find Garrett, my ex-husband, here. We argued. He hit me."

"We should get you assessed by a doctor. Make sure you're okay."

"I am a doctor," Drew says. I bite down a laugh. Drew is the sweetest guy, but clearly he feels slighted.

"Oh, sorry, sir." The officer nods.

"She'll need an X-ray. I think her cheekbone is broken."

Garrett's eyes widen. "I didn't hit her *that* hard."

"So you admit to hitting her?" the officer says.

Drew moves his gaze to me. "I'd say it was more like a punch than a slap. But on second thoughts, I don't think anything's broken."

A flash of anger appears in Garrett's eyes. Drew's just got him to confess in front of a cop, and there's no going back from that.

"I'm going to have to take you down to the station for questioning," the constable says.

"I want a lawyer."

"You'll need one," Drew says.

I wind up telling my story to the female officer. She's patient, and even though I just want to cry and crawl away, I get my version of events out.

Garrett scowls as he's led away by the cop, and I figure he's just lucky he's not in handcuffs.

"Right. That's him taken care of. Let's call a locksmith and then go to dinner," Drew says.

"I'm not supposed to change the locks according to our agreement," I whisper the words before realising just how silly they sound right now.

"Then you won't. I will."

James wraps his arms around me. "Let us take care of everything. Go sit in the living room."

I look up at him, my eyes filled with tears. "I'm so sorry that you have to deal with this."

"Mia, as long as you're safe, I don't care what I have to do. And I can tell you now he'll never get the chance to get close enough to hit you again." He kisses me gently before letting me go.

The living room is the same as the kitchen. The whole place is a mess. But I clear a spot on the couch and sit down.

I knew today seemed too good to be true, but I never thought it would come to this.

"Shit." James walks into the room and looks around. He pulls the ornaments that have been dumped off the couch and places a cushion down. "Here. Lie down. The locksmith is on their way."

I lie on the couch. "Can you check the rest of the house?"

He nods, stroking my hair and giving me a tender kiss. "I'll go and do that now. I'm sorry you came home to that. If I hadn't gone for a beer with Drew, I would have been here."

"It's not your fault."

When he disappears up the hall, Drew takes his place. "Let me take another look at you."

I don't think I've ever felt so cared for.

———

When the locksmith's changed the locks, I sit up again and survey the damage.

The few ornaments I had in here are shattered. There's glass on the carpet, and some of the cushions have been torn.

I guess at least now James and I get to start fresh.

Garrett never made it up the hallway. The bedrooms at least are fine, and we can sleep in our own bed tonight.

"Shall we go to dinner?" Drew smiles.

I shrug. "I'm not sure if it's a good idea."

"We're not going out to a restaurant, if you're worried about people seeing the bruising. Sonya's got some chef working for her tonight as a treat for us. It's just a dinner, but what rich families do."

I laugh. "I'd still like to come if the invitation is there, then. Sounds amazing."

"It will be. Besides, Hayley will want to mother-hen you."

"She's like that." James laughs.

Drew nods. "James is one of her chicks."

"I like Hayley. I'd love to see her again."

"Well, you might see her more often now you're part of the family," Drew says.

I grin. Part of a family. Despite our weekend away, I didn't completely feel it before. I do now.

And it's pretty damn good.

35

———

MIA

"HE DID *WHAT*?" Hayley's mouth falls open as we walk into the house behind Drew. She shifts her focus to me. "Oh, Mia. I'm so sorry. Are you okay?"

"Thanks to James and Drew, I'm fine."

Drew straightens. "It was me who got Garrett to confess to what he'd done."

I nod. "Yes, it was."

"Want a medal or something?" James asks, slipping an arm around my waist.

"No, he's just trying to impress his wife." Hayley snuggles into Drew's chest. "Not that he needs to."

"I'm already impressive?"

"Sometimes." She laughs.

He dips his head and kisses her, and it's so warm and affectionate. I love how much they clearly love each other. That kind of relationship's what I always wanted. It's what I have with James.

"Anyway, come through. Mum's got this chef cooking dinner, and there's going to be a ridiculous amount of food. I'm so glad you two could join us," Hayley says.

"It sounds amazing," I say.

"I'm so glad I have you to hang out with. Mum can be a bit out of touch, and it's so good to have a woman closer to my age around. Oh! I hope you guys can come and see us in Hamilton more often."

Grinning, I nod. "I'd love to. I haven't been to Hamilton in forever."

"Come up for the weekend. We'll leave the twins with the boys and go shopping."

"That sounds great."

Logan and Amelia walk into the entranceway, hand in hand with an older woman who I assume is Hayley's mother.

"Here are my babies." Drew squats and holds his arms open. They both run toward him, and I smile at those little legs running.

"Dad!" Logan yells.

"Dad!" Amelia follows suit.

Drew picks them up, balancing one on each hip. "I'm not sure how I'll cope when I can't hold both you guys like this." He laughs, planting kisses on the top of their heads. "Did you miss me?"

Amelia nods, resting her head in Drew's neck.

He leans his chin to rest on her head. "Oh, I love you two."

My heart swells watching them. I wanted children early on, but Garrett wanted to wait. And wait. By the time I'd had enough and walked, I knew I wouldn't have any of my own.

But at the same time, I was glad I hadn't had any with him. It would have made everything so much harder.

Now I have the right man, but it's too late for me to start trying. I've known that for a while. Apart from the potential medical issues for me, there's a much higher chance that something could go wrong for my child. I can't risk that.

"Come on, guys. Let's all go through here," Drew says and walks through a doorway to the right.

We follow him through to the living room. I can't get over how massive this house is. James had told me Hayley's parents were rich. It's breathtaking.

There are photos and ornaments everywhere. I sigh. *My poor broken house.*

"You okay?" James asks.

I nod. "I'm fine."

"Mia, this is my mother, Sonya," Hayley says. I turn to smile at the woman who'd appeared with the children a minute ago. An older man walks in behind her. "And this is my father, David."

"It's so good to meet you. Hayley was just filling us in on what happened. Are you alright? Do you need anything?" David asks.

I shake my head. "Thank you so much, but I'll be fine. I think I'd just like to forget about it for the night."

Sonya smiles. "That we can hopefully do." Her gaze moves to the side of my face. I'm sure it's swollen and probably bruised. I must look a sight. "I've got a cold pack if that would help."

"It might be a good idea, Sonya," Drew says. "Mia had a rest before we left, but we didn't put anything on it."

"And you call yourself a doctor." Sonya taps him on his arm before disappearing through a door.

I laugh.

"She loves me, really," Drew says.

All I can do is smile.

DINNER IS AMAZING. It's supposed to be five courses, but we struggle after three. There are a lot of leftovers.

"You're welcome to take whatever you want home," Sonya says. "Then you won't have to worry about cooking."

"I'd love that. Thank you," I say. "We've got a lot of cleaning up to do."

She frowns. "Let me know if you need any help. I'm so angry on your behalf."

"I appreciate it."

"Why don't you go and get some fresh air before dessert?"

"There's dessert?" Drew asks.

Sonya laughs. "We'll skip the last two courses and take a break, and then there's dessert. Trust me, you won't want to miss it."

"Are you trying to fatten me up, Mum?" Drew asks.

Hayley slaps him on the arm, and he shrugs.

I look down the table to the two high chairs. Amelia's picking at her dinner with her fingers. Logan is covered in what looks like the pureed potato we had with the second course.

"Those two are enjoying their food." I nod toward them.

Hayley laughs. "They'll be straight in the bath after this."

"Logan looks like he's having a lot of fun."

She sighs. "He's the one who likes playing with his food. He'll have eaten plenty too, though."

I smile. Logan and Amelia are so gorgeous, with their big blue eyes and dark hair like their parents. It does make me wonder what my children would look like if I had them. But I can't think that way.

It's too late.

James stands, and takes my hand. "Want to go and get some fresh air?"

"I'd love to. If I can walk."

He laughs, pulling me to my feet, and we walk out to the back deck.

"This place is beautiful."

"I've never been out here," James says. He wraps his arms around my waist, and I lean back against him.

"Really?"

He shrugs. "Drew and Hayley usually visit me. I hope tonight wasn't too stressful after what happened with Garrett."

I shake my head. "No. Everyone's been wonderful. And I love how peaceful it is out here."

"Sonya said we could stay the night if we wanted." James lets me go as I turn.

"Really? In that mansion?"

He laughs. "They have a spare room or two. I'm not worried. I had a glass of wine earlier, but nothing since so I can drive home."

"I kinda like the idea of staying. Going back to the house doesn't feel that good right now."

James presses a gentle kiss to my lips. "I'm sure. We could

always find another place to live for a while if we have to. Now we're out in the open."

I grin. "I feel so free."

"Me too." He grins. "The next time Cody Johnson says he'd like to fuck you, I can smack him for saying that about my girl."

My mouth falls open. "He said what?"

"Doctor Scott is so popular with the boys. They all think you're hot." James presses a kiss to my temple, and I snuggle into his chest. "But you are mine, and they can all bugger off."

I laugh, taking a deep breath. This place really is paradise. I'm looking forward to the day when I can escape the city and go somewhere where I can think.

And to having James by my side all of the time.

"I love this house. Do you think if I hide here, they'll ever find me?" I ask.

James laughs. "I'd have to sneak in to see you."

I drape my arms over his shoulders. "I like that we don't need to sneak around anymore."

James closes in on me, and presses the most gentle kiss on my lips. It leaves me wanting to cry.

This is the man I'm supposed to be with.

"If you two have finished canoodling out here, dessert's ready." Drew's voice is full of amusement.

"If that's the condition, we might skip dessert." James laughs.

"Oh, little brother. You do have it bad." Drew grins. "You've got good taste, though, so I'll forgive you. But seriously, you don't want to miss this."

It's not just one dessert; there's a selection. Pavlova,

chocolate mousse, the richest-looking chocolate cake I think I've ever seen, and then there's fruit and cheese.

I take a breath. I've always been the type to find space for dessert, but today, I don't know where to start.

"It's a bit overwhelming," James says.

"Might have to have a bit of everything." I pick up a plate. After filling it, I return to my seat.

Amelia squeals as she gets a small plate in front of her with some fruit. It doesn't take much to keep the kids happy.

"I'll show you your room after dinner if you're staying." Sonya smiles at me.

"What? They get to sleep in the same room? Remember when I first came here and you gave me a separate room to Hayley?" Drew laughs.

"Really?" James asks.

"Sonya tried to set Hayley up with some guy the same day Hayley brought me here to meet her parents."

Sonya blushes and laughs. "That was a long time ago." She takes a sip of her drink. "And, for the record, we love Hayley's choice."

"I should hope so." Hayley leans against Drew. "I love my choice too."

"We even made two beautiful grandbabies for you." Drew holds his hands up as if exasperated.

James shakes his head, and I laugh softly. "Drew, stop milking the guilt," James says.

"I'm allowed to make the most of it."

"He's always like this." James directs the comment to me, but out of the corner of my eye, I can see Hayley nodding.

"I'm not sure Drew will ever get over it." Hayley plants a kiss on Drew's temple.

"If I get hugs and kisses every time I mention it, I might have to talk about it more often."

"Don't you dare." She grins, pecking him on the lips. "Now let's get stuck into this food. It looks amazing."

THE BEDROOM IS BEAUTIFUL.

There's what looks like a king-sized bed against the far wall, covered in cushions. To the left is the en suite, and I gasp when I walk in.

A spa bath sits in the corner, more than big enough for the two of us. On the side is a bottle of bubble bath, along with shampoo and conditioner.

"I know I joked about it, but do you think they'd notice if I just moved in?"

James joins me in the bathroom doorway. "Woah. I would have been here a lot earlier if I'd known it was this nice. I'll ask Sonya if she can adopt me."

I laugh, burying my face in his chest. "This is exactly what I needed after today."

"Me too. It's perfect." He pauses. "Let's go back down and have that hot chocolate David said he'd make before having a bath."

"I like that idea."

James runs a finger along my jaw and raises my chin so my gaze meets his. "And then I want to go to bed and just hold you."

"I like that idea. I'm so glad we're here."

He nods. "I am too. I thought today was going pretty well, until …"

"Me too. Oh, I know there was gossip, but next week everything will be back to normal."

"I punched Cody. Before word gets back to you about that."

My mouth falls open. "What?"

"He said a few things he now regrets. Garrett saw it. Tried to turn Cody against me, but Cody basically told him where to go."

I swallow. "That might not have helped the situation."

"If I'd thought for one second he was going to go after you, I would have gone straight home and told Drew to meet me there."

Tears prick my eyes. "You two showed up. And that was all I needed. You were there for me, are there for me."

"Always," he whispers. "Isn't that what love's all about?"

I grin, and he kisses me. I know that he'll kiss me all night if I need it.

And that might just make everything better.

We walk down the stairs hand in hand and into the living room where Hayley's parents sit.

"Drew and Hayley are bathing the kids, but I'll go and get that hot chocolate I promised if you want it," David says.

"David makes the best hot chocolate with whipped cream and chocolate sprinkles," Sonya says.

I smile. "Sounds amazing."

"Is the room okay?" Sonya asks.

"It's gorgeous. Thank you so much," I say.

"You're welcome. We're happy to have you here."

I want to cry at how happy *I* am. To be part of such a big, loving family is wonderful.

36

COREY

I'll admit it's a little weird to get up and go to work every morning, but Tim's a good employer. He takes care of his staff, and everyone gets along.

The best part is coming home to Constance. With every day that passes, she copes a little better. The routine is easier for her now, I think because she's not constantly looking over her shoulder and worrying about taking care of me. She can focus on Eli and herself.

I don't mind coming home and cooking dinner either, and once I got that through to her, the pressure on her seemed to ease. If the baby needs feeding right as I get home, then that's what he gets.

My evenings are spent with her in my arms, or Eli, as Constance grabs some sleep. This new arrangement works well for all of us.

There's just one thing that makes me restless.

I want Constance to be my wife.

Every day I see that engagement ring on her finger, and it's not enough for me. I made a promise to her father that I'd marry her, and I'm not a man who breaks his promises.

I put my sleeping son to bed and walk back into the living room. We've had a great weekend.

Constance gives me a sleepy smile. It's been one of those days when Eli has just wanted to feed and feed. If he grows up to be anything like me, he'll go through a lot of growth spurts. But instead of freaking out and getting stressed, Con is handling it all like a pro.

"Let's get married."

She cocks an eyebrow at me and lifts her left hand. "I thought we did this? Have you got another ring for me?"

"No. I mean, let's get married as soon as possible."

"Clearly I'm really tired. I thought we were doing that anyway?"

I laugh. "It takes three days to get a marriage license. We know what we want to do. Why don't we go and apply tomorrow, and get married next weekend?"

Constance stares at me like I have two heads. "*Now* you want to rush?"

"You know me. When I want to do something, I do it."

She laughs. "I know, but …"

"I happen to know that Lily made you a dress. And it's time for you to show me."

"But there's no time."

"Sweetness, we can do it. I'll get Lily and Ginny on the case and we'll be sorted. Where do you want to get married? I thought the cove was nice for Drew's wedding."

She laughs. "There's no stopping you is there, Corey Campbell?"

"Not when it comes to you."

37

———————

MIA

COMING HOME IS like crashing to Earth.

But James and I get stuck in, and by Saturday evening, the kitchen and living room have been tidied and vacuumed, and everything Garrett trashed is in the bin.

After our amazing meal on Friday, we eat pizza on Saturday. On Sunday, we go shopping and buy our own crockery. At least the house can feel more like *us* now.

It's with a heavy heart that I go to work on Monday. But I was right. The class is back to normal, and I have to confess that I like the chatter today instead of the quiet whispers.

It's the longest day ever though, and I head back to my office when lectures are finished to tidy up a few things before I go home.

It doesn't take long to get everything done.

"Have you got a minute?"

My teeth grate as I hear Garrett's voice. He's leaning

against the frame in the open doorway of my office. "I do, but you're not supposed to be talking to me."

He nods. "I know. I'm sorry for what happened, Mia. I got carried away."

"That's what you used to say when you yelled at me. Minus the apology."

His Adam's apple bobs as he just stands there, staring.

"Maybe it was inevitable that you'd reach that point, Garrett. I just hoped that you wouldn't."

He nods. "I volunteered to take anger-management classes. The court will probably order them anyway, but I just wanted to say how sorry I was." Garrett licks his lips. "I love you so much, Mia, and I'm sorry."

"I appreciate your apology." The old me might have felt bad about the discomfort written all over his face, but not now. I spent years feeling like I wasn't good enough for him when the truth was the opposite. He was never good enough for me. "If you've finished, Garrett, I'm going home."

With a stiff nod, he takes a step back.

"And I would suggest that if you want to talk to me again, you do it through your lawyer. We're so done."

For the first time in a long time, there's emotion in his eyes. Real emotion. He's sad. But I'm not about to cave in any way. Garrett deserves everything that's happening to him.

"Okay." He takes a step back, and with a final look, disappears down the corridor.

I shut down the computer, and pick up my bag.

James is at home waiting for me, and if I know him, he'll have cooked dinner.

Before him, I didn't know what I was missing out on.

I'll never take what we have for granted.

I LOVE COMING HOME.

This house was always cold when Garrett and I lived here together. The atmosphere was always bitter and prickly.

It's been warm and welcoming since James has been here.

James stands in the kitchen, watching over the cooktop when I arrive. His whole face lights up with happiness.

I walk through and drop my bag on a dining room chair.

"Hey." He wraps his arms around my waist and pulls me to him.

I linger on his lips. "Hey, yourself."

"Good day?"

I nod. "Very. You killed that last assignment. I got your marks back today."

He grins. "At least the university knows I wasn't getting good marks for sleeping with the teacher."

Slapping his chest, I laugh. "They knew that before. You were achieving a long time before I came into your life."

"Then it just backs up how good you are at your job. I'm still learning." He lets go, returning to the cooktop.

I bite my bottom lip. "Garrett came to see me."

James's eyebrows knit. "Really? I thought he was supposed to stay away from you."

"Yeah, he is. He apologised. All it did was make me more angry."

James pinches my right shoulder, rubbing my neck with one hand. "Are you okay?"

"Just frustrated." I sigh. "He waited until his words didn't hurt me, you know? Where were all those apologies when he told me how useless and pathetic I was?"

James wraps his arms around my neck, pressing a kiss to my temple. "He was an idiot. I promise you'll never get any of that crap from me."

"I know. You are a million miles away from him." I turn my head. "I'm so grateful that we found each other."

"So am I."

"Can I ask you something?"

He turns. "Always."

"Are you sure this is what you want. I'm what you want?"

"Mia, I—"

"Let me finish. You're so young. I'm seventeen years' older than you. I know we've talked about this, but I can't start a family now. How are you going to feel when you're thirty being with a nearly fifty-year-old?"

His lips curve into a smile. God, how I love that smile. It lights up the room with youthful enthusiasm. "I'll still love you. You are everything I've ever wanted. Nothing else matters to me as long as I have you."

"No regrets?"

"Zero regrets. You're the best thing that ever happened to me, Mia Scott. And one day, I'll make you Mia Campbell, if I have anything to do with it."

My heart leaps. I want to be with James so much, and I want this to be a long-term commitment. I hadn't thought about marriage. "I like that idea."

"Really?"

I lean closer, hooking my arms over his shoulders. "I like the idea of everything with you."

He grins, and I get closer so I can kiss him. His eyes are so full of love, and his heart is on display. I love this. This is what a relationship should be like.

"By the way, Corey and Constance have set the date," he says.

"Really?" I smile.

"I hope you don't have any plans next weekend."

I gape at him. "What?"

"Apparently Corey's sick of waiting. They went and applied for the license today and they'll have it by the end of the week. They're getting married at the cove with the reception in Dad's backyard."

I grin. "That's beautiful."

"So, I figure we head out of town on Friday, and come back Sunday."

Nodding, I wrap my arms around his neck and hug him tight. "I'd love to. Those two are impulsive, huh?"

"Corey is. I'm not too sure about Constance, but they're so in love I think she'll be over the moon."

I let go of him, and he searches my face.

"What?" I ask.

"That'll be us one day."

38

MIA

THERE'S ONLY one other person I need to tell about James and me being out in the open: Kelly. I haven't seen her in forever.

She's back in the country, and while I was falling in love with James, she had her own hook-up and break-up story. But now I get to update her on my love life. It might take a while.

"Mia." Her tone is so warm when I call her. It makes me miss her all the more.

"Hey, Kelly. I wondered if you would be interested in a catch-up."

"I'd love to. When?"

"If you're free, tonight. Come around for dinner. James is cooking."

"I'd love to." She sounds excited. And I'm glad. I've missed her. "So, is it all official or are we keeping this a secret?"

"It's official."

She squeals. I love this woman. She's genuinely excited and happy for me, and I don't have enough people like that in my life. "How are things going with you?"

She sighs. "I'm by myself again, but you know that. I just want someone nice, you know?"

"Oh, I know."

"Anyway, I must go, but what time tonight?"

"Does six-thirty sound good?"

"Sounds wonderful. Can't wait."

Neither can I.

SHE'S at my door with a bottle of wine and a huge grin at six-thirty.

"Come in." I step back as she walks into the kitchen. "James is just getting changed."

Her expression tightens as she looks at me. "Who hit you? It wasn't your new man, was it? Because if it was, we are getting out of here, and he'll wear this bottle."

"No. It was Garrett."

Her eyebrows shoot up. "What? Really?"

I nod. "He didn't take the news about me declaring a relationship very well at all. Came 'round here, trashed the house, and got really upset."

"I can't believe he hit you." She huffs. "I mean, I knew he was a prick, but I never thought he'd get physical."

"Me either, but it happened. He tried to brush it off when the police came, but—"

"Wait. Stop. You called the police?"

"James did."

She shakes her head. "James called the police. What was he doing when Garrett hit you?"

"James wasn't here. He and his brother Drew showed up when I was arguing with Garrett. He'd already hit me. James called the police while Drew took care of me. He's a doctor."

Kelly holds her hands up as if in surrender. "It all sounds like a crazy time."

"It has been."

James walks into the kitchen, a smile on his face. "Is this Kelly?"

Kelly turns. Her mouth falls open as she looks James up and down. It probably helps that he's in dark jeans and a dress shirt. Mouth-watering.

"Nice. Mia said you have a brother?" She sounds hopeful.

I laugh. "He has four. And they're all taken."

Kelly sighs. "Shame. Maybe a younger man is what I need."

"Age doesn't matter," James says, slipping his arm around my waist. "It's finding someone who makes you happy."

"Awww, and he's sweet too. Maybe I need to be hanging around the university." Kelly grins.

"I've got a friend I could introduce you to." James grins.

I turn and stare at James. "Who?" He can't possibly be thinking of …

"Cody."

Laughing, I shake my head. "Oh, James. No."

"Who's Cody?" Kelly asks.

"One of my friends from uni. But I don't think he's after anything serious."

Kelly examines him closely. "Tell me more."

I LAUGH SO MUCH over dinner that my face aches. I massage my cheeks, tender from smiling so hard, and James rubs my arm. "Are you okay?"

Nodding, I lean toward him. "I'm fine. Just enjoying myself."

"Me too."

"I'm so happy to see you happy, Mia. I don't think I ever saw you like this with Garrett," Kelly says.

I let go of a contented sigh. "My life is very different now, that's for sure." I lick my lips. "Next year, the house will go up for sale, and James and I are moving back to his hometown."

"Really? I'm going to miss you."

"We can keep in touch. And you can always come and visit us. I'm not sure Copper Creek will be as lively as you like, but it's such a beautiful place." I reach for James's hand under the table. "And James's family is wonderful. They've been very welcoming."

"Have you told your parents about your divorce?"

James's grip on my hand tightens. He knows I hate talking about this. How do you mend a bridge that burned that long ego?

"No. I'm not really sure where to start. One day."

39

COREY

It's a very rare thing to find me wearing a suit.

Adam's wedding, Drew's wedding, Mum's funeral. I can count the number of times I've worn one on one hand.

Today, I wear one with pride.

Anything to make it perfect for Constance.

"Ready?" Adam asks. He's my best man, and the only one for the job.

"I was ready a long time ago."

He laughs. "You two are so good together. I'm glad you found her."

"Me too. I don't know what I'd do without her now."

Adam grips my shoulder. "I think you were just lucky to meet the right woman. Just like I was."

"I think you're right."

Everyone I love is here. Dad sits at the front with Eli in his arms. My brothers and their wives and partners are right behind him. I throw a wink at Ava, sitting beside Owen.

Lily and Ginny threw all their effort into this. They managed to get the company who did Drew's wedding to arrange the seats and the reception afterward, though this is so much smaller than Drew's wedding was.

A group of my friends are here, including Rob and Amy. It's perfect.

When the music starts, I look up.

She's here.

I hold my breath.

When we first met, she wore that drab, grey dress. I tore it from her body and burned it in the fireplace. The thought of that still makes me smile. It was that day she told me she was pregnant. I swore to myself then that I would never let her go again.

Now she's in a long, cream halter-neck dress.

She's breathtaking.

Her brown hair is down, and that makes me smile. I'd heard her discussing that with Lily. Lily's opinion was that she should wear it up to show off that graceful neck. But Constance knows I like it when she wears it down. She's done this for me.

My stomach flips as she walks past everyone I love and comes to a stop right in front of me.

"Wow," I say when she reaches me.

She smiles, her cheeks pinking. It doesn't matter how many times I tell her how gorgeous she is, she still blushes when I pay her a compliment. It's one of the things I love so much about her. She's so humble when the reality is that she doesn't know her own strength.

"You look so beautiful," I whisper.

Her smile grows. I'm so in love with her, and I want the whole world to know it.

The celebrant clears her throat, and we both look up.

"Corey and Constance are here to celebrate their love for one another, and to be joined in marriage …"

I don't even hear what comes next because all I can see is my bride. This day was always going to be overwhelming.

"The couple have written their own vows, which they'll now share with each other. Corey."

I turn to Constance. "Constance. I knew from the moment you walked into my life that you were something special. You make me feel whole, and you get me like no one else ever has. And you gave me the great gift that is our son, Eli. You're my whole heart, sweetness, and you will be for the rest of our days."

She looks at me through teary eyes. I just want to take her in my arms and kiss her.

Constance licks her lips. "Corey, when I met you I didn't know what to make of you." She smiles, and I squeeze her hands. "I soon learned that this mountain of a man was kind and caring, sweet and loving. And you were everything I ever wanted. I'm so grateful every day for coming through that fence and ending up in your arms. And I'll always want them around me."

"That can be arranged," I murmur.

"Can I have the rings?" The celebrant's voice breaks through, and I look at Adam.

He hands over the rings and steps back.

When Constance slides my ring on my finger, my chest feels like it's about to burst with pride. There's something quite primal about me placing her ring on in return. This is a symbol of my love, and a warning sign to anyone who even looks twice at her.

"Corey, you may kiss your bride."

I sweep her into my arms and claim her mouth. Everyone claps, but they fade into the background as I hold Constance tight. There was a time in my life when I had no plans for any day like this. As much as my solitude mattered to me, it was lonely on that mountain.

Now I have it all.

A wife. A son. A family of my own.

Everything I never thought I'd have.

AFTER PHOTOS, we head to Dad's place. We're not doing speeches or anything formal. All we wanted was to hang out with everyone we loved for a while.

There's food, and the one traditional thing we will do is cut a cake. Owen grumbled at having to put something together at the last minute, but after some teasing he outdid himself.

Once we've cut it, everyone swarms to eat cake and then the music starts.

"It's your turn next." I grin, looking at my brother.

Ginny pats Owen on the chest, and he nods. "We know. It won't be too far off."

"Won't it?" she asks.

He turns to her, disbelief on his face. "I thought we agreed."

She grins. "We did. Just testing."

Owen shifts his gaze back to me. "She's always testing me. It's the teacher in her."

I laugh. "Nothing wrong with keeping you on your toes."

Ginny nods. "There's a pop quiz later."

Owen just shakes his head, rolling his eyes. "Now you've done it."

"I haven't given you the rules yet. There are punishments when you get the questions wrong." She laughs.

I look between them. "You two keep that stuff behind doors. I don't want to know."

Owen kisses the top of her head. "No chance of any of that happening when there are children in the house."

"I dunno. Constance and I do quite well."

He shoves me. "Now look who's talking about what goes on behind closed doors."

Laughing, I take a seat and watch my wife. *My wife.* She's holding Eli, and dancing with Lily and Hayley. He's beaming at his beloved mother, and it makes my heart swell in response.

We're so far away from where we were when he was born. After all the upheaval in our lives, we're finally settled.

She turns, her eyes scanning the room, and I just know she's looking for me. Standing, I walk toward her.

"There you are."

I bend, giving her a lingering kiss on the lips.

"Are you two ready to go?" Lily asks. Eli's having his first sleepover tonight at Lily's place. He's so young, but it's just one night, and I trust Lily more than almost anyone else.

"You're that anxious to get your hands on him?" I ask.

She laughs. "Well, it's been a little while since I've had a baby in the house. It'll be good practice."

Con's mouth falls open. "You …?"

Lily nods. "It's not public knowledge. We just found out yesterday, and I didn't want to look like I was trying to overshadow your day. But it's time, and we're ready for one more. I think this'll be the last one, though."

"Congratulations." I lean over and peck her on the cheek. "Any time you do want to practice taking care of a baby, you know where we are. I could do with some alone time with Constance."

Constance snuggles in as I wrap an arm around her.

I press a kiss to the top of Eli's head. "Now. You be a good boy for Auntie Lily. And if you're going to take a dump, do it while Uncle Adam's holding you."

"Corey." Constance laughs. "That's so gross."

I shrug. "I'm sure Adam can deal with it."

"Oh, Adam's got to get used to changing nappies again anyway." Lily winks, and reaches for Eli.

With one last cuddle, Constance hands over the baby. I see the reluctance in her face, but once I get her home, I'm sure I can distract her for a few hours.

She'll have her hands and her body full of me.

I'M NOT sure if my truck is that romantic a vehicle to drive home from our wedding in, but it gets us there. Constance is already feeling Eli's absence. It's written all over her face.

When we come to a stop, she reaches for the door handle.

"Wait. I'll come around."

She laughs. "What are you doing?"

I climb out of my side, and walk around the truck,

opening the door. When she steps down, I scoop her into my arms.

"Corey ..."

"I'm carrying you over the threshold."

"Why? I live here." She buries her face in my neck.

"This is the first time you've been here as my wife, though. That's something special."

She raises her head and palms my cheek. "That's so sweet."

"That's the side of me you get right now."

"Right now?"

I lick my lips. "Well, once we get inside, I'm not sure if sweet is the word I'd use."

Constance laughs. "What words would you use?"

"Hungry. No, not hungry. Starving."

"You ate at the reception."

"I'm not hungry for food, Con."

Her eyes shine with happiness. "You'd better get me inside, then."

She laughs as I carry her up the steps to the house. I still have the keys in my hand, and balance her while I slide one into the lock and turn it. The handle is a bit trickier, but I get the door open and carry her inside.

Placing her gently on her feet, I grin as she cups my face. "Come here, Mr Campbell."

She presses her lips to mine.

"I have this problem." I sigh.

Her eyes fill with concern. "What's wrong? Are you okay?"

"I'm not sure if I can ever get enough of you."

Con's lips spread into a smile. "Well, it's funny you should mention that."

"Really?" I wrap my arms around her waist.

"I'm not sure if I can ever get enough of *you*."

"Is that right?"

"You constantly amaze me, Corey. You're such a good man who does whatever it takes to support his family. The family you didn't plan for."

I smile. I'd do anything for this woman. She's who I was always destined to be with—we were meant to be together.

"You gave me life, sweetness. You and Eli. I feel like I found myself when I found you."

Tears well in her eyes. "You always know what to say."

"It's easy with you. Everything's just so easy. Even when we argue, I know everything will be okay because you and me, we're for life."

I can't hold back anymore. I need her.

Just like I've always needed her.

LILY MADE SUCH A BEAUTIFUL DRESS. I manage not to tear it as I unzip Constance and push it to the floor.

She sighs. "I love that dress so much."

"You looked beautiful in it. But I have to say, the view is much better now you're out of it."

She laughs as I pick her up and deposit her gently on the bed. Her panties go flying one way, her bra the other. And I sink myself onto her pussy like I'm starving.

"Corey," she cries, her long fingers raking through my hair.

I roll onto my back. "Come here."

She straddles me, and I catch a glimpse of her wedding and engagement rings glittering in the dim light. She's mine. All mine.

I guide myself into her, and her lips part as she gasps. This is something I'll never get enough of—watching her fuck me, seeing that blissful look as she falls apart.

She throws her head back as I explore her with my thumb, stroking her clit, touching where my cock meets her pussy. With my other hand, I hold her hip. She rides me, rocks me, consumes me.

If I live to be a hundred, I'll never have enough of her.

She comes right before I do, falling beside me in a glorious mess of sweat and hair all over the place.

I laugh, pushing her hair off her face, finding her lips with mine. "Love you, wife."

She grins, letting out a pant as she tries to catch her breath. "Love you too, husband."

I pull her into my arms, and close my eyes.

This is my world right here.

Now and forever.

40

JAMES

COREY AND CONSTANCE left about half an hour ago, but the party continues without them. I sit at a table, and watch the dance floor.

Ava and Rose dance with Mia, who's having a ball. Lily gets control of the music, and Mia gasps at the kids when ABBA's "Dancing Queen" starts. I grin at Ava's giggle.

Holding hands, the three of them swing their arms. Mia spins them both around and back again. I love seeing her so happy. I love her.

She's laughing, and although the rest of the family slowly join them dancing, Mia is all I see. She's free of the past. I'm her future.

I stand, and make my way toward her. Her eyes widen as I approach, and she turns to the girls. "Look, it's Uncle James. Should we let him in to dance with us?"

Rose nods.

Ava shakes her head and giggles.

"I'm so hurt, Ava." I place one hand on my heart.

Owen swoops in, and Ava squeals as her father sweeps her into his arms. "There you are. We're going home. Say goodbye to James and Mia." He grins. "Will we see you before you head off?"

"Depends on how late we sleep in tomorrow."

He laughs. "Fair enough. If we don't, I'm sure we'll catch up again soon."

"Definitely."

With a wave, he carries Ava off over his shoulder, and Mia and I laugh as we watch. Rose runs toward Adam, and for a moment, I just watch her.

"Enjoying yourself?" Mia asks.

I nod. "It's been fun. The wedding was …" I fumble for words.

"Short and sweet?" she asks.

"Very Corey."

"He couldn't wait to get her out of here."

I grin. "I think I can understand that."

A slow song comes on, and I look up to see Lily wink at me

"Dance with me," I say.

I wrap my arms around Mia, holding her close, I move slowly.

"Marry me," I murmur in her ear.

"What?" She pulls back, her eyes seeming to search mine.

"I didn't plan on asking tonight, and I don't want to do one of those wanky public proposals where I embarrass you and you feel obligated to say yes."

Mia laughs.

"But I love you, and I want to spend my life with you."

She licks her lips and blinks away tears that have welled in her eyes. "I'd marry you in a heartbeat."

"Then, let's do it. Soon."

"After we move here. Let's have something like Corey and Constance did with the whole family."

I grin. "I love that idea."

"You've given me so much, James." She smiles a wistful smile. "You made me part of a family when I've been alone for so long. I want everybody with us."

I lean over and kiss her. It's tender and loving, and pretty chaste; we're considerate that there are kids are still around.

"I love you, Mia. I think I have since the night I found you in the car park. You were so sweet, and you never deserved any of the bad stuff. I promise you that you'll never get any of that from me."

She holds on tighter, and I close my eyes, resting my head on her shoulder as we dance.

Mia will be my wife.

41

JAMES

EVERY DAY, I worry about Garrett harassing Mia.

But every day, she comes home to me without further incident.

It might have something to do with him having to complete an anger-management course and the community service he was sentenced to. It'll be a stain on his record forever.

Somehow, we manage to make it to the end of the year, and the moment we've been waiting for creeps up quietly. We're both free to go and live our lives.

With a real estate agent trying to get top dollar for Mia's house, we pack up all our things and arrange a moving company to take them all to Copper Creek. To our new home.

It's been on the market for a couple of weeks, and there's a lot of interest. The auction's in a month, and then we'll know exactly how much she gets and how big our budget is to buy a place here.

In the meantime, none of that matters. We're together and she's safe. And in a month, her divorce will be final.

Nothing will stop us then.

WHEN ALL THE boxes have been brought in, we're left alone in our new place for the first time.

It's liberating.

"Oh, crap."

"What?" Mia asks.

"Owen locked the door to the bakery kitchen. No sneaking in for a loaf of bread."

Mia laughs, rolling her eyes. "That's probably a good thing."

"What if I want something sweet? For my sweet tooth?"

She sighs and shakes her head. "I guess you'll have to walk around and buy something."

When she turns away, I wrap my arms around her waist from behind and pull her into me.

"What are you doing?"

"You're sweet. I'll just nibble on you."

She shrieks with laughter, turning, her mouth falling open. "Do you think we'll have to keep quiet with your brother right next door during the day?"

I laugh. "I didn't think about that. That might be a problem. Maybe we can soundproof the bedroom?"

"At least they won't be here at night."

"No, but they start at something like four in the morning."

"What on earth would we be doing at four in the morning?" She grins.

"I can think of a few things."

Her eyes shine with happiness. "I love you, James Campbell."

"I love you too. Let's get the rest of this stuff unpacked."

There are still books to put on shelves, and pots and pans to put away, but for today we can get the basics out and set up so we'll be comfortable.

And tonight, we can sleep in our own bed.

AFTER A TAKEAWAY DINNER, I flop on the couch and flick on the television while Mia takes a bath. We'll sleep well. Today has been exhausting.

Closing my eyes, I drift off, sleep tugging at me.

The couch sinks, and I jolt awake, giving Mia a sleepy smile. "Hey. Nice bath?"

She nods. "It was just what I needed." She chews on her bottom lip, and I frown.

"Are you okay?"

"Umm. There's something I need to tell you."

She's pale, and my heart freezes.

"Mia, what's going on?"

Mia licks her lips. "You know how we said it was okay if we didn't have any children?"

"You want one?" I'd give her the moon if she wanted it.

"We're having one."

I stare at her. "What?"

She holds out a white stick. "This morning, I realised I was late. I'm never late. So, when we made our toilet stop …"

"You went into the supermarket to get snacks."

She nods. "And I bought a test."

I swallow hard. It didn't matter to me that we weren't planning on having children, but now it's right in front of me. I'll do whatever Mia needs to support her. "How do you feel about this?" I ask.

"That we've been through so much together, and this is just one more thing to add to our crazy relationship." She smiles. "How do you feel about it?"

I pull her into my arms. "I am insanely in love with you, and I promise to rub your feet when they're tired."

Mia laughs. "I'm sure it won't just be my feet that get tired."

"Hey, I'm an equal-opportunity rubber. I'll rub anything of yours."

She rests her head on my shoulder. "I'm happy. I think you'll be a good father."

"You'll be a great mother. We got the life we wanted, Mia. This is just icing on the cake."

"So, you're happy then?"

I nod. "Yeah. I am."

"Me too. I might be in shock, but I'll be okay."

"Are you sure?"

For a moment, she says nothing. She raises her head from my shoulder, and I see the fear in her eyes.

"Mia, if you're not sure …"

"I'm sure. I'm just scared."

I take her hand in mine. "I'll be with you the whole way."

She nods. "I know. I just wish I was even a few years' younger."

"We'll make sure you get the best of care. My brother's an obstetrician, you know."

A smile spreads across her lips. "I'm so lucky to have you, and your family."

"Our family. You're a part of us now."

Her smile grows. "I am, aren't I?"

I nod.

"I love you, James."

I lean over and plant a lingering kiss on her lips. "I love you too."

It's our first night together in our new home.

And we couldn't be happier.

42

JAMES

Eight months later

"HOW ARE YOU DOING, MIA?" Drew asks.

We must look a sight: Drew on one side of the bed, and me on the other, each holding one of Mia's hands.

"I'm okay."

He nods. "I think I should check your blood pressure again."

She smiles. "I'm glad you're here."

As he stands to grab the blood pressure cuff, he smiles at her. "Me too. I wouldn't want to be anywhere else right now."

Mia laughs. "Liar."

He shrugs. "The most important thing is that you and the baby are safe. I'm happy to be here."

Mia's pregnancy has been difficult. There were always going to be increased risks to both her and the baby simply because of her age. But Mia's struggled with her blood pressure the whole way through. There were also the repeated tests for gestational diabetes that were borderline, and now we've reached the point where she's in labour, she's bloated and exhausted, and we can't wait for the baby to be born.

Which is also why we're in Tauranga Hospital.

While we would have preferred a home birth, this is the safest place for her right now. Drew's not a part of the hospital staff helping her deliver the baby, but he's here as part of her support team. It was Mia's idea, and I just wanted her to be happy and safe.

He grins at her as he attaches the cuff to her arm.

"Can you stop flirting with my girl and check her blood pressure?" I ask.

"Hey, this is my bedside manner. I'll charm that baby out of her."

Mia giggles.

I narrow my eyes. "I'm so telling your wife on you."

He chuckles. "Hayley knows I only have eyes for her. Besides, your lady asked me to be by her side, and I'm not just here to check out her vag."

I gape at him. "Drew."

"I'll be at this end, little brother. You can watch your daughter being born. I promise you, it'll take your breath away, and nothing will ever be the same."

I shift my gaze to Mia. She's smiling at Drew, and her eyes are glistening with tears. I might be giving him shit, but I'm glad he's here to help reassure her.

"And you." He looks at Mia. "That baby is going to change your life."

"I can't wait. What's my blood pressure?" she asks.

"Higher than I'd like, but given it's been a few minutes since your last contraction, I'd say that'll be helping it rise."

As if on cue, it hits her. Mia's expression contorts, and she grips my hand tight.

"I've got you," I say.

I know when the pain fades a little as she gives me a small smile. "You always do," she whispers.

"Always."

"I'm so tired." She leans back on the pillows.

"I know you are, babe."

Drew's phone buzzes, and he picks it up off the cabinet beside the bed. "Hayley's after an update."

He taps his phone, sounding out the text. "Last check, she was at eight centimetres. BP still high. James accusing me of hitting on his girl. Love you."

Mia laughs before screwing up her face again. "You must drive her crazy."

"I try my best. If anything, she should be here with you. She's a great midwife. Though, I'm not sure if or when she'll be practicing again."

I cock an eyebrow. "I thought she was talking about going back when the twins were a bit older."

He nods, uncertainty crossing his face. "She was. But we'll have an addition to our family in about seven months' time. Don't you dare tell her that I told you that, though."

Mia lights up. "Really? That's wonderful."

He gives us a wistful smile. "We're both over the moon.

She went through a lot having the twins, and I just hope that this all goes smoothly."

The door opens, and Mia's midwife comes back in, followed by a doctor.

"Hi, Mia, I'm Doctor McRoberts. I hear you're having some blood pressure issues, so I'm here to help things go smoothly." He meets Drew's gaze. "Drew Campbell?"

"Hey, Jason." Drew grins.

Doctor McRoberts holds his hand out, and Drew shakes it. "Long time no see. If you're here, why am I?" He laughs.

"Mia's my sister-in-law. She wanted me here for moral support. I've been keeping an eye on her blood pressure." He nods toward me. "This is my brother, James."

I grin as I shake the doctor's hand. "Small world, then."

"We all end up at the same conferences, and go for a drink afterward." Drew laughs.

"Right, Mia. Let's have a look and see if this baby's ready to come out," Doctor McRoberts says.

"She was eight centimetres at the last check, but that was a while ago." Drew turns to Mia. "How are you doing?"

"You mean apart from the agonising pain every few minutes?"

He smiles. "Apart from that."

"Box of fluffies." Mia turns to me. She might hide from Drew, but she can't disguise the way she's really feeling to me. I know that face, those eyes.

"I'll just have a quick look and we'll see how close we are." The doctor says.

There's quiet for a moment.

"Mia? Do you feel like pushing?"

She nods.

"You're ten centimetres"

Mia nods. "I want to push."

Doctor McRoberts smiles. "Okay. Next contraction, push."

"You can do it, Mia," Drew says.

"How lucky am I?" she asks. "Two Campbell brothers with me."

"Don't you tell anyone else. They'll all be jealous." He grins.

She laughs. Then her face contorts, and I know the pain's hit her again.

"Okay, Mia. Let's go," Drew says.

Mia grabs my hand and Drew's, and squeezes.

It's the first of what seems like so many pushes. And with each one, we grow closer to our child.

I look at the clock. It feels like it's been hours for me, so for Mia it must seem like an eternity. In reality, it's been thirty minutes since she started pushing.

"That's it, Mia. Next push, she's out. I promise," Doctor McRoberts says.

"I hope so." Mia groans.

"You can do it," Drew says.

Mia bears down again, and in an instant, my whole life changes. Drew was right.

I see her.

I see the second our daughter comes out of Mia's body. It's gross, but beautiful. We made this little human.

She's worth everything. All the months of secrecy, the sneaking around to protect Mia, telling the world about us even if it meant losing everything. This little girl is our miracle.

"James? Is she okay?" Mia's tone is worried, and I realise I haven't said a word. No one has.

I nod. "Oh, God, Mia. In a minute you'll see what I do, and you'll see that she's more than okay. She's perfect." Tears prick my eyes.

"Congratulations, you two." I hear Drew, but I don't turn to look at him. I can't take my eyes off my little girl as she's placed on Mia's chest.

"James." She gasps.

Drew plants a kiss on Mia's forehead, and I look up as he walks around the bed. I take his extended hand, and he pulls me into a hug. "I'm so proud of you, little bro. I'll wait outside for a bit, leave you two to enjoy."

He pulls away. "She's beautiful, you guys. I'll text Hayley and let her know."

"Thanks for everything."

Drew smiles. "Any time."

I sit back down beside Mia. Seeing our child leaves me awestruck. *I'm her father.* I'd reconciled myself to this moment never happening, but I'm so glad that she's here.

"What do you think, Mackenzie?" Mia asks.

That was one name on a long list of names we couldn't agree on. "You want to call her Mackenzie?"

"I think it fits her." Mia grins. "She's amazing, James. We did this."

I nod. "We sure did. And I think her name is perfect."

The midwife leaves us to it for a little while until it's time for Mackenzie to feed. It takes a couple of attempts to get her latched onto Mia's breast, but once she does she feeds like a pro.

"That's my girl," Mia whispers, stroking Mackenzie's head.

I pull out my phone and take more photos. There's a part of me that still can't quite believe all of this. I've done the obligatory family text with pictures and stats, and my phone buzzes from the responses.

There's a tap on the door, and Doctor McRoberts pokes his head in. "Just checking on how things are going, and it all looks good. We'll keep you and baby overnight, and if everything's still fine in the morning, you can go home."

Mia nods. "Thank you."

"Congratulations, Mia, and you too, James." He nods before he closes the door.

Mia yawns.

"Want me to stay?" I ask.

"I'm not sure if they'll let you." She laughs softly. "I just want to get some sleep. It's still early. Go and have a drink with Drew or something."

"I'm not sure if I can leave." I grin.

"Go on. Go back to the hotel and get some sleep. When we get out, it's a long drive home."

Home.

Home to our little flat with the nursery waiting for our girl.

Home to our temporary place that just became somewhere to stay a little longer.

Home to our friends and family.

I can't wait to take my girls home.

Drew's waiting outside, talking to the doctor, when I walk out. He claps his hand on my shoulder and grins. "I was just saying to Jason that we should go for a drink. You in?"

I nod. "Mia told me to go out with you and then get some sleep."

"She needs time with the baby. It'll take a bit to get into their routine." Drew's brows furrow. "I still sometimes think about how hard it was on Hayley when our babies were in the NICU and she couldn't see them for a day or so. I'm glad things went well for Mia."

"So am I. That whole blood pressure thing was scary. But we knew it went with the territory." I let out a long breath. "Mia and Mackenzie are safe, and that's all that matters."

"Come on then. Let's go and celebrate, Dad." Drew grins.

We sit in the hotel bar, and for the first time all day I feel like I can relax. We've been stressed about Mia's health problems during these past few weeks.

Jason's really nice. He and Drew talk a bit of shop while I scroll through the photos I took, and when he leaves, Drew and I order one last drink and a pizza to share.

"I'm a dad."

Drew nods. "Yes. Yes, you are."

"She's such an angel, Drew. Her little fingers and toes—just perfect."

He picks up his glass, and I clink it with mine. "Are you sure? Did you count them all?"

"Are you trying to cast aspersions on my daughter?"

Drew laughs. "No, just winding you up. You guys did good. I'm proud of you."

"Thanks. And thanks for being here. I know it was a little weird of us to ask."

He shakes his head. "I'd rather be here when you needed me than not. If anything had gone wrong, there's no way I'd want to be back home and not able to help."

"You took such good care of Mia."

He shrugs. "I know you would do the same for me with Hayley if I asked."

I take a sip of my drink. "You bet I would. Congrats to you too. Another baby."

"It's just one this time. Which I'm thankful for." He leans back in his seat. "Less risk of what happened last time, but it doesn't make me less worried. I don't know what I'd do without her."

"You guys will be fine. I'm sure of it."

He's quiet for a moment. "I always wanted a big family, but this'll be the last one."

I nod. "Mackenzie will be our *only* one. Mia's not doing this again, and I'm happy for that. Hell, we didn't even think we'd have one at all."

"And now you have a beautiful little girl to love." He grins. "It's so worth it, James. The early days are hard, but one day she'll give you a dazzling smile, and you'll fall even deeper in love."

"I can't wait."

He sighs. "Just get as much sleep as you can. And make sure Mia gets a lot of rest. She needs it. That labour took a lot out of her."

"Of course. I can't wait to get home."

"I bet. At least at home you'll have uncles and aunts to help with the load. And Dad. Dad'll be over the moon to be there for the baby."

I grin. "I can't wait for him to meet her."

"It's an amazing feeling, that's for sure. Are Mia's parents close?"

I shake my head. "No, and they don't have a lot to do with her. They didn't approve of her past marriage."

"That's a shame. Maybe the little one will help bridge that gap."

"Maybe. She hasn't spoken in them for so long they don't know she's divorced. Or that she was pregnant."

He nods. "That's sad, but I think I can understand her reluctance if they rejected her. I hope it works out the way she wants it to."

"So do I. I think she's just scared of being rejected again."

The pizza disappears so fast, I think it barely touches the sides for either of us. But after his drink, Drew stands. "I'm going to my room. I could drive back tonight and skip the hotel, but after a couple of drinks and the excitement of seeing my niece being born, I could do with a good sleep. Besides, I need to call Hayley, and I'll need some privacy for that." He grips my shoulder. "I'm so proud of you. I hope you know that. We all are."

"Thanks, Drew. Good night."

"If I was you, I'd get some sleep too."

I nod. "I will."

I CAN'T LET GO of what Drew said.

Is Mackenzie what Mia needs to resurrect her relationship with her parents? Or has it been so broken for so long that there's no hope?

I don't know much about her parents, but I do know their names. After loading up the White Pages on my phone, I look up Stokes in Wellington.

There are a ton of hits.

I search my memory for their first names. Anthony and Meredith.

When I spot an Anthony and Meredith, I grin. Surely, it has to be them. I dial. Mia's already estranged from her parents. I can't make that worse. Surely.

"Anthony Stokes speaking."

I take a breath. "Hi, Mr Stokes. Are you Mia's father? Mia Scott?"

"I am. Is Mia okay?"

"You don't know me, but I'm James, Mia's partner."

There's silence for a minute. "James? You mean, she's not with Garrett anymore?"

"No. She hasn't been for quite some time. They're divorced."

I hear the hesitation in his voice. He hasn't spoken to his daughter in so long, and I don't want to push him too far. All I want to do is to tell him about the baby.

"What can I do for you, James?"

"Nothing, I guess. I just wanted you to know that you have a granddaughter. She was born this afternoon."

"I ... I ..." There's silence again, and I guess he's at a loss for what to say.

"I know it's not really any of my business, but I thought

I'd let you know. She's beautiful, and Mia and I are over the moon. Her name's Mackenzie."

"Thank you for calling." The emotion's clear in his voice now. "I appreciate it more than I can tell you. I'll let Mia's mother know."

"Thank you. If you want, I can leave my number if you want to get back in touch with Mia."

"I think I'd like that."

I can't help the grin on my face. "If you have email, I can email you through some photos."

"That would be wonderful."

I'm not sure if this will reconcile them, but I've got to give it a go. Right?

MIA'S LOOKING REFRESHED in the morning, despite a lack of sleep. Her blood pressure's back down, and we've got the okay to leave.

It's just as well. She's itching to get Mackenzie home and for us to just get on with it.

"Your bag's packed already?"

She laughs. "I'm so outta here. We have the okay to go, and I'm not hanging around."

I grin. "Fair enough. I haven't seen Drew this morning. I think he went home early."

"He popped in to say goodbye. One night away from Hayley and the kids was a lot for him to deal with."

"One night away from you sucked."

Her smile's radiant. "Well, tonight I plan on sleeping in

my own bed. With my boyfriend. And possibly my baby, if she has a night like last night."

"Was it that bad?"

Mia shakes her head. "She slept with me. It made it so much easier. I think we're going to use that Pepi-Pod after all so she can sleep with us." She twists her lips. "Just as well we have a big bed."

"Whatever you want, babe. I'm happy."

She turns back to her bag.

"But you might not be so happy when I tell you what I did last night."

She turns, her eyes blazing a hole in my forehead. "What did you do?"

"I called your parents."

Her mouth falls open. "You did what?"

"They disowned you because of Garrett, right? Well, you haven't been with him for nearly three years, and you just gave birth to their only grandchild."

Tears well in her eyes. "What did they say?"

"Your dad didn't know how to deal with it at first. But he took my number, and I have his email. I sent him some photos last night." I open my arms, enveloping her in them when she walks to me. "I don't know if anything will come of it, but it felt like the right thing to do."

"Thank you," she whispers. "I'm glad you did it. I wasn't sure if I could find the strength."

"You know my family is yours, but I had to try it."

She raises her face, a faint smile on her lips. "I love that you did. You made an effort, James, and that's more than *he* ever did."

"I'd do anything for you, Mia. Never forget that."

She nods. "So, when do we get married?"

EPILOGUE
JAMES

Five years later

I HAND the mallet to Lily, grinning when she struggles with the weight. "Want a hand?"

"Hell, no." She laughs.

This could only be her moment. We've spent weeks cleaning up, removing the overgrowth that covered this section. Now it's time to demolish the house, and Lily gets first hit.

"Thank you." Tears well in her eyes. Despite all the years that have passed, this must be so emotional for her.

"Go for it, babe. Knock that wall down." Adam places his palm on her back, and she takes a loud, long breath.

"Smack it hard." Corey winks at her, and she nods.

We back off as she holds up the mallet and swings it.

Crack!

The wooden cladding splinters when she hits it, and the sound echoes over the empty space. She's far from finished as she lifts the hammer and hits it again. The weight of the mallet seems to disappear as she lifts it, slamming it into the cracking wall over and over until there's a large hole.

"Babe," Adam says.

She drops the tool on the ground. Her face is red from the effort, and tears stream down her face.

He wraps his arms around her, and she clings to him. Everyone else falls silent as Lily sobs. Max joins them, his arms around Lily's waist, and Rose follows suit. Ben, their youngest, tries to wrap his arms around everyone, but ends up in the centre with his mother.

It's hard to watch, but equally hard to look away.

"Lily, do you want to have a go with the demolition equipment when it gets here?" I ask.

She nods. "You bet." Sniffing, she laughs, and Adam presses a kiss to her temple. They've come so far since he returned, and this has to be cathartic for Lily.

"I'll give you a call during the week. I'm getting professionals in, but I already asked them if you could have a go with the wrecking ball."

Her eyes widen. "Seriously?"

I shrug. "They thought a bulldozer would be enough, but I wanted to make it special for you."

Lily grins. "I'll pay for the upgrade."

"It's not costing a lot extra. And it'll be more fun this way, so don't worry about it."

"Thanks for thinking of my girl." Adam leans his head on hers.

"To be honest, it sounded like more fun to me too." I laugh. I can't wait.

———

Ava's holding court in the middle of the lawn. At eleven, she's very much the leader of all the Campbell children.

Violet follows her sister everywhere. Drew's children, Logan, Amelia, and Alexandra, don't get to see their cousins that often, so they hang onto Ava's every word. Corey's kids, Eli, Oscar, and Isla, are right there with them.

The only one missing is my Mackenzie. But she's at home with Mia while they talk on Skype to Mia's parents.

Watching the other kids makes me miss her.

We have such a good life here. We'd never planned to stay in Owen's apartment for five years, but Mackenzie's arrival threw us for a loop. I'm still at the garage, doing a mechanic apprenticeship with Adam, while Mia's onto her second text book.

We bought this place a year ago for next to nothing. After looking at all our options, this turned out to be the best one. We'll level the section and build what we want.

It's still central. We can walk to Owen's place, or Lily's from here. I'm only sorry my mother never got to see this.

She would have loved it. I'm sure all her grandchildren would have distracted her from trying to interfere in her children's lives.

But at the same time, if she was still alive, I know she would have struggled, in particular with my relationship with Mia. We just celebrated her forty-sixth birthday, and I'm more in love with my wife than ever.

Best of all, she's happy. I know I contribute to that, but Mia's thrived from having the freedom to be herself, to not have to look over her shoulder all the time. She'll never have to do that with me.

"Daddy."

I turn, and hold my arms open as Mackenzie leaps. Catching her, I twirl around while peppering her face with kisses. "Hey. It's nice to see you. I thought you were coming later."

She beams. "We finished our Skype with Nana and Poppa."

"Did you? Are they good?"

She nods.

"Mum and Dad are fine. They're excited to come up in a few weeks, check the block of land out." I can see the nerves in Mia's eyes. It's been a long road, rebuilding her relationship with her parents, but now we see each other every few months. Each time feels like we're getting closer and closer to bridging the gap between us.

"Mackenzie and I wanted to see how you were doing with the demolition." Mia plants a lingering kiss on my lips, and I swing Mackenzie to my hip to slip my other arm around my wife's waist. She leans her head on my shoulder.

"Well, Lily made a start. That big hole in the wall belongs to her."

"Where is she now?"

"She went inside with Adam. I think she wants the chance to say goodbye before it gets knocked down." I sigh. "This house was such a big part of her life."

"It's probably good for her to confront it before it's destroyed."

I nod. "I'm so glad we're the ones doing the destroying."

"I can't wait until we have our new house built."

"Daddy, put me down." Mackenzie wiggles, and I drop her gently to the ground. She runs toward Ava.

"Being here is so good for her," Mia says.

"Good for us too."

Mia moves in front of me, and wraps her arms around my waist. "You've given me so much, James. You gave me the family I never thought I'd have."

I press my forehead to hers. "You two are my everything."

"I'm only sorry we can't have any more children."

I shrug. "Mackenzie's fine. She's surrounded by her cousins, and she has two parents who love her and each other. What else does she need?"

Her lips curl into a smile. "I guess you're right."

"And soon enough we'll have a home with plenty of room for her to grow up in."

Mia shifts her gaze back to the house. "I can't wait."

It's been a long day.

We haven't done much in the way of demolition. Giving Lily the mallet was symbolic, but such a powerful thing to help her get her past with this place out of her system. She said goodbye to her childhood home, and the place where her mother traumatised her.

Once the house is gone, then Corey and his crew will move in and start construction on our new place. He completed a building apprenticeship, and now he's running his own little business while his mate, Tim, focuses on Carlstown.

Today was good. We have these family gatherings fairly often, but with us living in Owen's old flat still, it's not often that Mia and I host them. Once we have our new house built, it'll make things easier.

Mackenzie's fast asleep after an afternoon of running around in the sun with her cousins. She was so tired, she barely made it through dinner. Mia had to put a very tired girl into her pyjamas. She'll no doubt be up at some ridiculous hour of the morning tomorrow.

When Mia appears in the doorway, I move over on the couch and pat the seat.

"Turn around and face that end of the couch," she says. She sits sideways, and I follow suit, placing myself between her thighs with my back to her.

Mia massages my shoulders, her gentle hands relaxing me as I lean back.

"Today was good," I say. "I'm glad we're building on that property."

"I can't wait to get the house built and us moved in. As much as I've appreciated having this place for free, the thought of finally being in our own home fills me with joy."

"Do you know what else can fill you with joy?" Turning, I meet her gaze. One of her eyebrows is raised higher than the other, and she's got this look on her face that tells me she's not sure she wants to hear the answer.

"Do I want to know?"

"Me." I pounce, pushing her back on the couch as she shrieks with laughter.

"Shhh, you'll wake Mackenzie." I laugh.

"Nothing is going to wake that child. Trust me." Her eyes shine with happiness as I lean over to kiss her.

Lifting her legs so she's lying on the couch, I position myself on top of her.

"What are you doing?" Her tone is full of amusement.

"Loving you."

She purses her lips. "You're so good at doing it."

"You're so easy to love."

"Teacher's pet," she murmurs right before I plant a kiss on her lips.

"Always."

BONUS CHAPTER
LILY

I squeeze Adam's hand as I take a deep breath and we walk down the stairs together. The house is a mess, but the concrete steps that lead to what used to be my mother's sewing room are still intact.

My head feels lighter the farther down we go.

"Anytime you want out, tell me and we'll leave." Adam's presence is reassuring. He's been by my side since I've been back, and has done everything to support me and our family. I don't know if I could do this without him.

I take the final step and look around.

The door's been closed for I don't know how long, and the room is musty and damp. People have been using the house above to sleep rough, and I hope to God none of them have stayed down here.

There's still such a bad feel about this place.

The sight of the built-in cupboards floods my memory with thoughts of my mother's fabric collection. All her sewing gear was in here before her breakdown. I spent hours in this room looking at the different colours, feeling the variety of textures, and admiring the clothes she made so many years ago.

"I never thought I'd come back here."

Adam envelops me in his arms, and I breathe him in. He's so familiar, and I love him more than I ever have.

He loves me.

He gets me.

He knows what it's like to be afraid of the dark.

"Are you okay?" The words rumble in his chest. He makes me feel so safe.

"I'm fine. I'll be glad when it's all demolished."

"Me too." He kisses the top of my head. "I'm glad you got to say a final farewell to the place."

"So am I." Tears well, and when I close my eyes, one escapes down my cheek. "I wish she was still here. Despite everything, I wish she could meet the kids. I wish she could know the happiness we have together."

"I know, babe."

When the other tears follow, we say nothing. He just holds me, and I say a silent goodbye to the home where I worked so hard to keep my mother on track, where I never really felt loved. It's the place I last saw when I left for the hospital, pregnant with Max and not even knowing.

I was a frightened eighteen-year-old who survived something other people might not.

And then I never stopped fighting.

Until I got Adam back.

The warmth of the sunlight greets me as we walk out together, hand in hand.

"Mum, can we go inside and take a look?" Max asks.

"I'd rather you didn't. It's not safe." I reach up to stroke his chin. Max is the same height as his father, but where Adam has muscle, Max is lean. I love my son and our other children more than words can say.

"Sophie wanted to see."

I shift my gaze to Max's girlfriend. He met her on a trip to Carlstown, and they've been inseparable ever since. She's a sweet, quiet girl who reminds me a lot of me when I was younger. And she looks at Max like he hung the moon.

"I appreciate your interest, Sophie, but this house has a lot of bad memories for me. Once it's gone, I'll be glad."

She smiles, the dimples in her cheeks popping up. "I understand, Mrs Campbell."

"Why don't we get this barbecue going? I bet everyone's dying for lunch. Want to help me, Sophie?" Adam asks.

"Sure." She flashes Max a smile. Adam leans over and kisses me on the cheek.

I let out a breath as he walks away with her.

"Mum?"

I turn back to Max. "Yes?"

"I'm glad this place is being demolished too. I'm sorry for what your mother did."

Tears well in my eyes. I tried so hard to protect Max from the truth, but over the years he's learned what happened. I always made sure he knew just how special it made him, and how desperately I loved him. Max always came first. "I know you are, sweetheart. But you know what? It's all good now."

He wraps his arms around me. "I'm glad Dad came back. You're so happy with him."

"You all make me so happy. This house feels like a distant memory."

Max grins. "Remember the zombies, Mum?"

"How can I forget?" I laugh.

He lets go of me, forming claws with his hands, and swipes the air. It takes me back to when he was still a kid and we were both scared of the dark. All those lonely nights when I couldn't see how things would get better.

Then Adam came back and made all the bad go away.

We'll never get back the twelve years we were apart, but we've built so much since we've been together.

I claw my hands and wave them in the air.

Max and I both laugh, and I know I'll always treasure these moments. Moments no one else can ever understand but Max and me.

When I look over toward the barbecue, Adam's eyes meet mine. He's watching Max and me with so much pride on his face. It makes my heart swell.

I love my husband more than I can say.

And he loves me.

Our house is quiet. It's not that late, and the kids are all in bed asleep.

From the doorway, I take in the peace that is our bedroom. There are so many memories here. Memories we've made as a family.

This is the house that Adam bought us when he came

home, and our first real family home. Rose and Ben were born in this house. It's the house we'll grow old in. Together.

Nothing traumatic will ever happen in our home. Not if I can help it. My children are safe, and always will be when I'm around.

The soft lights mounted on our bedroom wall flicker on when I press the switch. My heart swells. That was Adam's doing, so I'd never have to be afraid of the dark again. Since then, I've never been afraid.

We were two broken people who put each other back together.

I close my eyes as he surrounds me from behind, his strong arms wrapping around my waist. He buries his face in my neck and takes a deep breath. I love this man with all of my heart, and nothing is sweeter than simply being with him.

"What are you doing?" he asks.

"Just thinking about how lucky I am. Seeing the old house brought back a lot of memories, but I have so many better ones now."

He lets me go, and I turn to face him.

"Thank you for being with me today." I palm his cheek, and he turns his face to kiss my hand.

"I'll always be with you when you need me. You make me whole, Lily Campbell."

I smile. I'll always love being called that when for so long I never thought it would be possible. "That's how I feel about you, too."

"Nothing's ever going to separate us now. You know that, right?"

I wrap my arms around his waist and rest my head on his

chest. "I know." I sigh. "This. Us. It's for life. What happened back then is a distant memory. I'm still not entirely sure how I survived it."

He strokes my hair. "I'll always regret my leaving. I hurt you so much. You must have hated me, and yet you let me back in again. I'll be grateful for the rest of my life for that."

"I'm not sure I ever hated you. But I am glad that when you came back you didn't give up on me." I lean back and smile. "And I know now that no matter what, you're here for me and our children."

He bends his head and kisses me. His kiss is gentle and slow.

He's everything I ever wanted.

And he's all mine.

———

Thank you for reading! The Campbell family story doesn't quite end here. Set five years after the Teacher's Pet epilogue, join the brothers for Christmas, and celebrate a very special arrival.

Click here to read A Very Campbell Christmas now

ALSO BY WENDY SMITH

Coming Home

Doctor's Orders

Baker's Dozen

Hunter's Mark

Teacher's Pet

A Very Campbell Christmas

Fall and Rise Duet

Falling

Rising

Fall and Rise - The Complete Duet

The Aeon Series

Game On

Build a Nerd

Bar None

Coming 2022 Love on Site

Hollywood Kiwis Series

Common Ground

Even Ground

Under Ground

Rocky Ground

Coming Soon Solid Ground

Stand alones

For the Love of Chloe

Only Ever You

The Friends Duet

Loving Rowan

Three Days

The Forever Series

Something Real

The Right One

Unexpected

Chances Series

Another Chance

Taking Chances

Lifetime Series

In a Lifetime

In an Instant

In a Heartbeat

In the End

At the Start

ABOUT THE AUTHOR

Wendy Smith published as Ariadne Wayne for three years before deciding she didn't want to be someone else all the time. She's an Apple Books and Nook bestselling author, whose book In the End, written as Ariadne Wayne, was named one of Apple's best books of 2017. All her stories come with a quirky sense of humour , and she cries over everything.

Find me online
www.wendysmith.co.nz
wendy@wendysmith.co.nz